A WEEK OF THIS

(a novel in seven days)

A WEEK OF THIS

(a novel in seven days)

NATHAN WHITLOCK

ECW Press

Published by ECW Press
2120 Queen Street East, Suite 200, Toronto, Ontario, Canada M4E 1E2

This is a work of fiction. Names, characters, places, and incidents either are the product of the author's imagination or are used fictitiously, and any resemblance to actual persons, living or dead, business establishments, events, or locales is entirely coincidental.

Library and Archives Canada Cataloguing in Publication

Whitlock, Nathan
A week of this : a novel in seven days / Nathan Whitlock.

ISBN 978-1-77041-036-7
Also issued as: 978-1-55490-815-8 (PDF); 978-1-55490-317-7 (EPUB)
Originally published in hardcover in 2008 (ISBN 978-1-55022-815-1)

I. Title.

PS8645.H566W44 2011   C813'.6   C2011-902950-2

**FT
Pbk**

Editor: Michael Holmes / a misFit book
BackLit editor: Jennifer Knoch
Cover and text design: Ingrid Paulson
Cover image: mamarosa/photocase.com
Typesetting and production: Rachel Ironstone
Printing: Webcom 5 4 3 2 1

This book is set in Adobe Caslon

The publication of *A Week of This* has been generously supported by the Canada Council for the Arts, which last year invested $20.1 million in writing and publishing throughout Canada, by the Ontario Arts Council, by the OMDC Book Fund, an initiative of the Ontario Media Development Corporation, and by the Government of Canada through the Canada Book Fund.

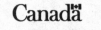

Printed and bound in Canada

"Actual life is full of false clues and signposts that lead nowhere. With infinite effort we nerve ourselves for a crisis that never comes."

– E.M. Forster, Howard's End

for Ciabh

(WEDNESDAY)

Everything in Dunbridge was dead by October. The backyard gardens that had scaled old mop handles and broken hockey sticks throughout the summer, spreading up and out in a green lurch for the sky, now fell back in a withered heap. Leaves left a print of themselves on the sidewalk, looking trapped under ice. Colours everywhere were fading, as if the whole town were painted onto cement.

About a week before winter really hit, a woman walked her dog through a grey morning to the park at the end of her street. Her dog, a German shepherd with a puckered scar over its right hind leg, moved forward with its tongue out, looking like it didn't expect ever to return to the warm house and the warm blanket it had just left. Damp leaves brushed against its side, and it cheered up a little, thinking it was about to be let free to pursue the smells invading its nose – not as vividly as they used to, but still strong enough to start its tail wagging in anticipation. The woman stopped at the park entrance and tightened her grip on the leash. The air was cold and sharp; she would go no further. "Just go, sweetie," she said. "It's freezing; mummy's cold." The jacket she was wearing wouldn't close around her chest. It was her son's – she hadn't yet dug her own out from the basement. She looked at the trees and tried not to think about cigarettes.

"Come on, Diamond, just fucking *go*."

The time of parks was nearly up – there hadn't been any kids in this one since school started. For weeks she'd seen only other dog owners; they would stamp impatiently and look around as if worried about snipers. Locks were appearing on the doors of the public washrooms. All of a sudden no one believed in summer anymore.

A man appeared without a dog on the arched bridge spanning the creek. He wore a heavy, blue parka with the hood up and was walking fast, sending billows of agitated white breath ahead of him. The woman stepped back and pulled Diamond – who was already going into a squat – between herself and the man. He was wearing wool mittens like a little boy. He stopped when he saw her, then turned around and went quickly back over the bridge and across to the far side of the park. Wind came through after him and got under the woman's jacket. By the time they got home she'd already decided Diamond was going to have to make do with the backyard from now on.

"Watch the park," she told her son later, "there's some freaks hanging around in there."

"Oh yeah?" her son asked.

"Some big retarded guy."

"Oh," he said, disappointed.

The man in the parka sat and rested on a bench covered over in brown leaves, feeling their dampness coming through the seat of his pants. He'd walked nearly the entire length of Dunbridge that morning, tramping through every cold park like Jack Frost in mittens. Now he was feeling hungry, the side of his face was throbbing, and he still had to get ready for work in a few hours. He decided to give himself exactly two more minutes of rest before starting again, and even checked his broad-faced watch to mark the time. Squirrels ran up and sniffed at the shrunken-head apples on the ground all around him. He took off one mitt and got to work on the inside of his nose. More wind came through, bringing the last of the leaves down. The park was naked and waiting. Though it looked like it could, Ken decided it wasn't going to snow that day.

THURSDAY

Patrick's alarm spoke up in the silence of the bedroom, coming alive in mid-sentence to promise "Hotel California" and classic Billy Joel. Patrick let it all get absorbed into the broken logic of his dreams. It always took him a few minutes to get all the way upright, drag his legs over the side, and let his feet curl unhappily on the bedroom carpet. The pull of the bed was so strong that he didn't reach to turn off the clock radio until his wife started to groan and move beside him. Then, once the world was silent again, another minute of sitting in the dark to gather strength and courage. He tried to clear some of the room's dry air out of his throat.

"Get up," Manda said from under the blanket.

"Sorry."

It was earlier than usual. Patrick wanted to get a start on sorting the mountain of stock sitting in the back of the store. He had been putting it off for days. It wasn't as if he didn't have time – the store was open six days a week and he was alone there all six, from open til close. He couldn't really afford not to be open Sundays, too, but Manda had been ready to walk out after a year of him being there every single day, and he was secretly happy for the excuse not to be.

"You're not like some Chinese guy or whatever," she told him, "with fourteen kids in the back and your grandparents. You don't have to kill yourself."

The store wasn't killing him – not quickly anyway. He'd worked at jobs that had literally torn the skin off his knuckles and singed his eyebrows, that had got into the flat muscles in his back and into his shoulders like rust or dry rot, ruining them, weakening them from the inside out. He'd had jobs that could have been done by animals, that *should* have been done by animals; no one would ever let animals work under those conditions. A couple of times a year, especially when it was cold out, a serrated cough would settle into his chest, and he would think about clouds of white dust from demolished walls or rooms filling with silver-backed smoke from machines kept alive for too long and fed with syrupy homemade fuels.

Active Sports was his own, at least. There were days when, after standing behind the counter for the entire day, or restocking shelves with shoes or baseball gloves or the rest of it, he'd catch himself vaguely wishing to be sent home early, but mostly the reality that the little store was *his* sat with him like an animal sidekick: there to help him out and boost his mood when he needed it, but mostly just mocking him and making a mess of things. For a while, his friend Danny had helped him out, but when business died back down, Patrick had been forced to lay him off. That was around Labour Day, more than a month ago. It never used to bother Patrick to be there so much. It had always felt as though he were building something. But after letting Danny go it felt as though he were only there to oversee the place's collapse. Before, there had never been anything to it: the store was an end in itself. Now, when he turned on the lights each morning, he felt as though those lights were drawing their energy directly from him. Draining him. If one was flickering, it was because his exhaustion had seeped so deeply into him he could almost feel his muscles loosening their grip on his bones. Patrick knew he was going to fall apart in that place. It had eliminated all of his savings – Manda's, too, not that she had much to begin with – and dropped them both into a smooth-walled pit of debt that got deeper every month.

The part Patrick had been liking most lately – the part Danny had hated – was doing things like fitting a girl for figure skates or going through a bin of baseball bats with a kid who was just joining his first team. Older kids would come in and stand there talking to Patrick about different kinds of sticks, or all of the stupid new rules that had been brought in at the Junior-A level. At these moments the exhaustion would disappear, the knots in Patrick's back would loosen and uncoil.

He knew better than to talk about this to Manda. Any time he did she gave him a blast, accusing him of trying to guilt her into having kids and of having dangerously sentimental ideas about what having a kid was really like, which was probably true.

"You want the one in her little dress," Manda told him. "Or the one you teach to skate or ride a bike or some shit like that. But you don't want the one that's up all night screaming or getting drunk or getting molested or running away from home." She looked at him with a mixture of scorn and panic. "You don't get it: you can fuck your kids up so bad if you don't know what you're doing. And *you*," she said, softening a little, but not prepared to withhold the final judgment, "do *not* know what you're doing. Ever."

His sentimental fantasies remained, however, and he was ashamed to admit they were exactly the kind of thing that Manda accused him of. It was at night when he was most susceptible to these thoughts, especially while he was closing the store: he'd start thinking vaguely about what awaited him at home, and whether there should be more. But in the morning he was ready to concede that Manda was right. He couldn't imagine, as he pulled himself out of bed, trying to carry any extra weight.

He closed his eyes and put his head back as if about to sniff the air. Instead, he held his breath for half a minute before letting it seep out through his teeth as quietly as he could. He felt he needed ropes around his arms and legs, and little men pulling them like in that cartoon, just so he could get anywhere.

Patrick had to fight through three layers of shower curtain to get to the knob and start the water. Once it got going and he could sense the steam coming from behind the many plastic veils blocking his sight, he got undressed, sliding himself under and letting the water pummel him for a minute before trying to find a more gentle setting on the shower head. Patrick used to think that the awful feeling he had in the morning was a temporary state, a phase he was going though, a bad patch – in his real life he was still healthy and full of vigour. Now he knew he was wrong: *this* was his real life, a life of fatigue.

The water hit the cut on his thumb where he had gouged himself opening a crate a couple of days before. The sting of it made him hiss and pull his hand to his chest. The cut was clean, but it was long; it looked like a bite from something small and nasty. He forced himself to hold the thumb under the hot water until his eyes teared up, until he could barely see. Even after he pulled his hand away it took a few minutes for his eyes to calm themselves.

Hours later, Manda stood in the doorway of her stepbrother's apartment, trying to locate the source of a smell. Marcus lived on the second floor, above a store, at the top of an outdoor flight of stairs. This smell, which hit her full in the face every time she came over, was like the building's bad breath. It exhaled on her the minute she opened the door and she'd have to take a step back. A plant stood beside her, just inside the kitchen, reaching up to her knees. She had bought it to bring some colour to Marcus's life. Its leaves drooped, and the whole thing leaned forward like an exhausted child, embarrassed and wanting to go home.

"How does it stink so bad in here?" she called out.

She felt a little giddy all of a sudden – she sometimes found herself invigorated by failure, even the failure of the air to smell good. Her hair was wet from the rain; it slumped and made her look older than she was. She was only two years away from turning forty and nearly done shedding all resemblance to her younger self. In the last couple of years she had stopped letting her bleached dirty-blonde hair snake down her back, cutting it herself to just below her shoulders. It was almost a relief not to be girly anymore, to trim off that last connection. She had always *felt* hard, so now she *looked* hard.

"Marcus, it really stinks! What is it?"

There were empty cases of beer on the landing. Marcus hardly ever drank: they had been there since before he moved in. The boxes were faded, warped, and broken at the seams. Brown bottles leaned out of the split corners, their clear bellies full of cigarette butts. Nothing frustrated her more than this, this wilful paralysis. She saw it in Marcus, she saw it in Patrick, she saw it in everybody she knew. She tried to hunt it down and kill it in herself, but it gripped her from the inside and slowed her down. She wanted to cough hard sometimes, to cough up this fog. Instead, she shouted it down.

"These are so *gross*, Marcus. You're gonna have to get rid of them sometime. Get Patrick to help you."

She walked through Marcus's apartment into the living room, staying clear of the couch where Marcus lay, and of his long, pink feet pointing crookedly at the ceiling. It looked like he'd been on the couch all morning watching TV. It was almost noon; the fishing shows were starting. Manda walked deliberately in front of the TV to see if Marcus would object, to see if he was even watching it anymore. She kicked at a pair of socks that were mashed together on the floor and held her keys defensively out in front of her, as if ready for something to peel itself from the wall and fly at her. The air was like the inside of a scuba tank. Manda liked to make clear how awful she thought the place had become – how awful he'd *let it* become. "This used to be a cool little apartment," she'd tell him. She hardly ever came over anymore, and when she did, she couldn't help but condemn it.

"This is why your mom doesn't come around. She thinks it's full of mold and doesn't want to get sick from it."

"She doesn't like the stairs," Marcus countered sleepily. "She doesn't give a shit how the place smells – *her* house is like an ashtray, you know that. She just can't get up the stairs easy. She almost went down on her back a couple times."

Marcus's hair flopped down over his forehead like an omelette. He didn't get up.

"She told me that, too," Manda said. She pulled at the living room window, and her fingernails crunched the baked corpses of wasps and flies. The window wouldn't budge.

"It smells dead," she added. "Do these windows even open?"

"Not usually."

"Oh, but wait!" Manda said suddenly, and out she went while Marcus hid himself further under his blanket. He was sure she would bring in some new thing for her house, and he was so *sick* of looking at chairs and paint samples. Instead, she walked back in with her whole upper half magically transformed into a plant.

"Move all that," she said from behind the thing's leaves. She bent her knees in the direction of the trunk he used as a coffee table. Manda flopped the plant on the trunk and stepped back without taking her eyes off it. "For *colour*," she said in a serious tone, as if colour were something he was being rewarded for, like bravery. "You need some green in here."

She went looking for some water for the plant, expecting to find evidence of a week's worth of meals in the kitchen and maybe a few dark things running under the fridge, but there was just one plate and a knife in the sink. The cupboard doors were all closed.

"Has Kelly been over?" she asked through the door.

"She's in the shower right now," came the answer.

Manda came back fast into the living room. "Is she? Why didn't you tell me? I almost walked in there."

Marcus only gave her a sarcastic look.

"Oh shut up," she said.

"As if I wouldn't have said anything."

"You probably wouldn't have. I only asked because it's so clean in your kitchen," she said. "It's a miracle."

Marcus had been seeing a woman for a few months now, a little blonde. Manda was surprised at first at the difference in their ages – he was thirty-six; Kelly looked at least ten years younger. The only real problem with Kelly was that she had a kid, a little boy whose father had fucked off long ago. Manda tried to hold her tongue – she wanted Marcus to be happy; he hadn't been in a serious relationship since just after high school – but she just couldn't do it.

"Can this go somewhere else?" Marcus asked, pointing at the plant. It looked pathetic sitting there, as if waiting to be thrown out the window.

"Oh, you're so friggin helpless," Manda said and lifted the plant again. She carried it to the bathroom. "You're sure Kelly's not here now," she shouted over her shoulder. Marcus threw his hand up to give her the finger, but let his arm drop back down without following through. On the TV a man in a camouflage hunting jacket had just landed a huge bass that kicked water at the camera with its tail. "Nothing to it," the man said, the whole heavy fish hooked by the gill onto one of his fat fingers. By the time Manda returned he had thrown it back in the water.

"So keep it somewhere where there's lots of light."

"How about outside?"

"You're funny."

Manda had her jacket on and looked ready to go, but she made no move to leave. She was still holding her keys in her hand. She looked almost as though she'd forgotten the way back out.

"Are you supposed to be working?"

Manda lay her palms flat against her forehead. "Oh fuck, when am I not?" she said.

"So what's going on with Ken?" Marcus asked her through a yawn. "He doesn't like his new place?"

Manda had her keys out again and almost dropped them. "What? You were talking to him? When? He isn't calling me back."

"I saw him yesterday – no, Tuesday. He was in a weird mood." *Not that you could tell*, he wanted to add. Manda's brother was more than a little fucked up. The whole side of his face had been burned when he was a kid, and he was slow in the head. Not quite fully retarded, but unable to get his brain moving sometimes. He spoke and acted like someone who'd just been fished out from under the ice: his head was half-frozen all the time. Margaret, Marcus's mother and Manda's stepmother, used to say: "There's nothing wrong with Ken, he's just a little behind the times." When they were teenagers, Manda would leave the room whenever her stepmother said something like that. She used to stomp out of the room for pretty much anything, actually, but especially when it involved Ken.

"Where'd you see him?" Manda asked Marcus.

"Somewhere. Downtown. I asked him about the new place, and he told me he hated it. Wasn't he all excited to move before?"

"He hates moving, but he had to get out of the last place so bad. Oh Christ, Marcus, you remember all that." Manda's eyes went wide. "Well look, if you see him again, tell him to fucking call me back. It's stupid. Anyway, I have to get going."

On the fishing show they were doing a quick montage of strikes that made the whole thing look more exciting than fishing had ever been, ever. Tails kept thrashing at the water and slapping against the side of the boat. The camera's lens got beaded up with water in all the commotion. The water looked like some kind of frothy oil. Manda had never been on a boat in her life. She refused. Seeing the kinds of things they were pulling out of the water just confirmed it: huge and sleek, with stretched, grimacing mouths. She couldn't watch any more.

"Don't let that plant die," she yelled from the kitchen. "Get Kelly to take care of it or something – she can use all her mothering skills."

"What the fuck is that supposed to mean?" Marcus asked, trying to see where she had gone, but she was already out the door and down the stairs.

All Manda had on was her windbreaker – she never wore enough when it got cold. She'd push the sleeves up hard to the elbows as if ready to dig in and start kneading the cold air with her bare fingers. She wanted to grapple with it, to get the better of it. Manda opened up in the fall; it revived her. When everybody was feeling the chill, she was out in her backyard in a sweatshirt, cheerfully hacking down the last of her small garden, dragging the dead stems into piles and pushing the whole thing into the giant composter at the back of the yard. It looked big enough to curl up and sleep in. That black box seethed with warmth and activity the entire winter. Even in a long cold snap, in the most desperate stretch of February, Manda knew there was a warm, humid heart beating slowly at the centre of all those densely packed carrot peelings and bread crusts and coffee grounds. There were colonies of tiny creatures in there, living in highways of slick mulch, waiting for the sun and waiting for her to come and lift the lid and set them all loose into free soil. She had no kids and no pets, but back there she was a mother to millions.

The call-centre where Manda worked sat above a bridal store that never seemed to be open. There was dust on the shoulders and heads of the mannequins, the dead-eyed brides and frozen flower girls. Manda hadn't worn a dress like any of the ones in the window when she married Patrick, so it always pleased her to see them looking rotten. Many of the stores along Dunbridge's main strip were like this, dark and quiet. There was a whole stretch of pawn shops near the old movie theatre. Only they and the dollar stores were thriving – the mall and the new Wal-Mart having sucked everything else out to the highway. The movie theatre itself was sealed up and being used as storage for an army surplus store.

With a chocolate bar and a can of Diet Coke she'd bought to get her through the afternoon, Manda started up the stairs to the office. Cheryl and Lana, two of the women she worked with, were coming down at the same time. All three made half-hearted jokes about having to squeeze past each other, though they all knew Cheryl was the reason. Manda had never been thin, and Lana had put on weight since she quit smoking, but Cheryl was just huge. When Lana walked with her, she looked like her trainer, as if Cheryl were about to mount a unicycle and ride around in circles. Manda had to press against the wall while the other two went down single-file.

"I'm not *that* late, am I?" Manda asked when she got above the other two. "Who's on the phones?"

"Just Jessica," Cheryl said, and made a face that showed how well she thought the new girl was doing on her own.

"So Sean's having a shit-fit?"

The other two were already at the door and didn't hear Manda's question over the sound of traffic.

The office was just one big, open room with a small kitchen in the front and an enclosed room in the back that Sean, the manager, used as his own office. The room had been the sewing and repair room for the bridal store; there were still rectangular outlines of the machines on the floor and holes where they'd been bolted in. In the gaps between the wooden slats were millions of tiny pins. Sometimes Manda had to pull them out of the soles of her shoes when she got home at night.

Once inside, Manda could hear Jessica trying to complete a reservation, but couldn't see the girl behind her cubicle wall. The new girl kept trying to confirm a credit card number: she would slowly recite it, then pause to be told that she'd got it wrong again. She sounded as if she were giving coordinates or trying to break a code. Sean came out of his office just as Manda was walking by, and they both stood there for a while, staring toward Jessica's cubicle, from which again came the sound of the same nine numbers being read out in a slightly different order. Sean looked at Manda, curled his lips back over his teeth, and soundlessly strangled the empty air in front of him.

"Then why'd you friggin hire her?" Manda muttered after he had gone back into his office. The answer likely involved a combination of his love of stupid young women and Dunbridge's laughably shallow labour pool – he probably hired the first person who could work a computer. The people Manda saw when she came for her own interview looked less than a generation away from the tractor. The woman who had waited next to her admitted she couldn't make any sense of the company's want ad, though she assumed that computers were somehow involved. "I just figger they'll show me what they need me to be doin' and that'll be it," the woman told her with a nervous laugh. Manda had been in Dunbridge almost two-thirds of her life, but she still sometimes felt like she was living in some kind of pilgrim village.

Manda had her headset on and was about to start taking reservations when she realized she was still wearing her damp windbreaker. Jessica was just finishing her call when she heard someone hiss out a swear. She stood up to see who was around, but Manda had already disappeared. The new girl sat down more slowly than she had stood up, looking with dull panic at the red light flashing on her phone.

Always after his stepsister came over Marcus felt as if he'd had his hair violently combed the wrong way and his teeth flossed against his will. He threw off his blanket and let his thighs breathe before going to look for something to wear. The fishing shows were over; the only thing on was a health show for old people where everyone seemed to be whispering. Marcus had promised his uncle Sinc he would call in to see if he was needed at all at the furniture warehouse. He had no real interest in hauling couches around any time soon, but he'd been complaining to his mother that Sinc wasn't giving him any hours, so he figured he should at least *act* like he wanted to work. He also had to drop by the rink in the next day or two to make sure he had the ice booked for the hockey team he coached. He'd forgotten last time.

Marcus kept all his clothes in milk crates wired together and stacked up against his bedroom wall. He could have got a dresser off his uncle cheap, but couldn't face trying to get the thing up the stairs. Anyway, he liked the look of all his clothes folded and piled in these red and blue crates: in an instant he could see everything he owned. Most of the furniture in the apartment was left over from the previous tenants, who had taken off on the rent. The silliest crap, the posters of jazz musicians and flute-playing panthers, Marcus threw out as soon as he got there, but the legacy of the deadbeat tenants was still in the rectangles of unfaded paint on the walls and in the layout of the rooms, which Marcus was too lazy and superstitious to change. They could have moved back in anytime without much trouble. He even gave in and used the shrunken discs of soap and the dregs of the shampoo left in the bathroom when he was too broke to buy his own. There were cans of things with scalps of grey dust on the top shelves over the sink; he left those alone. Most of it was coconut milk, which he couldn't think of any use for, though he wondered for a while if he was supposed to bathe in it.

The only piece of furniture he brought with him from his mother's house was the bed he'd slept in since he was twelve. The headboard was speckled with stickers of rotting eyeballs, random stars and comets, and the face of Darth Vader, to which a sixteen-year-old Marcus had added a full beard and a giant, smouldering cigarette. The bed drooped badly in the centre like an old horse; he had to swim for the edge when he woke up in the morning. Marcus had broken its back with his loyalty and with the extra sixty or seventy pounds he'd put on since he was a kid. The bed was loyal to him, too, though it wheezed with relief and settled back like an old dog when Marcus got out of it.

Almost everything Marcus wore dated back, like his bed, to his teens, or was a reasonable facsimile of the kind of thing he'd worn back then. At the laundromat down the street he would pull the scraps of underwear and T-shirts out from the machines, and they would feel to him like a minor illness, a damp cough that he couldn't get rid of and had simply gotten used to.

It was cold in the bathroom: Marcus couldn't ever get the small window above the toilet to close all the way. He kept a dishtowel jammed into the crack but there was still a rim of frost around the sill in the winter. He ran the shower hot for a while to steam up the room before getting in. He didn't dare lean against the sink or the whole thing would have come out of the wall in a spray of defeated plaster. There were towels on the floor; Marcus moved them with his foot into a more organized-looking shape, then bent down to select one to use when he was done his shower, one dry and clean enough.

When he reached in to check the water, something stroked his arm, something cold and leathery like the wing of a bat. He jumped back and had to stifle a scream. It was the plant: Manda had put it in the tub and forgotten it there. Marcus hauled the whole thing out in his underwear, swearing at the touch of the cold leaves on his neck and arms. He carried it into the kitchen and dropped it hard on floor, hoping the plastic pot would split and he could put the whole thing out on the street. It certainly didn't look like it wanted to live with him. Or at all. As though it were only staying alive out of fear of what Manda would do to it if it started to droop and yellow. So many things seemed to tiptoe around her, afraid of awakening her wrath. Marcus hated to see the way Patrick let her whip him into place. He seemed like a tough enough guy – if *he* couldn't stand up to Manda, how would Marcus?

When they were kids, Manda had treated Marcus like a retard. She even called him that obsessively, which used to overwhelm his mind with a pre-teen sense of injustice and bitter irony, given the way Ken was. She used to lock Marcus out of the house in his underwear and come running into his room when he was sleeping to pummel him in his bed. His mother would tell him not to pay any attention to Manda's behaviour, that she was still "adjusting." Manda was always fighting with her father, always running away or coming home drunk or out of her mind on something in the middle of the night. It was only after she left home that Manda and Marcus were able to talk to each other at all. Over the past ten years, they'd achieved a wary form of friendship. Marcus suspected that this had happened

| 17 |

out of a combination of Patrick's long hours at the store and Manda's hating just about everyone else in Dunbridge. Whatever it was, he didn't actually mind too much – he didn't exactly have a lot of choice himself.

Marcus moved slowly. He wanted to get out, but the apartment sapped his will. He stood in the shower too long, and the dense calluses that hulled his feet peeled off in yellow strips like foreign candy. Standing on the mat, he nearly dripped dry before reaching for the towel with a shudder. He stared at the blue-handled toothbrush in his hand and at the brush with the orange handle still hanging in its slot, unable for a moment to say which one was his, and which had been there when he first moved in. The orange brush had a swollen elbow joint and its bristles were splayed flat as if by a violent force; he dropped it down into the wastebasket, into the clouds of crumpled tissue strung together with bloodied dental floss. He plucked at the wispy bridge threatening to unite his eyebrows, his contorted reflection in the mirror edging into a mocking self-consciousness. *A monobrow: this is what I've come to.* He was regressing, squandering his inheritance as a modern human being. Hair would flow out of his ears, his cock would shrivel and blanch. He drove a tight cone of tissue into each nostril.

If he died, he wondered, how long would it take for his body to be found? He'd been living here for years – cold in the winter, hot in the summer, cowed by the low ceilings. The electrical outlets bulged and smoked in a rainstorm. The very air exhausted him and slowed his thinking. At night he dreamed of lonely missions to Jupiter in a cramped capsule. In some documentary he'd seen on TV they'd shown paintings by a colour-blind man – all desperate greys and blacks, iron fruit in charred bowls. The same thing was happening here, he thought: his apartment was making him colour-blind. The food in his fridge was rotting, and his shower curtain was made of snakeskin. He was becoming mummified. The walls crinkled if you touched them – layers of paint over old wallpaper.

And yet, when he'd first moved into this place, Manda had been jealous. She used to come around and sit in the kitchen to complain about the tiny, one-bedroom apartment she and Patrick were living in at the time. Marcus knew she coveted his apartment; he waited for her to suggest a trade. The suggestion never came, probably because Patrick's mother was sick and it was obvious she wasn't going to last much longer. When she went, it was clear Patrick's dad would follow pretty quickly. Which he did. That meant they got the house. Marcus could never get over how crazy Manda had become about that house. Before Patrick's father died, she would tell Marcus she didn't ever want to live there. She acted like the house was a sentence. It was rotten, she told him, and way out in the worst end of Dunbridge, practically out in the country. "It's so *old*, but not even cool-old," she said. "It's just a big shack. I'd almost be happier staying where we are." Marcus knew she'd tried a couple of times, when they'd first got married, to talk Patrick into moving out of Dunbridge, closer to Toronto, even right into Toronto, but Patrick had the store and was still taking care of his dad.

Marcus didn't know how serious Manda had ever been about leaving. Allen, her own dad, the guy who'd brought her from Toronto to Dunbridge in the first place, was sick, and Ken was pretty helpless without her. This web of sick and dying people was trapping her. Marcus thought he'd caught her a couple of times looking at him as if he, too, were one of the people keeping her there, another sticky strand of the web. And yet, she'd had her moment of total helplessness, too – not that she'd ever admit it. She had never, ever acknowledged the fact that Marcus's mom had taken in Manda, her dad, and Ken, when all three were pretty much fucked. Most of the shit that had gone down in their lives was because of Manda's mother – who was a crazy bitch, from what Marcus had been told about her – and it was because of her that Allen wanted to get out of Toronto so bad. Lucky for him – and for Manda and Ken – that Margaret fell in love with him at the right time and said they could all live together like some kind of emotionally broken Brady Bunch. Manda never showed any gratitude for it; she never thanked Marcus's mom. She certainly never thanked Marcus for doing such a good job of getting used to the fact that, right in the middle of puberty, he had acquired a stepfather hiding out from his fucked-up ex-wife, a stepbrother who might well have been a zombie, and a stepsister who was angry and violent all the time. They weren't the Brady Bunch, they were the fucking Addams Family.

It looked cold out, so Marcus pulled thick, wool socks over his thin, white ones. He didn't have winter boots; the heels had fallen off the pair he'd worn last year. He tried to fix one of his baseball caps. The brim was tearing away from the rest of the hat, and the electrical tape wasn't holding.

Marcus walked through town and down to the marina. He refused to go straight to his uncle's store, even if it meant killing time walking around town, looking like Ken. At the far end of the park, dump trucks and diggers were converting the swamps next to the water into level land for a new soccer field. Right now it looked like they were unearthing a muddy mass grave. Shocked groups of seagulls oversaw the grim job. He walked along the gravel road that went by all the baseball diamonds and ended in a small parking lot. The grey brick building of the snack bar was boarded up tight. In the summer, he would sometimes buy an armload of popsicles and Mr. Freezies from a girl with Karla Homolka eyes who had a tiny TV the size of a lunchbox propped up behind the counter.

Someone had drawn onto the side of the building the most realistic-looking set of cock and balls Marcus had ever seen.

With a different-coloured marker, and with a lot less care, someone else had drawn a spurt of cum arcing up and across the board in lazy teardrops. Whenever he was out with Manda and they came across something like this, she would say something sarcastic about all the artistic talent in Dunbridge that was going to waste. She meant it as a joke, but in this case Marcus thought it was true: the balls, in their gnarl of pubic hair, were so realistic they looked like they'd be warm to the touch.

He checked his watch: he'd been out walking for almost an hour already. He turned and headed out of the park in the direction of his uncle's store, his back already aching from the coming weight of discount furniture. Stray seagulls glided in and landed along his path, pacing him with their thin legs and looking up at him quizzically as if he were about to pronounce on something uniquely important to scavenging birds.

The air in Manda's office was hot by the end of the day; the walls of her cubicle seemed to lean in on her a little. Sean had forbidden them from opening the windows. When Cheryl, who suffered the most, insisted on opening them a crack anyway, he'd had them all sealed shut. She had to bring in a small fan for her desk to blow in her face all day. Manda could hear its tiny whine rising and falling as it slowly shook its head at her workmate on the other side of the divider. It was putting her to sleep. After the third time she'd caught herself almost nodding off with her fingers on the keyboard, Manda called over: "Chinese food."

"Oh, don't tempt me," Cheryl replied. "I can't."

"I can!" Lana shouted from behind the other cubicle wall.

Manda ignored the other woman for the moment. "Why not?" she asked Cheryl.

There was a sound of a great weight being shifted and an office chair being relieved of its unfair burden, and then Cheryl came walking slowly around the cubicles to where Manda was sitting. Manda had time to respond to an e-mail while Cheryl made her way around.

"We're finally putting in a shower upstairs. Jim's supposed to meet the guys, but I want to be there when they start ripping up the bathroom to make sure they do it right."

"You've been talking about that since last year," Manda said. She felt a twinge of jealousy at the thought of Cheryl's house being redone.

"Well, I finally told Jim I was sick of going all the way downstairs just to shower. I almost broke my neck. And I hate taking baths."

"Oh, I love baths!" Lana cooed, coming round to join the conversation. Manda suddenly noticed that Jessica, the new girl, had appeared next to Cheryl. She was at least a few weeks away from being acknowledged as part of the office, and no one knew if she was even going to last that long, so the three women mostly ignored her.

"I'd love some Chinese buffet," Lana said. Jessica said nothing – she must have known she was considered a non-entity.

After work, Manda and Lana walked down to The Golden Dragon, pretty much the only restaurant on Dunbridge's main strip that hadn't been shut down or taken over by men and women using it as a *de facto* afternoon drinking hole. As they sat down, Manda started giggling.

"Oh, I just had a really mean thought."

"What is it?" Lana asked, already smiling.

"It's so mean: I just thought of Cheryl sloshing around in her bathtub."

Lana looked hurt. "That's not fair," she said. "She's been trying to lose weight. It's not easy."

"I know, I know," Manda said, a little annoyed at Lana for spoiling the funny mental image she had built up. (The new clawfoot tub, its legs straining at the weight like a beast of burden).

The waitress brought them tea and two pairs of chopsticks. Lana and Manda only had to nod to let her know they were there for the buffet. Everyone was. Manda sometimes wondered why they bothered with a regular menu; there was nothing on it that wasn't already available at the buffet.

"What do you think of Jessica?" Lana asked.

"I think she's kind of useless."

"Yeah. . . ." Lana said, trailing off.

"I don't think she's going to last. Even Sean can't stand her."

"But if she goes, then what?"

"Someone better, I hope, though you never know with Sean."

Lana leaned in to whisper, which bothered Manda. As if anyone was listening, or cared what Lana had to say even if they were.

"She told me she wants to have a baby."

"Who? Cheryl?" That *would* have been shocking news. Cheryl hated kids. *Hated* them.

Lana let out a high laugh. "No! Jessica! My god, can you imagine?"

"What, is she married?"

"No, not yet. You don't have to be, you know."

"No shit. Are you serious? Can you see that little girl lasting a day with a baby?"

"Well, she told me she wants to have a baby before she's thirty. I think it's sweet."

"Don't talk about babies," Manda said. "Patrick's going on about that again."

"Patrick wants a baby?" The bright look on Lana's face told Manda she wasn't going to get much sympathy from her.

"He wants *babies* – as in more than one. Like I'm just going to quit my job and stay at home until I'm sixty. I can't handle that shit. I'm not a baby person, I don't think."

"Oh, *I* am."

Lana was single and had never had a baby, but at that moment she looked as though she could happily eat one whole.

They lined up at the buffet and filled their warmed plates with everything that looked edible. At the far end of the buffet there were a lot of slippery-looking things on a bed of crushed ice, chunks of pineapple and little bowls of strawberries. Lana used her knife to look at the underside of the watermelon slices, but Manda only said, "I don't have *time* for fruit," and headed back to their table with her load. Lana followed her, smiling at her plate like it was a pet she was bringing home from the pound.

"I feel so guilty about using a fork," Lana said with her mouth full of rice and noodles. "I always think I should be using chopsticks when I'm here."

"So? Use your fingers."

"So why does Patrick want a little baby all of a sudden?"

Manda noticed that "little," but decided to let it go. "I think he has a thing where, now that his dad is dead, it's like *safe* to have kids. He never really said much about it before Ronnie died." Manda pulled a chicken ball away from her mouth as if it contained some drug meant to convince her of the joys of motherhood. "No, I am *not* going to be stuck at home all the time with a screaming kid. He wants to have one so bad, but it's not like he's going to help a lot."

Lana put on a knowing face. "I bet if you had one, Patrick would want to be the one to take care of it. He seems like the type."

"No, Patrick is his dad's son, through and through. I don't believe I just said that, but it's true. He'd want me at home with a hundred babies running around while he's at the store. And then when he comes home, there's dinner and everything ready, and the house is spotless, and he'll just sit in his little Ronnie chair and tell me to keep the kids quiet while he watches TV."

"I don't think Patrick would be like that."

"Are you joking? He's already like that half the time! It drives me crazy." Manda shook her head, clearly reconsidering. "Oh, I'm going to hell: Patrick's not like that. He could never be Ronnie."

"Patrick's a sweetie!" Lana protested.

"He *is* a sweetie – Jesus, Lana, don't say *sweetie* – he can be super-sweet, but he's got just enough Ronnie in him to make you want to strangle him."

Manda had cleared her plate and was waiting impatiently for Lana to finish so they could go back again. It was frustrating to watch Lana pick at every little thing, then put the fork down as if resting between each bite. *At least Cheryl eats*, Manda thought. Plus, Cheryl would have known exactly what Manda was talking about with babies. Manda gave up waiting for Lana and carried her plate to the buffet alone. She filled half her plate with steamed vegetables so that she could say she hadn't eaten only fried things, and stacked the other half with chicken balls and pork-fried rice. There was music playing in the restaurant at such a low volume it could have been coming from next door. The tune sounded familiar, a plinky instrumental version of some song Manda hadn't heard in a long time. She stood stock-still in front of a steaming mound of vermicelli with a vague frown on her face, fighting to bring the name of the song and maybe some of the lyrics back by force of will. Without realizing it, she had closed her eyes and started to sway.

"Do you know this one?" she asked Lana back at the table. The song was almost over, but could still be heard over the sound of waiters moving dishes and the kitchen workers replenishing the buffet.

Lana held her drink in mid-air and listened. She started to giggle. "I saw this thing – I think it was a joke – where people could get these computer chips put in their brain that played their favourite song all the time, but only you could hear it." Lana touched her temples with the tips of her fingers. She did it without thinking, then checked her fingers quickly to see if she had inadvertently dabbed soy sauce on her forehead. "One guy went crazy at the end – it was *so* funny."

Manda knew what was coming next: Lana never missed an opportunity to get a party-game going in the middle of a conversation.

"What song would you pick if you could?"

"I wouldn't pick anything. You just said the guy went crazy – I would too, same song in my head all the time."

Lana made a face of feigned exasperation. "No, but if you did, though, which song would you pick?"

"Nothing. A dial tone."

Lana ignored her. "I'd pick something by Celine Dion," she said. Manda pretended to faint in her chair; Lana ignored that, too. "Something where she does someone else's song. She has such a powerful voice, she can sing *anything*."

"Patrick had 'True Colors' playing in the truck the other day. Cyndi Lauper? I could have killed him."

"That's so romantic. It's such a beautiful song. I want that at my wedding, whenever *that* is."

"It drove me crazy for like two days."

"Maybe Patrick's a bit sappy."

"My god, he's like Mr. Roboto half the time, but when he starts with the having-a-baby shit . . ." Manda spun her remaining noodles onto her fork and prepared to push the whole thing into her mouth out of spite.

The streetlights were already on when they left the restaurant. It was raining again, and cold. Manda offered Lana a ride home, but she declined when Manda told her they'd have to go all the way over to Marcus's apartment to retrieve the truck. "I'd end up walking farther than if I just went straight home," Lana said. She stood there for another minute as if waiting for Manda to offer her a piggyback.

Manda was feeling good from all the food in her stomach – she needed Chinese buffet at least once a month, she decided – but within minutes of leaving Lana and the restaurant, her thoughts were on the house, and her good mood just melted away. The paint store at the top of the hill was closing as she passed. Just seeing paint cans filled her with frustration: she'd barely made a dent in the house in four years, it felt like. A couple of days ago, she'd seen a place with exactly the kind of white-rock garden she wanted. She thought about driving past with Patrick that night. The owners of the garden were Chinese or Japanese, Manda guessed – there were all kinds of symbols on their front door, and pretty Asian wind chimes hanging above it – but it'd be dark enough so that Patrick wouldn't notice. If he thought she was trying to do something Chinese to their house, he would freak. He thought anything more than the basic square of Astroturf was too much.

Two streetlights were out on Marcus's street, another was flickering. The windows of his apartment were dark – she imagined him still laying there half-nude on the couch, too lazy to get up and turn on a light. She had to go down a dark alleyway to get the truck, which she'd left earlier in the tight parking space beyond his stairs. She felt a chill stepping into the darkness. She couldn't even see the truck from the street. She used to make fun of Ronnie's obsession with people getting raped; the old guy wouldn't let Patrick's poor mother go to the doctor because he was convinced they would put her to sleep and molest her while she was under. "He's got that on the brain," Manda had told Patrick at the time. It got less funny when his mother finally did go see a doctor and found that a storm of cancer had been eating away at her the whole time. Manda could never figure out why Patrick didn't immediately go and kick the shit out of his father for that. She would have. Poor woman.

The exterior of the truck was beaded all over with water, meaning Patrick had gotten it waxed recently. They had no money for their own home, but he could afford to buff up the truck. *His* priorities were clear. As she backed the truck out of the alley she shouted "Fucking hell!" and almost hit the brakes when she realized that she'd been humming "True Colors" for the last twenty minutes.

Patrick was already pulling the accordioned wall across the front of his store and locking up when Manda called. The mall was dark and quiet; they had cut the canned music a few minutes ago. He had to run to get the phone, almost knocking over one of the big shoe displays he'd pulled back inside earlier. His clumsiness looked wrong on someone his size. He was under six feet, but broad-chested and muscular, with a face that seemed to conceal all vulnerability under an inch of impassive skin and bone. Even when he played hockey as a teenager he was a klutz.

He caught the phone on the last ring before the voice mail would have picked it up. Whenever Manda got the store's voice mail, she would leave long, obnoxious messages, swearing her head off and being as crude as possible to let Patrick know she was joking, but he always understood he was supposed to recognize that she really was a little pissed off about it.

"I'm outside, babe. Truck's warm."

He could hear the radio on loud in the background. He wondered if there'd be anything to eat when he got home; he'd skipped dinner. He didn't mind making himself something to eat, but Manda had a habit of leaving it to the last minute to get groceries. Maybe only canned tuna and bread awaited him.

"Hey Manda?"

She'd already hung up.

With everything pretty much done he went through his usual half-minute of paralysis, standing and waiting for a gust of mental wind to push him toward closing up completely and going home. When Patrick first opened the store, he vowed always to stay open a few minutes later than his posted hours and not get into the habit of packing up twenty minutes before closing if it was quiet. He thought this sense of commitment would be felt at some subconscious level by everybody who came into his place, and they would respond in kind by showing him a similar sense of loyalty. In the last few months, however, he had started getting everything ready to go so that he could lock the front at exactly nine o'clock and be home by nine-fifteen. He was turning forty-two in a month, and was secretly wondering what else he would start to let slide.

In the back parking lot, the pavement was wet and reflective like oil. Someone had pushed a stolen shopping cart up to the back door of his store; Patrick gave it a kick and it clattered all the way to the next door. He wasn't wearing a jacket, so the sudden cold hit him with a shiver. He wondered if it was cold enough for people to start thinking about Christmas presents, despite the fact that the mall would still be choked with pictures of witches and ghosts for another week.

Manda flashed the headlights of the truck at him as if they were making some kind of illegal drop. Walking across the lot he got tangled in a plastic bag that had come blowing across and wrapped itself around his knees like a jellyfish. Manda gave a quick honk of the horn when she saw him almost trip, but he ignored that. He pretended to look for the moon that should have been just coming over the edge of the mall's roof but was sealed behind a thick dome of cloud.

"Having a little trouble there, babe?" she asked him as he climbed into the truck.

"People are always chucking shit back here," he said.

Once they were out of the parking lot Manda turned the music back up. She took the longer way home, skirting the north end of Dunbridge where there were still small dairy farms and two-room houses right by the road that looked like they were being absorbed by the trees.

"Where are we going?"

"Something I want to show you. Two seconds."

"I need to eat something."

"Two seconds."

They drove past Marcus's apartment, and Patrick worried they were meeting her stepbrother; he had nothing against the guy – though he thought Marcus was a bit of a waste – but it was late, and Patrick didn't feel like talking to anyone.

"That's Darren's new place," Patrick said, pointing at a bungalow with all the lights on and no curtains in the windows. Darren was a friend of his from school who had come to their wedding. Though Patrick had never made a conscious decision to eliminate Darren from his life, he'd only run into the guy a few times since. Every time, Darren would make a big deal about them getting together for beers or something as soon as possible. Patrick would reply, "Definitely, definitely," but even as he was saying it he knew it probably would never happen. He couldn't think of any reason why not – their friendship just seemed obsolete, somehow. Darren was married now, too, with two kids, one from before the marriage and one from after, a girl and a boy.

"Since when do they have a house?"

"They bought that last year. Wanted me to help him move, but . . ."

Manda slowed the truck almost to a stop to look at the house. The curtainless window made it look wide-eyed and hysterical in the dark.

"Looks like they're still moving in," she said. "Look at that yard: it's all mud."

"His girl's almost three."

"That tree's going to come over."

A woman walked past the living room window – Darren's wife, probably, though it was hard to tell.

"You can see right in there," Manda said. "That would drive me crazy."

They came to the end of the street, which Manda was now convinced was the wrong one.

"Well, it's totally gone," she said.

"What are we looking for?"

"Nothing, never mind. A rock garden. I didn't dream it."

They drove past Nun's Hill, where Patrick used to go sledding as a kid. Near the hospital they had to stop for a train. The stoplights at the end of their street kept appearing and reappearing between the cars. Manda sometimes leapt across the tracks almost as soon as the last car had cleared their front bumper, but tonight she waited until the lights had stopped flashing and the clanging was silent, then drove gently over the tracks as if out of concern for some delicate cargo.

"Hey, we were close tonight," she said as they got going again. "Only two numbers off."

Patrick looked asleep but he was listening. "How much was this one for? Was this the big one?"

"No, that's on Friday. Christ, if we ever came so close on *that* one I think I would lose my fucking mind. This was only for a couple million."

"*Only*, eh?"

"I was thinking while it was on about what we would do if we won," Manda said.

"Buy a new truck."

"Oh come on, fuck – we can do better than that! No, I was

| 31 |

thinking we can finish the house finally, or buy a new one. Doesn't even have to be here; we could probably buy a place in Florida if we wanted."

"Ever been to Florida?"

"I haven't won a million dollars yet."

It started to rain again. They passed Patrick's old schoolyard. All of the old playground equipment had been replaced with giant tubes and climbers that looked like they were built for infants. Most of the trees were gone, even the big one shaped like a Y they used to climb up and jump from. His first broken bone – his first two, in fact: his collar and his arm. Ronnie had wanted to swat him for being so stupid. Manda wouldn't believe it when Patrick told her, but there'd been an old van with no tires in the playground when he was in kindergarten. He could remember fighting to sit in the driver's seat and crank the steering wheel back and forth like the wheel on a ship. The school hadn't even taken out the windows; someone eventually smashed them and they would wrestle in the back with glass underfoot. He could show her right where it had been. He could see the spot from the road.

"You know what I was thinking?" Patrick asked. "If we ever have a kid some day, I was thinking we could have it in the house if it's all finished." He kept his eyes closed, but he knew Manda was looking at him.

"Where do you think the baby would be, in the garage?"

"No, I mean like *having* it in the house," he said. "In the bedroom or whatever. Do the whole thing at home and have the doctor there and everything."

"You mean like actually deliver a baby in our house? What are you talking about?"

"People do it," Patrick said.

"Yeah, hippies and people out in the friggin bush, maybe. Where is this coming from?"

"Nowhere. I just said it, that's all. I'm tired."

Manda kept looking over at him as she drove, half-expecting him to burst out laughing.

"You'd want all that going on in our room, in the room where we sleep, with all these people in there, and me screaming my friggin head off?" she asked him. "And all this blood and everything going all over the place? That sounds good to you?"

"We'd cover everything. With paper or whatever."

Manda started laughing. "You don't put paper down when you're having a kid! You're not carving a jack-o'-lantern. Come on, babe. Haven't you ever seen a kid being born?"

"No. Not yet."

That was low, her face told him. *A low blow.* They didn't speak for the rest of the ride home.

FRIDAY

Manda wanted to give the bedroom ceiling the finger for staring down at her first thing in the morning. Drowned under the heavy duvet and curved like a shrimp around the empty space where Patrick had been only a few minutes ago, she felt as though the room were full of people who had only just gone silent. They were waiting for some sign from her. She threw up a bare arm to wave them off. The curtains on the bedroom window were swollen eyelids, barely letting in any light, so she couldn't tell what kind of day it was going to be. The furnace was breathing up from the floor, ruffling the fronds of carpet that had grown up to the edge of the vent.

Manda didn't actually need to be awake this early. She'd booked the day off. But Patrick had been truly pathetic about the alarm that morning. When he finally got it to stop buzzing he must have hit the sleep button because it went off again ten minutes later, when he was already in the shower. Manda was forced to drag herself across the bed by her fingertips and slap the little black clock like it was an insect that wouldn't die. Almost instantly she was back under the covers, but full of the grim certainty that she was up for good.

Getting out of bed she almost knocked the phone off the side table with her elbow. Patrick hated having a phone in the room; he said that just having it there, just knowing it *could* ring, would keep him up, which Manda thought was stupid. She told him so and told him she needed the phone, and that was that.

One of the things she was waiting to hear was that Allen, her father, had died. When Allen had his stroke she didn't hear about it until the next morning; Patrick had come into the bedroom with his hair wet and his face all white. "Fuck," was all she could say when he told her. "Fuck fuck fuck." She was waiting now for the final call, though who knew how long that would take to arrive. Margaret had told Manda recently that Allen was forgetting things and falling down and waking up in the morning fighting for breath.

The rumble of the shower went on and on in the next room. Showers were just about the only place where Patrick indulged himself, which was why he hadn't really protested her buying a fancy shower-bath combo even though it was more than they could afford. Buying a simpler one could have allowed them to make serious inroads on the kitchen and maybe even the living room, which still looked as if Patrick's father could have walked in from beyond the grave and started demanding the TV be put back to The History Channel for his nightly dose of mail-shirts and Nazi rallies and masses of bare-backed slaves.

Manda got up and knocked on the bathroom door. "You've been in there like twenty minutes," she yelled. "You're gonna use up all the hot water."

"All right," Patrick yelled back. Within a few seconds the thundering in the walls ceased. The door clicked, and he padded out, pursued by faint steam and wrapped in a thick towel. "Yours," he said, and disappeared into the bedroom to get dressed.

"The wallpaper's starting to curl up at the corners, you know," Manda said after him.

She followed him and sat on the bed while he got dressed. It was dark in there except for the lamp on the bedside table. Patrick pulled at a pair of jeans that were caught by the leg in the drawer. He was looking older, she thought, unless it was just the light. She'd been wanting him to grow his hair out a little in the back, the way he had it in the high-school pictures of him she'd seen. He just made a face at the idea. He didn't lift weights or exercise much anymore, but he was still heavy and muscular. If he ever started getting fat she would make him eat less and walk to the mall more, maybe ride a bike. There was grey hair around his ears now. Manda wondered what would happen if he grew a beard, if it would come out all white. She wondered when his pubic hair would turn, and if she'd be able to stand it when it did. She looked but couldn't tell, in the dimness of the bedroom, what state it was in now.

When they first got married, they used to lie naked together for hours, sometimes daring each other not to get dressed for the entire day if neither of them had to go to work. When they'd first started going out, Patrick had a habit of feeling around for his underwear almost the instant they'd finished fucking, but Manda had eventually cured him of that. She used to make him let her rub her hands all over him as he lay there. She would curl her fingers into his hair while he fought back laughter. (The consequences of laughing were severe, sex-wise: she wasn't afraid to use her teeth.) He had the body of an Olympic wrestler without hardly doing anything to earn it. Ronnie had been muscular, too. Even Patrick's mother had looked tough to Manda. Seeing him naked now reminded her how long it had been since they'd lain together all day. Years.

"You look exhausted," Manda told him. "Not that you look a hell of a lot different any other time."

"That's nice," he said, still trying to pull on his jeans: they wouldn't yield to his feet.

"Seriously, why don't you go back to sleep for an hour, babe?" she asked. She didn't like to see him this tired. "I'll wake you up around ten and drive you in."

He suddenly stood straight and stared at the wall as if he'd been shot with a tranquilizer gun; Manda expected him to go all glassy and fall forward onto the bed. Instead, he started slapping at his pockets.

"Have you seen it?"

"Which?"

"My wallet."

The two of them went on a ten-minute hunt through the house, Manda retracing his probable steps while Patrick made frustrated lunges into corners and closets he hadn't been near in days, trying to catch the missing wallet off guard. Manda finally found it lodged in the front seat of the truck, hidden under a pile of new baseball caps. Manda laughed at how it looked in there: as if Patrick had been driving around luring boys into his truck to kill and dispose of, leaving only their hats.

"There, you've got your wallet," she said, handing it over with much ceremony at the doorstep. "Can we relax now, or have you lost your keys, too?"

"I need to get moving."

"You're not even going to eat anything? Aw, don't eat at that place in the mall – the last time you had breakfast there you shit all day."

"I feel sorry for that guy. No one ever eats there."

"Cuz everyone gets the shits, now stop."

Patrick let Manda persuade him out of his jacket and he followed her to the kitchen.

"What's going on today that's special, babe?" she asked him.

He told her about how his back room was choked with boxes, how he couldn't even get at his little washroom and was forced to use the one in the mall.

"Can't you get Danny in to help you? Just for the weekend?"

"Danny's working up at the Irving station now; they have him on nights. Anyway, I think he's still pissed at me."

Manda's annoyance shot up at the same time, and with the same speed, as the toast.

"He's gotta get over himself," she hissed. "He could barely work a friggin *cash register* and you had him trained up to open the place all by himself." She scraped the toast with butter, then spread on sour marmalade, a liking Patrick had inherited from Ronnie.

"He wouldn't have that job now if you hadn't given him a chance," she went on, handing him the toast as if the proof of her words were written there in marmalade. "He was a mess – you gave him a chance."

Patrick shrugged. He knew he could never redeem Danny in Manda's eyes. She hated his sloppiness and his sullen ingratitude. She couldn't ever stand ingratitude, but especially coming from Danny. She saw him as someone who had had it easy growing up but who had fucked it all up out of sheer laziness and stubbornness. He leeched off of Patrick, probably more than she was even aware of.

"What about Marcus? He isn't working much at his uncle's, so he could use the money. You could pay him cash. Actually, just give him a new pair of running shoes and you won't have to pay him at all."

"Maybe."

Patrick ended up eating four pieces of toast, which made Manda glow with vindication. After he left, she cleaned up the kitchen and took her coffee into the living room to watch some morning TV. Though it wasn't the best place to see the screen, she sat on the couch instead of Ronnie's old chair. With Patrick gone, the house seemed to get colder, as if aware that Manda did not belong.

Manda was surprised to discover she had planned nothing for herself for the day. She had vague thoughts about looking at paint samples for the back room upstairs or at carpet samples for the living room, but she had done this so many times – she was tired of trying to make decisions in a vacuum while they waited for extra money to shake loose from their otherwise drum-tight finances. She was sick of putting together hypothetical rooms. She blamed the house for being so old that even the smallest renovations were expensive. Just like an old man, she thought: it fought back with the sheer inflexibility of age. Patrick's father had lived here for nearly a year on his own after his wife died and had obviously taught the place a few things. He had de-feminized it, drawn out whatever warmth it had, making it bitter and recalcitrant. It didn't matter, though: just as she had with the old man, she would win out over this house. She could be colder and harder, she would meet stubbornness and inflex-ibility with an axe. If a room refused to be reformed, if its dimensions or its strange fixtures made it too difficult to update, then she'd just knock out a wall to make a new room. Or maybe just knock out the wall and wait a couple of weeks before staunching the wound with plaster and paint, leaving the hole open and raw to teach the house a lesson.

The room Manda tried not to ever think about was the one down the hallway from their bedroom, the one with the full-on hole in the ceiling. She used to see that room as evidence of the raw deal they got when they decided – when *Patrick* decided – to move into the house instead of selling it after Ronnie died. She'd actually burst out laughing when she first caught sight of the hole. Repairing it was yet one more thing that remained hypothetical until the money started coming back in. The chunk of money they'd originally put aside for renovation had dried up fast. All of it had come from selling Ronnie's hunting cabin up north, though some of that money had been funnelled into the store. Manda was scared to look at her credit card bills now. She just put a hundred-dollar cheque in the mail every month without even knowing if this was doing anything to reduce the debt. She told herself that she would very soon have to look at that debt head-on, but right now it would have discouraged her completely to know its true dimensions.

They couldn't agree on what to do with the room once the hole was repaired. She knew the kind of room Patrick wanted: one with animals and glow-in-the-dark stars on the wall. A shallow closet with a cute door. All the electrical outlets gagged with plastic so they couldn't bite little fingers. She imagined him standing in there and silently filling the space with his fantasies of trouble-free fatherhood. In his mind he must have seen CindyLoo Who asleep on a blanket being held aloft at each corner by an angel. She thought about finding some black paint in the basement and painting a crude cartoon portrait of her ovaries – six feet high – on the back wall of the room. It would shut him up about babies for a while at least. And if Ronnie's bitter old ghost really was still in the house, it might be enough to make him move on for good. She was tempted.

Manda wanted new things in the house; she wanted to chew through the layers of used-up life deposited everywhere by Patrick and his parents in their four decades of living in the place. She wanted to get down to the bare soil of walls and windows and then grow all new rooms, rooms that were conspicuous in their newness.

The bedroom was the warm centre of Manda's lair, where the eggs should have been laid. What Patrick had come out with the night before, about having a baby in the house – she was still mad at him for it, but it almost made sense in a twisted way. She'd worked hard to make their bedroom into a kind of soft mitt that held her and Patrick as they slept, so why not make that a baby's first experience of the world, instead of some awful place full of people coughing and dying? If she ever did have a kid she wouldn't want to be stuck in a hospital, especially not the one in Dunbridge, and it wasn't like she'd have much choice. She'd had fainting spells a couple of years ago and had gone in to get herself checked out. She ended up having to stay two nights while they looked for the cause. They never found anything, which made her feel deeply betrayed: she'd avoided hospitals for so long, now here she was making this gesture of trust, and all they can do is throw her into a depressing room with a woman who moaned all night. And then, after all that, they let Manda leave without even telling her what was wrong. "Stress," was all the doctor could come up with.

Stress. Manda had said the word acidly all the way home. "That's what my dad used to call a ketchup answer: you can use it on anything. How long did he have to go to school for that? Stress. Never again, I'm telling you."

It was just after nine in the morning, but as bright out as it was going to get all day. Outside, Manda could see an October sky, rusty and scraped. It didn't depress her. It certainly didn't make her feel old or remind her she was going to die or anything like that. To her it looked clean and clear and dry – there was *room* in that sky. Room to breathe. It wasn't a sky that lay close to the ground and stifled you. That's what happened in the summer in Dunbridge – the sky became a blue dome that penned them in like animals. She wanted the sky blocked out by buildings, like it was in Toronto. Patrick would always say that it was *there* that he felt like an animal, but that wasn't true: you could hide in those canyons of shadow, and not feel like your every move was on display for the neighbours, for the police, or for whoever or whatever was staring down. She thought there was something wrong and reptilian about summer-worship: too much lying around, too much passivity. She was warm-blooded; she didn't need to lie around on the sand like a lizard to stay alive. Patrick used to go to Wasaga Beach as a kid and was always bugging her to go, but Manda hated raw sunlight and the kind of crowds that went to the beach in the peak season. Plus, she was afraid of the water (though she'd never admit that to Patrick). She wouldn't have minded going now, when it was cold and the beaches were deserted and the sand was too damp and cold to just sit around on. They could have gone for a walk and collected driftwood to use in the yard and looked across water nibbled white from the wind. You had to respect the water when it was this cold out. When it burned your skin to step in, when the whole stretch of it was black and agitated – that was when water did what it was *supposed* to.

Manda, still in her bathrobe and her socks, felt a draft coming from somewhere. Patrick had left without locking the front door, and the thing had slipped open again. The house was so old that everything had to be locked shut or it would hang open all day like the mouth of a dumb kid. Manda could shut a window and a cabinet door would click free. She went on missions throughout the house, shutting all those mouths. As she swung the front door closed she caught sight of the mailman coming up their front walk. Without thinking, she slammed it shut on his wave.

"Sorry, I only saw you there at the last minute," she said to the man now standing on the walkway and looking through his bag. He held out a small packet of letters bound in an elastic band. He was standing a few steps from the door, right where he had stopped when Manda had shut it. He wouldn't come any closer, so Manda was forced to come out of the house in her socks to retrieve the letters.

"Is that it, no cash?" she asked him as she looked at all the return addresses. "Too bad, eh?"

He took a minute to pull his gloves back on. Theirs was the last house on that side of the street. He had a few minutes' walk before the next delivery.

"If there's freezing rain you need to salt this walkway," he said, pointing down at the row of paving stones under his feet in case she thought he was referring to somebody else's front walk. "It's supposed to freeze up this week," he added, so she wouldn't think he was telling her this just because.

"I use sand usually," Manda replied. "Salt's bad for the grass and the garden."

He closed the flap on his bag and started turning away.

"Sand doesn't do it," he said. "If there's no salt then I am not obligated to come up the walk. By law I don't have to, meaning you'll have to put a box at the end of the driveway or pick your mail up at the post office on Victoria Street. That's the law."

She was stunned for a second. "Excuse me, but we *always* put sand down and there has *never* been a problem before."

The man only shrugged with his gloved hands way up in the air to show her how relevant he found that information.

For almost a minute, she allowed all her irritation to be directed at his receding figure; she tried to focus it, to sharpen it to a deadly point so that it would pierce his jacket and scar his back. She gave up standing outside when the soles of her sock-feet started to burn on the pavement. She felt like getting the hose and turning the walk into a skating rink.

A young man wearing a toque that sat up straight off the top of his head like a vertical windsock pushed another loveseat to the back of the truck and onto the ramp, then sat in it and pretended to doze while the ramp lowered him to the warehouse floor at the back of Sinc's store. When the ramp hit the floor with a bump, he woke up and looked around. "Fuck," he said with a lazy smile. "I thought I was at home and my girlfriend was coming over to give me a blow job."

Marcus smiled but couldn't make himself laugh – he'd been

watching Jacob perform variations on this routine since they'd started unloading the truck a few hours ago. He sat on a crate kneading the muscles in his arm and trying to sit straight enough to not disturb the invisible shark teeth embedded in his spine. The truck they were unloading was only half-empty. They had barely made a dent in it the day before, spending most of their time clearing space in the warehouse. Jacob had given him a drive home, which meant a lot of gripping the dashboard as he drove through the most tenuous of yellow lights while volunteering all the squishy details of some recent sexual encounter that always sounded suspiciously effortless. They were both back in by ten that morning, as per Sinc's instructions.

"We're gonna be fucked once we get all these loveseats in here," Marcus said when his uncle came back to check on them. "We'll have no room to move around."

"Bullshit," Sinc said, rolling up his sleeves to help Jacob stack one recliner on top of another.

"That's amazing," Marcus said, looking around the warehouse, his eyes wide with mock wonder. "You said 'bullshit' and all of a sudden there's *twice* as much room back here. I don't know why I was worried; do that again."

"Have you two precious little girls pulled that kitchen-set out and put it in the van yet?"

"We're not delivering any of this today, are we?" Marcus asked, feeling something slump within him. He had been hoping to get out of there by early afternoon. If they had to drive around making deliveries he wouldn't get home until late again.

Sinc held his arms far apart and smiled. "You don't want to leave already, do you? You've got better things to do?"

"Yeah well, you're not keeping me here late tonight. That was *bullshit* last night."

"What was bullshit?"

"Us being here til fucking ten o'clock."

Sinc pretended to stagger back in shock. "Oh I'm *sorry*," he said. "I didn't know I was making you all sleepy keeping you here so late. I didn't know you had more exciting things to do."

Marcus shrugged. "I don't," he said. "Let's just get it done so we're not here til fucking midnight." He had an instinctual sense of how far to push it with his uncle. He knew he could easily be replaced with someone bigger and stronger.

"Have you at least found me any steel-toe boots that fit?" Marcus asked. He had only his running shoes. They looked pale and vulnerable next to all the heavy furniture. "I don't want to crush my foot and have to sue you."

"You sue me and I'll fucking lock you in a wardrobe and drop you in the fucking river. I have to get back out front. Pete's probably got another piece sold, so be ready to do a little light lifting, ladies."

While Jacob took a break to smoke a joint just outside the warehouse entrance, Marcus went into the office and closed the door behind him. His right arm felt like it had been torn loose, his back was on fire. Still, working for Sinc was actually one of the better jobs he'd ever had. He'd spent two years driving a van around, delivering bundles of newspapers. One night, the van hit an icy patch, slid into the ditch, and rolled onto its roof. Marcus was hit in the face with heavy bundles of newsprint and had to pull himself out the passenger's side door to limp home. He refused to get back in the van again, and even let his driver's licence expire so that he never had to – and never could – get another driving job. Since then he'd been living off the honorarium they paid him as a coach and the shifts he picked up at Sinc's store.

Marcus called Kelly on the office phone, but her machine picked up after half a ring. Jacob knocked angrily on the office window and made furious jerking-off motions with both hands, so Marcus hung up without leaving a message.

"You fucking guy," Jacob said when he came back out. "We have to move a desk, and you're in there making calls. Next time *I'll* go have a little rest and leave you with all the shit."

"You went for a smoke!"

"I had like *two* puffs. I've got nothing til we get paid and I have to make it last. That's why I'm not sharing."

The desks were jammed in behind a wall of refrigerators. They would all have to be moved out and then moved back into place. Marcus couldn't believe it. It took them a few minutes to move even one fridge. Marcus wanted to check inside them to see if they were filled with cinder blocks. They moved two more and took another break.

"Hey Marcus," Jacob said. "Pete told me you're fucking a woman with a kid. Is that true? Are you that fucking desperate?"

"I'm always that desperate," Marcus said, pulling off his gloves. "Anyway, Pete got it wrong: I'm fucking the mother *and* the kid."

Jacob howled, as Marcus knew he would. He had learned long ago never to resist anything that Jacob or his uncle threw at him. Same with the boys he coached. Better to just take the shit and wait for them to get bored or for the storm to move on.

A few hours later, Sinc sent them out to start making deliveries. Jacob scraped the side of the van against the wall on their way out of the warehouse and almost drove over a concrete parking divider. The back of the van was jammed with furniture, three deliveries' worth. They drove out under a distressed-metal sky, looking for the first house on the list hidden somewhere in the irregular coils and twists of a new subdivision on the other side of the highway. Marcus had a hard time getting any actual heat off the van's heater, and Jacob kept cracking the window to smoke. Marcus rang the bell at the first house, which looked exactly like every other house within sight, but had to come back empty-handed.

"Nobody," he said when he got back in the van.

"Fuck it, let's leave it all in the driveway."

They waited for twenty minutes, trading elaborate guesses about what they would find if they broke into the house.

The next house was closer to town. On the way, they passed Kelly walking alone, but the fact didn't register in Marcus's tired mind until they were almost around the next corner. She must have been on her way to pick up her son at the babysitter's. She didn't look like she was coming from work; Marcus immediately regretted the probable loss of an entire day together without the kid around. He could have told Jacob to stop but he didn't. Anyway, Jacob was too busy trying to retrieve an unlit cigarette from under his thigh. Another time, Marcus thought.

Manda was outside the Dunbridge Public Library. It had a big sign that said "Main Branch," though it was the *only* branch. Patrick had told her about a bookmobile that used to visit schools when he was a kid, but nobody had seen it for decades. It was probably on blocks in someone's yard out in the boonies like every other bus that died of old age. She waited at the bottom of the wheelchair ramp while an old man brought himself down slowly, his chair's electric motor whining at the strain. "Need a hand, there?" she asked, but he didn't look up. She had to press up against the wall of the building to let him pass. The chair had clearly become a kind of friend to the man, his trusted mule. There were stickers all over the thing, and tassels hanging off the arm rests. A bright orange triangle hung from the back of his seat, the kind that hung off the back of tractors when they drove along the side of a highway. Manda tried to imagine where he took the thing that he needed such a huge sign like that.

There was an after-school story group inside the library, spooking the old folks who usually hung around all day and forcing them out of the chairs they liked best to doze in. It was warm and shadowy inside. The library put old and damaged paperbacks in a milk crate by the door and sold them off for twenty-five cents a pop. Manda would scoop up armloads of them at a time, careful to let the Harlequins and the outright trash drop back in the crate. Sometimes she got lucky with a fat, old Atwood or a John Irving bound in yellowing layers of Scotch tape, its spine broken but strong enough for one more reading. That day, she was looking in the stacks for a novel they'd been talking about on the radio for a week now, one about the building of the Bloor Viaduct in Toronto. She'd heard the title a dozen times but could never remember it right.

The only thing she knew about the Bloor Viaduct was that it was a suicide magnet. She wondered if there'd be anything about *that* in the book. An old boyfriend of hers, a hockey player, had thrown himself off the thing a few years ago. She hadn't seen him for nearly fifteen years before that – she didn't even hear he was dead until weeks later when she ran into someone she knew from school. The information was passed on in the same gossipy tone that would have been used to tell her who was getting a divorce because her husband was a drunk, or which of their old teachers had turned out to be gay after all. Manda had sucked in her breath and made shocked noises, all the while trying to remember what the guy looked like.

Suicide was just another part of the background of life in Dunbridge, a regrettable but common occurrence on the same level as drownings in the Coldwater River and accidents on the highway. For a while, the town had acquired a reputation for them: for athletes being found in the woods with a note, a borrowed gun, and a face turned to black jelly. For heavy metal pacts that went awry and left one friend dead in a mess in the car with the stereo still on full blast and the other crawling back along the highway with a blown-off jaw. There were at least three picked-on fat girls who had trusted all their dead weight to an extension cord tied tight to the ceiling of a tool shed or a garage. Manda remembered obsessing over them when her father first brought her to Dunbridge. She would fantasize about being the one to come across the body of a suicide. She didn't know what she would have done if she had – in the fantasy she only stole the note and ran off.

They'd even had a scare with Patrick's little sister, apparently. Patrick never gave Manda the details, but she knew it involved pills and had something to do with his father. Sara had moved out of the house and out of the province as soon as she was old enough – probably even a little earlier than that. She was in B.C. now; Manda had never met her. She hadn't even come back for their wedding – Patrick said there was no point in inviting her while Ronnie was still alive. She lived out there with four kids by two different dads and never had much contact with Patrick. Every once in a while Patrick asked what the birthdays were for Sara's kids, and Manda had to remind him she had no idea. It bothered him to know so little about his nephews. Sara left Dunbridge in such a mess, he said, that he never pushed her to keep in touch. That was almost twenty years ago. Patrick said they were always changing houses and apartments – sometimes with one of the fathers, sometimes without.

Manda tried to imagine what life was like for those four kids. Living like that had almost killed her own father. Maybe it still would: maybe what her father was going through now was a kind of delayed reaction from the years he'd spent keeping Manda and Ken out of their mother's clutches, fighting her in court, doing everything he could to make sure she was stripped of all rights. Manda tried to talk about it with him a couple of times, but he usually acted like he was a veteran being dragged out to visit his old foxhole. Other times he just ignored the question or simply shrugged it off. Margaret had told Manda that her father used to talk about her mother when they first moved in, but that he forced himself to stop because it made him so angry.

"I think Allen's just glad it's all over and that you and Ken are fine and all grown up and happy where you are," she'd said.

Manda didn't believe a word of this, though she knew the woman was saying it out of good intentions. It was the last part of what Margaret had said, however, that particularly bugged her. It went to the heart of a question she had been asking her father since they'd first started coming to this town, a question he reacted to with either jokes or impatience, but which he could never answer to her satisfaction: what were they *doing* way up in Dunbridge? She and Ken had grown up ten minutes away from a subway station, surrounded by noise and kids, and he had taken them to live in a house in the middle of a muddy field. Ken had been taken from a place where people had mental and physical problems that made his own look like nothing. On the street they used to live on there was a man who always smelled like shit – like actual *shit* – and who walked like a crab trying to make an evolutionary leap. Dunbridge had its fair share of freaks and mental-cases, but they were local, they grew up there, which made all the difference. Everyone had all the time in the world to get used to them. Ken showed up and he was like a monster coming out of the woods. The one blessing was that he was big, and therefore hard to knock down.

Manda, when she first got here, had the opposite problem to Ken: instead of moving too slow, she always felt as though her mind was spinning too fast all the time. The things she used to try to slow it down – booze, drugs, sex, fights with other girls

– just made her situation worse. She simply refused to accept that her life had been completely changed, and that she was now living in the kind of place that used to make her bored to even hear about. She very quickly became Manda the Crazy Slut and Manda the Mean, Nasty Bitch and Manda the Weirdo Freak Who's Probably a Dyke. The only friends she made were as skittish and messed-up as she was – girls who'd been fingered by their dads, or whose mothers had tried to yank out all their hair with their bare hands because they'd peed their new shorts on the way to the store. Girls who burnt things into their arms and who had pale scratches on their wrists, leftovers from half-hearted suicide attempts with a Swiss Army knife. Girls who couldn't stop talking hypothetically about the taste of their own menstrual blood. Not that any of this endeared them to Manda. She used to come down hard on them, even the ones she genuinely liked, eating one alive every few months, beating the crap out of them or publicly humiliating them so badly the Swiss Army knives came out again.

Allen had acted as if coming to Dunbridge had solved his children's problems, and that Manda's behaviour was worse for the ingratitude it displayed. It was then that Manda began to formulate her belief that having a kid was an extreme form of selfishness. You have this baby, this helpless thing that didn't ask to be there, didn't ask to be pulled from your vagina, and it is your hostage, your slave. Short of killing and raping it – and even there, exceptions would be made based on extenuating circumstances – you could do with that kid whatever you liked. You control it, you fill its mind with whatever ideas you want, you push it where you want to go, and then you get to stand there and demand gratitude. It used to sicken her, the very idea. Every time she heard of someone getting pregnant, she would think: here was another person going to all the trouble of creating a life to fill a hole in their own.

After spending a maddening ten minutes looking for the book in the library's dark aisles, Manda asked one of the workers to help her find it. Turns out she had the author's name written down wrong: not enough A's and too many O's. The photo on the back cover made him look Greek.

"That's a good one," the woman behind the counter said, smiling hungrily and pointing at the book in Manda's hands.

"Is it? I keep hearing about it, so who knows. How are you, Anne?"

"Oh it's wonderful," Anne said, still not taking her eyes off the book. "His best, I think. Just beautiful."

Anne was an old friend of Margaret's – she sometimes asked Manda: "How's your mum?" And Manda would once again have to correct her: "*Stepmother;* she's fine." Anne had been working at the library since forever, the kind of woman who looked like she'd collapse in a panic if she ever left the building. Manda used to imagine her sleeping in the attic, above the encyclopedias. She was deaf in one ear: her voice had a kind, dead limp to it. You could almost measure the passage of time by how far her hearing aid had receded into her ear, the technology having improved and become more compact each time she got a new one. Manda liked her because she was always friendly to Ken, who sometimes came in to look at magazines all day if he had nothing else to do.

"It's hard to find anything good, nothing that bores me to death," Manda said. "I don't have the time, you know?"

Anne shook her head and looked almost genuinely concerned.

"So what's Patrick up to?" she asked, resuming her card-sorting as she spoke.

"Oh he's, you know, busy with the store."

"That's right: I was going to ask you about that. How is it going out there? He must be very busy this time of year. I see boys playing hockey on my street all the time now."

"You should tell them all to shop at his store," Manda said quietly.

"Oh what's that?" Anne asked, craning her head like a bird and reaching up to move her hearing aid with the tip of her finger, though it'd been a long time since she'd worn one that needed jostling.

"Hey, have you seen Ken in the last couple of days?" Manda asked her. "Have you been working?"

Anne put down the cards to think.

"I was in Monday and Tuesday," she said. "Wednesdays I have off. And I was here last night – I switched shifts with Sonia because she wanted to go see her sister's new baby."

"Was Ken in at all?"

"You know, I don't remember seeing him. Do you want me to ask someone else here? Sonia or Terry – they may have seen him."

"No it's alright, we just keep missing each other."

But Anne was already turning around in her chair to find another librarian.

"Terry, have you seen Manda's brother in the last couple of days? He's the big fella with –" Manda saw Anne raise her hand to the side of her face but then catch herself and lower the hand after making only a slight wave in the direction of her cheek. "He reads magazines sometimes. Manda's brother."

Terry shook her head.

"Terry hasn't seen him, Manda. Do you want me to ask Sonia? We could go in and ask Mr. Price. He's in his office I think – or around, anyway."

"No it's fine. Thanks, Anne."

"Well if I see him . . ."

"Thanks."

When Manda got outside she tried calling Ken on her cell

phone. It rang six or seven times before the machine picked it up and a male voice recited, in a slow and hesitant monotone, the number she had just dialed and asked that she leave a message "after the beat."

"*Beep*," Manda said almost involuntarily, correcting the recorded voice for the third time that week, and maybe the hundredth time that year.

"Ken, it's Manda. I'm just out at the library – how's it going? Everything okay? Marcus says he talked to you the other day. Give me a call on my cell when you get this, okay? I just want to say hi. Or just call me back at home and leave a message if you're not going to be around. If you want to come over, that's great. Patrick's working, but he'll be home by nine-thirty or around that. So give me a ring. I haven't seen you! Just come by, or I can pick you up in the truck whenever you want. Come over for dinner, or whatever. I have to go get a few things now. Give me a ring, anyway. It's Manda. Ken?"

That night, Patrick forced himself to keep the store open until after nine. It had been a better day than usual: some families came in to equip their kids with skates, and one of the coaches Marcus knew called to price some jerseys. He sat behind the counter with some of the wholesale catalogues until Derek the security guard came by to check why his lights were still on.

"You having a sleepover there, Pat?"

"Ah, you know." Patrick was too tired to come up with something funny, so he left it at that.

Derek picked up a cross-trainer and held it at arm's length, making a big show of trying to figure out what made it so special that it cost more than a hundred dollars.

"I'm just waiting for Manda to pick me up," Patrick said. He'd only just realized that she was overdue to call.

Derek picked up another expensive shoe for a quick look, refusing to let himself be impressed: "Ninety bucks? For a shoe?"

"It's what it costs, I guess," Patrick said with a yawn and started packing up. "I don't make the rules, thank fucking god."

Outside, there was a shopping cart rammed up against his door again. Patrick ran it into a hedge, then went back to wait for Manda. He had stupidly left his jacket in the store. He stood with his back against the wall and let his gaze fall on a dark-looking truck parked right at the back of the lot.

What Derek did with the running shoes was the *exact* kind of thing Ronnie would have done if he'd lived to see the store open. Ronnie'd missed the opening by less than a month. He never even came out to see the place while Patrick was getting it ready, but in his defence, he'd had a lot on his mind. He may have even known he wasn't going to last much longer. Ronnie could complain for hours about non-existent drafts or phone calls that came ten minutes later than expected, but being at the very lip of death was exactly the kind of thing he'd keep his mouth shut up about. He'd fallen off a ladder and twisted his ankle badly when Patrick was ten. The entire weekend was spent yelling at Patrick's mother for repeatedly slipping pillows under his leg while he watched TV. By the Monday, his foot was as big as a shoe box and the colour of jam, so he agreed to drive himself to the hospital. They found out that not only had he fractured a bone in his ankle, but that one of his toes was mashed up, too. After that, all he could talk about was how long he'd waited to see a doctor, and how much it itched under his cast. On the week he died his only complaint was an old one about how many stray cats there were in the neighbourhood now that so many of the houses around them were empty. Plus his pension cheque was a few days late.

After his mother died, Patrick hung out at the house a lot to keep his father company and to help deal with her things. Ronnie had struggled with his grief as if with an adversary who was constantly trying to get the better of him. Patrick never saw him cry or get maudlin, but every once in a while he would hear him yell "Fuck off!" and he would find him in the backyard, holding an orange garbage bag that kept vomiting up the dry leaves it was being fed. He refused to help Patrick clear out his wife's sewing room: he just stood in the hallway, smirking and shaking his head, as boxes and furniture were carried out. "Oh yeah, *that*," he'd snickered as the pale-green sewing machine was wheeled out, all antique shoulders and elbows. Patrick would make his father dinner – usually spaghetti, the only thing Ronnie would agree to, and one of the only things Patrick could make – and the two of them would watch TV until Ronnie fell asleep in his chair.

After that, Patrick tried to stay the night at the house at least once a week, but he had already leased the space for the store and was busy setting the place up and talking to suppliers, so he couldn't stay there as much as he wanted to. Manda started to get impatient with him going to see his father all the time. "Ronnie's no baby, Pat," she told him. "Christ, you took it harder than he did, probably. In a couple of months he'll probably be glad to have the house to himself."

"I don't know how long he's going to last," Patrick said. "He looks like shit."

"That's because he has to do everything for himself for the first time in his life. Probably eats beans on toast all the time when you're not there."

But Patrick was right: Ronnie didn't last long. Patrick found him sitting dead on the couch in front of the TV one evening. Ronnie had on his T-shirt from the '76 Olympics and a pair of pajama bottoms that were pebbled with toast crumbs. He was hunched forward, as if grief had been waiting for just that moment to get him hard in the stomach and knock him right out of his own life.

With both parents gone, Patrick had felt the house slump around him. When it rained, the acicular slivers of water would sting the front of the house and run down the living room window like tears, and the thin maples next to the house would lash the siding while the furnace moaned in the basement. Patrick convinced Manda to let them move in almost right away, though she had been pushing to stay in their apartment while they got the house ready. He didn't tell her that he thought the place needed people in it.

Patrick tried to remember if he'd ever actually invited his dad out to see the empty space he was frantically converting into Active Sports. He was sure he had, and if he hadn't, it was only because Ronnie made it clear the invitation would not be accepted, or because Patrick was already sick of the man shaking his head and chuckling at the pointlessness and waste involved.

As he thought about all this, the truck in the back parking lot grew more and more familiar, taking shape and becoming three-dimensional. It took another few seconds for Patrick to connect this truck with the memory of driving himself to the mall that morning. Out of embarrassment, he walked over to disentangle the shopping cart from the hedge and force it farther into the ditch, almost sliding in after it and putting a rip in the side of his pants.

Marcus went straight to Kelly's apartment from the warehouse. It was cold, and he hugged himself the whole way like a hurt little boy. Jacob had refused to give him a ride, and Marcus didn't really want him knowing where Kelly lived, anyway. Not that he didn't trust her, but he didn't trust Jacob at all. Never lead a wolf back to your burrow. As he waited on her porch for the door to open, he thought again that the advantage of going out with a single mother was that she was almost always guaranteed to be home. And so she was. She led him upstairs, picking up tiny hats and shoes and toys on the way. She turned around and dramatically put her finger to her lips as they entered her living room, pointing to where Mark was asleep under a blanket on the couch. Marcus could see only a bright red sprig of the boy's hair coming out of the top of the blanket. He looked dead.

"He's been having nightmares the last couple of nights," Kelly whispered, carefully lifting Mark's sleeping form and carrying him to his bed.

"Me too," Marcus said, and went looking in her kitchen for something to eat.

"I don't know how long he'll stay down but I hope all night," she said when she came back. She had her hair back in a ponytail, which Marcus always thought made her look sixteen. He tried not to think how old and collapsed he looked beside her. She looked too small and thin and young to be even capable of childbirth, but the proof was asleep down the hall. She sat at the table with him, holding her forehead in her hand and trying not to yawn.

"Oh fuck, sorry," she said, unable to stop a big one from coming up and stretching her mouth wide. "I'm so tired. I hope to god Mark sleeps tonight. This is like two weeks now."

Marcus felt he should ask something about Mark, but with the boy asleep, he felt that to keep talking about him was to waste the small amount of time they had alone together.

"I saw you walking around earlier," he said.

Kelly instinctively looked toward the living room window, a little alarmed. "In here?" she asked. "What were you doing?"

"I was spying on you, obviously. I watched you pee and take a shower. . . . No!" he shouted, laughing at the look on her face. "I was delivering furniture, and you were walking somewhere."

Kelly laughed a little with relief but was clearly still a little troubled.

"I'm sorry," she said. "I'm just . . . I just get nervous about the idea of someone watching me and Mark. It bugs me, I don't know. I'm being stupid."

"Who would watch you?"

They sat together on the couch to watch TV. She leaned her head against his shoulder and put her feet up, clearly about to fall asleep. "Turn it to whatever you want," she told him. "I'm not even sure what this is." Marcus struggled with the remote control, which was the size of a brick and bristled with unmarked buttons. He kept getting led to unwanted channels. Kelly had a satellite hook-up she shared with the family downstairs. Watching TV at her place had brought before his eyes whole genres of shows he'd never even imagined. Kelly fell asleep on his shoulder. "I'm so sorry," she said, when he nudged her. He walked her to bed, holding her shoulders lightly from behind. She was asleep almost before he got in with her.

Mark started whimpering at three in the morning; Kelly got out of bed and went down the hall to his room. Marcus woke up at the shifting in the mattress and at the voices in the distance, but his mind only idled, still corrupted by sleep and dreams. Kelly came back for clean sheets from her bedroom closet.

"Mark peed the bed," she whispered. "He said he was dreaming that robots were chasing him, but they were tunnelling underground so he couldn't see them." She paused out of pride in the imaginativeness of her son's nightmare, with its tangled, toddler complexity. "He wants me to sleep with him, so you go back to sleep."

Marcus didn't need to be told: he was halfway there before she'd even crept back out of the room and pulled the door closed.

SATURDAY

The same man walked past Active Sports three times. His short black hair was dyed blonde on the top – like yellow icing – and he was wearing wraparound sunglasses attached to a rubber tube that ran around the back of his neck. Patrick could see a grin swimming just under those glasses, trying to find a hold in the rest of the face. On the first two passes Patrick was dealing with a customer, a woman who took a long time trying to pick exactly the right basketball jersey for her son before deciding that what he *really* wanted were some new video games. The third time the man walked by, the woman was gone and Patrick was alone in the store. The man stopped and stared in at him.

"Hey," Patrick said with friendly neutrality.

The man didn't respond right away but took a step forward, stopping at the threshold and looking up at the sign overhead.

"Pat Murphy," he said, and the grin finally locked.

"What's that?"

"Your name's Pat Murphy, right?"

"No: Mercer."

"Oh shit, that's right," the man said, pulling his sunglasses off as if ready now to introduce his eyes. They were strangely round and red and looked as though they were about to pop out. "Ronnie *Mercer* – I kept thinking it was Murphy for some reason. You're his son, right? Ronnie? Your name's Pat?"

"Patrick, but yeah. You knew my dad?"

The man looked like he wasn't much older than Patrick.

"Ronnie Mercer, holy shit. I haven't thought about that guy in – whatever, twenty years, I think. More."

The man stopped to stare at Patrick again, and the life in his face turned inward for a second while he went through a quick mental gallery. When it came back, he reached out to shake Patrick's hand.

"Holy shit," he said. "Ronnie was our teacher in high-school gym. I recognized you from when you used to come and hang out. I'm Brad Severin. Used to be Bradley. You still look a bit like you did. I couldn't believe it when I saw you – I can't believe I even recognized you."

"Wow, that was – I was like eleven or twelve."

The schools in Dunbridge had been desperate for teachers, so Ronnie had filled a gap for a couple of years teaching gym part-time. Patrick remembered walking over to the high school every day to get a ride home. He would go in through the back entrance of the gym and stash his jacket and knapsack under one of the benches and shoot hoops until the team came out of the change room looking beaten and fearful before they'd even put their hands on a ball. Ronnie's voice pursued them out, and he'd emerge with two stopwatches around his neck and his hands stuffed deep into his pants pockets. Patrick would climb into the bleachers with his homework. He could remember the musty smell of the place, old sweat and dirty canvas, and always feeling hungry.

"Who were you? Were you on one of his teams?" Patrick asked.

"Yeah, for maybe about five minutes. Ha ha! No, I was playing basketball for a while, but I had to quit. Christ, that guy – he'd have us outside, whatever weather. Running around, shouting at us. Everybody's slipping on the ice in their running shoes, you know? Just these little canvas jobs with the white soles. You know, the cheap fuckers. Not like these you got here, right? He was such a character."

Brad looked around for something to sit on, and settled for leaning against a bin of hockey sticks. Patrick was sure the whole thing would be crushed or toppled by his weight. The sticks closest to Brad's back slid away in a panic.

"What's he doing now, old Ronnie? He must be a hundred years old."

"Died a couple of years ago, actually."

"Oh shit, sorry buddy. That was stupid of me."

"Don't worry about it."

"He wasn't that old was he? Was it cancer or something?"

"No: heart." Patrick tapped his chest with his thumb. "Some other shit, too, but mostly that."

"Well sorry, eh? Is your mother still around?"

"Not anymore. She went before him, actually. Might have been part of it."

Brad shook his head. "That's rough, eh? They do that a lot, though, these old couples that have been together forever – one after the other. I had an aunt and uncle like that. One died, then *boom*! My daughter's gerbils just did the same thing just a little while ago."

"Anyway," he went in a slightly brighter tone, "I was just here visiting my sister. We're living down in Brampton these days and I don't really come up much. Me and Susan. You wouldn't know Susan, I guess, she was probably older than you. Same school. My folks are with us in Brampton now. My sister's out in one of those new places by the highway. You know the ones I mean? There was just like fields out there when we were growing up. I guess that's what happens – you go away and they start putting new stuff in."

Brad talked for a while about all the changes he had spotted on his last few visits to Dunbridge, changes that Patrick was fully aware of, having witnessed most of them occur. Still, it was good to kill some time – the day had been slow so far – and this sudden link to his own past was a nice surprise. It was good to talk to someone who knew Ronnie. Patrick hardly saw anyone from when he was growing up. The ones still around he lost touch with over the years he spent setting up the store.

"This place is alright," Brad said, fingering some jerseys. "How long you been working here?"

"I opened it up four years ago; four years last month, actually. It's been a pain in the ass, but you know," Patrick shrugged and looked around at the store, temporarily forgiving it for draining him of his energy and money. "It's mine, so I can't complain too much."

"This place is yours? Hey shit, congratulations. You're your own boss – so am I, actually. God, it's exhausting, isn't it? And I just have this little office in the basement."

"Oh yeah?"

Brad nodded. "Web design. Commercial sites and that kind of thing."

Patrick started nodding, too, not knowing what else to say about it.

"So you're still living here, eh?" Brad asked him.

"Yeah, in my parents' old house. We moved into it after. We're still fixing it up. My wife is."

"Susan and I tried to sell my folks' house, thinking we'd get enough to buy something in Brampton. What a pain in the ass! Sold it for almost nothing. They've got guys sleeping in fucking bank machines in Toronto – they should all come up here and live like fucking *kings*. Put them all on a bus."

"That's the *last* thing we need."

Brad laughed and reached out to shake Patrick's hand again

and slap him on the shoulder. "Listen buddy, I gotta go find my kids before they start stealing shit; they're practically in a gang already. You got any kids?"

"Not yet."

"Well, trust me on this: you don't want to be chasing them around when you're sixty. And have a boy first – tell your wife that. Way easier. And nice job on the store. Seriously."

Brad was almost knocked over on his way out by the same woman that had been in earlier, running back in to see if she had left her gloves behind. She and Patrick looked for them around the store for nearly five minutes. Before she left, Patrick managed to secure from her a semi-firm promise to come back before Christmas to buy skates.

Marcus awoke late in the morning in a bedroom completely unlike his own. This room was painted white, its window was curtained with real curtains (instead of a blanket) and had a dream-catcher hanging in the centre of it. This room had a painting of a ballet dancer on one wall and a full-sized wardrobe against another. There were stickers on the door of the wardrobe, bright fruit that fell through empty, wooden space. There was a chair in the corner stacked with laundry. On the very top of the stack a toy knight with a million joints stood half-a-foot high, with arms akimbo and a broad axe in one hand. It was warm, there was a furnace humming somewhere, and when the sunlight hit the white wall opposite it gave the illusion of a sunny, summer day.

Marcus drifted into reluctant wakefulness and stretched himself diagonally from corner to corner so that he could not be removed. The bed was deep and wide and covered in blankets that were both heavy and light. His toes pushed against the bottom of the sheets, and he was surprised to feel resistance – he hadn't known tucked-in sheets in years. The bed smelled like lemon, the room like pine. There were more toys on the night table – there was a *night table* – and a pair of glasses with silver-flecked frames stared back at him. Marcus picked up the glasses and made his most severe Charlie Chan face, scrunching up his eyes and bucking out his teeth. The room looked even sharper and whiter with the glasses on. He tried looking through them the wrong way to see if the clean, white room receded, but it was still there – a little warped, but still blissful. He heard Mark's muffled voice on the other side of the door, and Kelly's voice trying to keep him quiet while taking the air out of a fight – about the need to pee, as far as he could tell, though he couldn't make out whether the boy was for or against.

Kelly had the whole second and third floor of the house, a big one in the older part of town, down near the river. She had some deal where the apartment was paid for by the family of her son's absentee father in exchange for her not asking for more in terms of support. Or maybe they owned the house. Marcus was a little murky on most of the details, but there was one fact he could never get out of his head.

"You live here for nothing?" he asked her more than once the first time he saw the place.

"It's not like I'm a welfare case," she replied, a little more angrily each time until she finally insisted he drop it.

Beyond the apartment being large, clean, and free of charge, there was something else that had confronted Marcus the first time he came over: Mark. Before that, Kelly's son had only been a shy presence, barely visible behind his mother's legs, but on his own turf he became a real being with a voice and a pair of acute eyes and ears, all of which came as a small shock to Marcus, who hadn't fully absorbed the idea that his new girlfriend had a four-year-old son until the exact moment that Mark came running in to meet his mummy's new friend.

"What kind of car do you drive?" the boy had shouted before Marcus had a chance to fake a warm hello. And then, before he had a chance to answer: "Neil drives a jeep!" Marcus took this as a complete *non sequitur* until Kelly told him that Neil was Mark's father, and that he indeed drove a jeep.

"I just walk," Marcus told the boy, but Mark had already lost interest in cars and become stuck on the coincidence of their first names. He started wandering around the apartment chanting, "Hey Mark! Hey Marcus! Hey Mark! Hey Marcus!" Marcus had wanted to wander around the place, too: he'd been inside for less than three minutes and he already could feel an intense calm and relaxation coming over him. He started to understand how decisions got made in the real world, how people assessed their situation and moved forward, how things got *done*.

Lying in Kelly's bed, Marcus felt as though his skin had melted off him in the night. His own bed at home was heavy with shed skin, dust, and bugs, but this one seemed to float on the floor. When he put his feet onto the carpet there was no shock of cold air: Kelly's apartment was warm in every corner. It was only when he was here that Marcus realized how much time he spent tensed up in a perpetual shiver.

Kelly's clock said it was already after ten; he'd had more than nine hours of uninterrupted sleep. He imagined this was what it felt like to have a total blood transfusion – he was cleaned out and rebuilt. His eyes didn't even hurt. He pulled his jeans on and went out into the hallway to see if Kelly had made anything for breakfast. Just outside the door he found a semi-circle of dinosaurs facing into the room.

"They're guarding," a voice said, and Marcus jumped. Mark was standing at the end of the hallway with his back against the wall. He was still in his pajamas and his feet were bare.

"Guarding me? Thanks, man," Marcus said.

Mark didn't smile, and Marcus realized the boy meant guarding *against* him. He raised one foot up like Godzilla and roared quietly before bringing it back down – gently enough so he wouldn't break anything – on the back of a plastic Triceratops.

"No!" Mark yelled, but Marcus raised his foot again and gave another quiet roar. Mark squealed and ran into the bathroom where Kelly was picking up towels.

"I was only *joking*, fuck," Marcus said when he heard the howl of accusations being made against him. Kelly came out of the bathroom with yellow dish gloves on her hands. Mark was behind her legs. He was pinching her on the backs of her thighs.

"Don't hurt mummy, please," she told him patiently. "Can you *not*?!" she shouted when he wouldn't stop. He pulled his hands back but didn't take his eyes off Marcus.

"I didn't want him to wake you up," she said.

"I'm up now."

"Sorry, I tried to keep him quiet for as long as I could, but he's been up since six-thirty."

"Oh fuck, really?"

Mark sucked in air like he'd just been burned, and he tried to hide an involuntary smile behind his hands.

"He said *fuck*!"

"Sorry," Marcus said. "I forgot that's a rule. Don't say it, okay buddy?"

Mark looked ready to keel over from scandalized pleasure.

"Mum!"

"Sweetie, mummy wants to talk to her friend Marcus for a minute. Can you pick these all up and put them away where they're supposed to go, please?" When Mark looked like he was going to cry, she gave in: "Okay, just go watch some more cartoons and mummy will be in in a minute."

Mark looked at both of them with intense suspicion, but couldn't resist the call of the hyuk-hyuking voices that could be heard coming faintly from the TV in the living room.

"He's been acting totally weird since he found out you were sleeping in there," Kelly said. "He wouldn't even talk to me for a while this morning. I'm already wiped."

Marcus was annoyed at the idea that there was something sinister in the sleep he'd just had.

"I've slept here *tons* of times."

"You're usually up before he is, I guess. He's always seen you in the kitchen or the living room when he gets up, so maybe he always thought you came over early in the morning."

"He's freaked out because I slept here?"

"In my bed."

"So? So what?" Marcus couldn't hide his annoyance anymore: they were spending way too much time on this. "What's the difference if I sleep in your bed?"

Kelly just stepped forward into Marcus's arms and put her head against his shoulder.

"I'm so tired," she said, snuggling into him. He smiled as he wriggled and resisted her.

"Can I get a shower at least? I was lifting shit all day yesterday."

Kelly gave him a friendly sniff. "You don't stink."

"You're too nice."

In the shower, Marcus brought the water to the very edge of his pain threshold to let it burn off all the remaining ache from the day before. Kelly's towels were thick and broad; he could dry himself by simply holding one around him and standing in the lingering steam. He regretted having to put his old clothes on, and he thought again about leaving a clean pair of jeans, socks, and underwear at Kelly's place just in case. He wondered if she would go for it. She pushed him sometimes to talk about where the two of them were going, and he could sense she wanted something more formal between them, but at the same time she always seemed wary about him getting too comfortable in her apartment. There was always a pause when he stayed over late watching movies and suggested that he should just stay there instead of walking home.

"How does your back feel?" Kelly asked him when he came into the kitchen. He felt he was bringing with him a halo of pleasure from the shower and was puzzled that she couldn't sense it. Mark ran in from the living room to grab a cup of juice. He gave Marcus a toothy grin that was half-snarl and ran back to the TV.

"It's fine . . . now," Marcus said, not quite ready to let go of this source of sympathy. "I really wasn't going to make it all the way home last night."

"Oh, poor thing. Why does he keep you there so late? Isn't he your uncle? I wish I could get you something at the bakery."

"That would be wicked. Can you check? I'd rather be lifting hot dog buns all day. Seriously."

She handed Marcus a bag of bread, and he loaded the toaster. Even *toast* tasted better at her house. Mark heard the toaster button thunk down and came running back in, yelling "Toast! Toast! Toast! Peanut butter and honey, please!" He stopped when he saw who was manning the toaster, but Marcus tried to play on his initial enthusiasm.

"We can split these if you want," he said. "You can have peanut butter, and I'll have Cheese Whiz on mine, right?"

Mark just looked at Kelly: "Mum, I want my *own* toast."

"Whatever," she said, dispersing all potential conflict by waving her hands in front of her. "I'll make you toast, your *own* toast. You go watch your cartoons."

When Mark had gone back to the TV, Marcus turned on her. "What, he won't even share my toast?"

"I know, I know," she said quickly. "He's just . . . I'm sorry, Marcus, he's trying."

Kelly took a cup out to Mark and pushed in beside him on the couch. Marcus was busy trying to get the *Dunbridge Examiner* to stand up and stay open on the table in front of him: he kept pulling at it and slapping it down, trying to read the sports to see if anything was happening in his league. He stopped when he came across a familiar face in one of the photos in the news section. A young man was standing with one hand on a cheque the size of a beach towel while an old man wearing a beret and a dozen medals did the same at the other end. Conrad, the younger man, was the captain of Marcus's team years and years ago; he still held the record for assists in the league. Marcus took the paper into the living room, where he was amazed all over again at how open and filled with light the apartment was. Mark, sitting on his mother's lap, twisted around and stuck his head up when Marcus walked into the room.

"Owie honey, don't push," Kelly said.

"Hey there's a guy in here I know," Marcus said, holding the newspaper out.

Kelly didn't look away from the TV. "Oh yeah?" she asked, and jumped a little when her son got his fingers into her ribs.

"This guy Conrad. Played on one of my teams – the captain, actually, for a while. Anyway, he's in here –"

"Mom!" Mark shouted.

"Ow, Mark, stop it."

Marcus gave up. He finished the last of his toast and his juice and poured himself a cup of coffee from the pot Kelly had made. He carried the coffee and newspaper back into Kelly's bedroom and lay down with his cup within reach on the night table. He sometimes wondered just how many kids had passed through his teams. He'd been coaching on and off for more than ten years, so it had to be nearly a hundred. Sixty or seventy at least. He was in touch with almost none of them now, aside from the ones currently playing for him. A few he said hello to when he saw them on the street, but that was it. In any given year there were only five or six players who would hang out at his apartment before practices or games, and only a couple more that he would talk to much at the rink, so most of the players he probably wouldn't even recognize. No, that wasn't true: he remembered them all. He would always recognize a former player, even if he couldn't remember the name. Eventually, he figured, he would be coaching their children. Either that or he would quit, maybe at the end of this season. He mulled the idea over, as he did every year.

Kelly knocked on the door, waking Marcus up. He couldn't have been asleep for more than five minutes; the bed had seduced him.

"I'm so sorry," she said, creeping into the room. "I have to help serve at a wedding this afternoon and I need to get Mark to Estelle's."

She sat on the bed and rubbed his leg while he looked around in a daze for his coffee. He tried to twist himself off the bed, but his back and shoulders were hurting again.

"Mark's just in his room picking which toys to bring," Kelly told him.

Marcus could never understand why she thought he needed to know where her son was and what he was doing every second of the day.

"I don't even know if I can walk home now," he said. "I'm all seized up again. I thought I was okay, but no."

Kelly's hand stopped rubbing but stayed on his leg.

"I really need to get going, sorry. Is there like a cab or something. . . . How bad is it?"

Marcus lay back on the bed. "I don't know, it might start spasming. How long are you're going to be at this thing? I could just hang out here til you get back. If you're back at like seven, that's nothing. I could watch a movie or something until my back is better."

"What, with Mark?"

"No, I mean – well, I guess – but you've already set it up with the babysitter and everything, and he knows her better. No, I mean I could just hang out here and you drop Mark off like you planned, and I'll even make you both dinner when you get back, spaghetti or something. You have any spaghetti?"

Mark came running down the hallway, looking for his mother. From the noise his feet made on the floor Marcus imagined his legs stretched out straight like a tin man unable to bend his knees. The boy found them in the bedroom, and Kelly stretched out her arms for a hug.

"Mark honey, would you like to stay here this afternoon with Marcus?"

"You know what?" Marcus said quickly, before Mark could answer. "With my back like this I don't think I can really watch him, you know? I might even have to take a muscle relaxant, which will just knock me out."

"I wanna go to Estelle's," Mark said.

"Okay, well . . . okay," Kelly said.

"So should I just hang out here? Make you guys supper?"

Kelly picked Mark up and carried him to the door.

"Today's not good, actually. He didn't sleep well and neither did I, so I don't know. Estelle has a key and she might need to come here. It's really not a good idea today. Is that cool? I'm sorry."

Marcus threw off the blankets. "Fine, fine."

"Maybe next time. I'm just . . ."

"Whatever."

Marcus left Kelly's apartment as soon as he could. It was just cold enough outside to add injury to insult. There was no reason why he, Kelly's supposed boyfriend, should be walking home to his depressing apartment instead of hanging out at hers while she was out. Clearly he didn't hold that kind of position in her life yet. Marcus felt like he was a luxury in Kelly's life, something impractical, something to have around only when the circumstances were exactly right and there was nothing else going on. When she wasn't working, she was with Mark, and she spoke about her time with Mark as of a sacred duty. She kept her cell phone near her when she was out with Marcus, just in case the babysitter called. Marcus always had the urge to throw the thing away or at least secretly turn it off. It stared at them with Mark's eyes, forever on the verge of having a fit and summoning her home. Their relationship was a privilege granted with extreme reluctance by a four-year-old who was liable to suddenly withdraw it on a whim. She was a Pharaoh's slave, buried alive deep in the tomb of her boy-king master.

The first thing Marcus did when he got home was climb out onto the fire escape, armed with a hacksaw he had borrowed from Patrick months earlier to bite through the locks holding two rusting ten-speed bikes that were taking up all the space out there. It was something he'd been meaning to do since he'd moved in, but now they would suffer for his sour mood. It took him ten minutes to get through the locks. Once free, the bikes toppled. Marcus decided to let them rust out there for another couple of days – he was tempted to just drop them over the side of the railing. A boy and a girl, both of them belonging to the owner of the store downstairs, were playing in the junk-filled yard out back. They wore identical winter jackets and boots. The girl dumped a pail of milky liquid onto the stones around the edge of the yard and into some empty pop cans she had lined up on the ground, while the boy threaded a string through two lawn chairs and tied it to the back of his bike. His plan seemed to be to take off fast and drag the chairs behind him. He sat on the bike for a few minutes without moving, then dismounted and disappeared inside, furiously scratching at his scalp. Across the alley, new cement tumbled noisily within the belly of a mixer. A man stood near the mixer like a bored bingo caller, trying to ignore the big machine's rotations.

Marcus's first few weeks in this apartment had felt triumphant. He'd walked around on the bare floors in steel-toe boots he'd borrowed from Sinc, loving the sound his stomping made. He'd slept on the couch for a while until his stepfather was able to bring the bed over from the house. There was a corner streetlight just outside one of the living room windows that illuminated the whole place at night. He'd pinned up a heavy blanket to block out the light, but pulled it down again when he found himself bothered by how dark the room got and by the sound of the mice in the walls gathering their courage. In the mornings a grey squirrel stood at the top of a telephone pole and screeched insults at him.

The triumphant feeling lasted only a couple of months. Money was always a problem. More and more the squirrel seemed to be admonishing him for having made the mistake of moving out of his mother's basement.

Marcus stepped hard against the back wheel of one of the bikes, bending the spokes with the heel of his shoe and rendering it unusable. He knew before he'd even stepped back through the window that he would never move them.

Manda was asleep on the couch when Patrick pulled into the driveway. She awoke at the sound of the engine and opened her eyes to the light of the truck's headlights doing quick violence to the walls and pictures. The lights gathered in the corner of the ceiling and leapt back through the glass as the truck cleared the corner of the house. For a few seconds she lay there, confused by the darkness of the room. She had lain down while it was still light out, thinking she would read a bit before Patrick got home. Her mental clock was missing an hour – she felt like a time-travelling visitor from the immediate past. She yawned and got up. By the time he came in through the back door, she was already moving through the house, closing curtains and clicking on lights. She kissed him and immediately put her hand to her lips as if stung.

"You need to shave, my god."

"I *did* shave."

"You need to shave again."

Manda cleared some newspapers and magazines off the kitchen table and discovered a dried-up bowl of cereal underneath it all. The day had escaped her, she'd done nothing with it. She used to feel as though every minute that went by left its mark on her, cut her as it ticked over, but now it was as though days and weeks were just a muddy flow. It didn't seem to matter what she did – throw herself into some job or just stand there letting it go by – nothing left its mark anymore. She was all scar tissue, like one of those thousand-year-old whales that wash up on a beach to rot.

"I've been trying to read *this*," she said, picking her library book off the floor and holding it out to Patrick. "And you know what? It put me right to sleep. Look: I'm only like twenty pages in and it's boring as all hell."

Patrick read the back cover. He made a face like he was reading about some unnecessarily strange and useless animal, something that only lays its eggs every twenty years, and in some ridiculous place like the tears of a horse. The look only intensified when he opened the book at random and read a few sentences. He quickly closed it again, and after taking a peek at the author's photo out of a sense of morbid curiosity, he handed the book back, a truth he had believed in since he was a kid – *fuck* books – having once again been affirmed through direct experience.

"You didn't run into Ken today, did you?" Manda asked him.

"How would I do that unless he came into the store?"

"He sometimes walks out to the mall, I don't know," she said. "I thought maybe if you'd seen him on the way home or something."

"Then I probably would have stopped to give him a ride."

Patrick tried to find something to eat in the fridge but gave up and settled on unsealing a can of cashews. There was no commitment to any definite action in his movements – he stood in front of the fridge as if waiting for the can to dissolve in his hands. Manda had to put her hand on his elbow to move him out of the way.

"Some guy who Ronnie used to coach came in today," Patrick said.

Manda stopped and waited for the rest, but Patrick looked as if he'd forgotten who had begun the story.

"*And*?" she asked, prompting him.

"He said he recognized me from when I was a kid. Is that weird?"

"Someone Ronnie coached?" It always surprised Manda that other people had memories of Ronnie that weren't of him just sitting around the living room eating crackers and bitching about everything, calling everybody on the TV a faggot. The idea of him out in the world, functioning like a human being – it was hard to digest.

"What was this guy, a hundred? How old were you when Ronnie was doing that?"

"He said I still look a lot like I did when I was a kid."

"I've seen pictures of you as a kid, and you looked like a little midget version of yourself. Like instead of growing up you just got inflated. It's so cute. How did he know where to find you?"

"I don't think he was looking for me. He just walked by the store and I guess recognized me."

"It's not surprising he remembered *Ronnie*, anyway. I can just imagine what it must have been like to be taught by him. He probably brought his gun to school, just in case some fat kid couldn't do like a *million* push-ups."

Patrick got angry. "This guy was saying shit like that, but you know what? My dad was a good teacher and a good coach. He was only ever an asshole at home. I'm sick of everyone talking about the guy like he's a fucking monster! He did a lot of shitty things, but that doesn't mean he's a fucking *Nazi*, for fuck's sake."

Manda stopped filling the pot with water and walked over to Patrick, putting a hand on his back. It was hard and tight under his shirt, as if he were bound tight in his own vulcanized muscles.

"I was just *joking*, Patrick. I'm sorry."

"I'm having a shower," Patrick said, and left the room.

"Don't forget Marcus is coming! It's almost seven," she called after him, but there was no response. She felt like shit for upsetting him. She'd forgotten how sensitive he could be about his parents. He was like a former prisoner-of-war who liked to remind people that, however much his captors had tormented him with bamboo stakes and hungry rats, they at least kept him alive, giving him alone the right to hate them. She wished she had kept her mouth shut, but it wasn't as if what she had said wasn't true: everything Patrick had told her about his sister just confirmed it.

A spume of steam came from the pot. Manda lifted the lid and started jabbing fistfuls of thin, uncooked spaghetti into the turbulent water. The doorbell rang, but she ignored it until she had enough pasta in there to feed herself, Patrick, and Marcus, and maybe have some left over for tomorrow. When the pot was bristling with spaghetti, she went to answer the door.

"Where's Patrick?" Marcus asked, following her back into

the kitchen. The tips of his ears were bright red and he was bouncing a little on his feet to get the blood moving.

"He's pissed at me now."

Manda took a can of Coke out of the fridge and handed it to Marcus, along with half a bag of white bread. Marcus liked to ball the slices up with his fingers and eat them like doughnuts; it was the only way to keep him from whining about dinner.

"What'd you do?"

"I said some shit about Ronnie and he got all –" Manda made two fists and shook them in front of herself like jackhammers. She liked to exaggerate Patrick's anger. He'd been fighting all his life to stifle the temper he'd inherited from his father; it was now nothing more than a sick animal inside him that snapped impotently when roused. Manda knew why he had to do it, and she admired him for it, but she saw what it cost him to not be able to put his fist through the wall whenever he liked.

"He got mad cuz of Ronnie? Since when? I thought he hated his dad."

"He does, but you know, it's his dad and everything. He's touchy."

"I only met the guy a couple of times and *I* hated him. He scared the shit out of me."

"He didn't scare *me*, but I know what you mean. Patrick's just weird about it. He feels bad about the whole thing with his mother, and the store, and Ronnie, and everything."

"His dad was a prick about the store, wasn't he? What's in that bowl?"

Marcus had finished the bread and was looking around for something else.

"That's cereal from this morning. You're welcome to have it if you like. No, Ronnie was a prick about everything. Look at Patrick's sister: I bet she ends up with twelve kids. She's probably only happy when she's knocked up."

Marcus started giggling. "Kelly showed me a photo of herself when she was pregnant," he said. "She had this *huge* belly, and her head was so small and her arms were so skinny she looked like a kangaroo."

"I can't even picture it."

"You should see it, it's hilarious. It looks like a joke."

"I didn't know you're into that kind of thing."

"Seriously? I'm totally into that. I hang out in maternity wards. I get my milk straight from the source."

"God! You probably do."

"You're just jealous."

"Oh boy, trust me – I *never* want to look like that."

Manda puffed out her cheeks. She lifted the pot and dumped all of the pasta into the strainer spanning the open mouth of the sink. The explosion of steam made her take a step back.

"What's Kelly doing these days?"

Some part of her knew better than to ask, but she was too curious. She kept waiting to have her suspicions confirmed. Whatever else she thought of her stepbrother, she knew he was a sucker for anyone who looked like she might take care of him. She didn't want him to get hurt, and not just because she'd be the one who had to listen to him whimper for six months. Her protective instincts became unnaturally sharp at the first sign of a threat.

"I was there today, actually," Marcus said, with feigned neutrality. "I slept over there last night, and she had some job she had to go to."

"Was her kid there?"

Not seeing the trap, Marcus opened up: "He's always there! And he was acting like a fucking crackhead! I sleep over there at least once a week, but this time, because he got up before me, and I was in her bedroom or something, he gets all freaky and won't even look at me. Which doesn't bother me, to be honest, but Kelly starts getting all freaky about it, too. He's got her wrapped around his little finger."

"You're surprised? I hope he's the only one."

Marcus finally clued in to where she was leading him. "What's that supposed to mean?"

"Do you babysit?"

"No, do you?"

They heard Patrick walking over their heads, having finished his shower, and they went silent, as if out of respect for some grieving victim in their midst. Marcus ducked into the living room to catch a glimpse of the pre-game show. Manda took a drink from the can Marcus had left on the table. Patrick stamped once on the floor, probably struggling with his pants. Marcus hooted in the other room: someone on the other team was out with a groin injury.

"I still haven't heard from Ken," Manda said when Marcus came back in. "I think I've called him like ten times, and nothing."

"Jesus, give the poor guy a break. He's probably walking to Florida right now. Or the North Pole. You're treating him like a kid."

"He's probably scared now to call me back cuz he thinks I'm mad at him." Manda got herself a beer and sat with Marcus. "I *am* mad at him. He's being fucking useless. As usual."

"He probably forgot how to turn left and is going in circles," Marcus said.

Manda had to swallow fast before she choked on a laugh.

"Like two months ago, I brought him a whole pile of new socks," she said, "and he wouldn't wear them because they were grey. The ones he had on were grey just from dirt! But no, he will only wear *white* socks. Grey socks, that's just *so* crazy. I got so mad, I just left them there. I felt like throwing them on his bed and telling him to make puppets or something."

"I'd pay to see that puppet show. Can you imagine? It'd be like the Muppets on acid. Or heroin, more like."

"You're going to hell," Manda laughed.

Patrick came in the room and had the fridge open before either of them even noticed he was there. He got a beer out and almost cut his hand open trying to twist off the cap.

"Need some help there, buddy?" Marcus asked him.

"Why's he going to hell?" Patrick asked Manda, ignoring Marcus's taunt.

"Because he's been molesting the boys on his hockey team again."

Marcus made himself look as wide-eyed and innocent as a cartoon lamb. "Only the pretty ones!" he said.

"See? He's going to hell."

"They make me do it, I swear to god!"

Patrick put his bottle down and made a disgusted face, as if the joke had soured the beer on his tongue. "That's just fucking *sick*."

"Ever happen to you, babe?"

"Yeah, you played hockey, didn't you?"

"Patrick was the coach's favourite, with his big muscles and long eyelashes."

Patrick had to endure this kind of thing whenever Marcus and Manda got together: they got sick of taking shots at each other and went looking for fresh blood. He just shook his head and went to look at the TV. Some kind of 'Classic Moment in Hockey' was on now – grey men, most of them dead, with crew cuts instead of helmets, chasing each other over what looked like hard white limestone while the camera struggled to keep up. Patrick tried to think if he'd ever seen this particular moment before. Ronnie used to watch this kind of thing in silence. He would snort if his son ever guessed at what it was and guessed wrong, though Patrick secretly suspected that the old man never knew what it was until they said, either. It was a playoff – that much he could tell. He muted the screen before they said it. Half the players on the ice looked like Ronnie to him, the Ronnie from photo albums and pictures hanging around the house when he was growing up – same stiff hair, same angry eyes, same hard face.

Manda was laughing soundlessly when Patrick walked into the kitchen. Marcus looked almost scandalized. Patrick felt he should walk right back out again – whatever it was, it couldn't be good.

"You told Manda she should have a baby in your bedroom?" Marcus said, the look of scandal now turning sharper and more sarcastic. "In your *bedroom*?"

"Oh for fuck's sake, I was joking."

"I'm sorry, babe," Manda said, finally getting her breath back. "It was just so . . . *weird*. I don't know. I had to tell him."

"Were you joking?"

"Obviously."

"No you weren't, you were one hundred per cent serious."

Marcus could see Patrick was not liking this, so he changed the subject to the upcoming game. Manda served out spaghetti on three large plates and dumped bright red sauce on each. She took a long sip of Patrick's beer and went to get another one for herself. She didn't sit down, but stood leaning against the counter with her drink while the other two ate. Marcus took a piece of bread, covered it with pasta and sauce, and folded it over like a sandwich.

"Are you not having this?" Patrick asked her. He was already on his second plate.

"I will in a sec," she said, raising her beer as explanation. "You wouldn't believe this girl they have at my work now, Marcus. Patrick, I've told you about her."

Patrick looked puzzled for a moment, trying to remember. "Is she a dunce?" Marcus asked.

"Oh my god, she can't even answer a friggin phone," Manda said. "I honestly don't know where they find these people."

"And the best part is," she went on, with growing heat, "she's supposed to be thinking about having a kid."

"So what?" Marcus asked. "Isn't that good? Doesn't that get rid of her?"

"No, because she'll get her year."

"What year?"

"Her year's maternity!" Manda said. "And then they have to hire her back."

"That's fucked up! Why don't they just fire her as soon as she says she's pregnant?"

"Can't," Patrick said.

"That's fucked."

Patrick shrugged his shoulders. "People do it."

"You should totally get pregnant now, Manda," Marcus offered. "If you're gonna get a whole year off? For sure. I would."

"Yeah, thanks."

Patrick took his plate into the living room. "On!" he shouted, and someone on the TV blew an air horn. Marcus grabbed his plate and followed him in. Patrick was behind the big set, jiggling the cable to get rid of the ghostly image of another channel that was floating over the white ice. Manda stayed in the kitchen to eat and finish the beer she was working on. Marcus came back to get more bread.

"The spaghetti's good," he said. "Are you watching with us?"

"Soon."

As if it had been waiting just for him, "O Canada" started just as Marcus returned to the living room.

"You might want to see this," Marcus called. "It's that guy you like."

Manda left her plate and took her beer in. The lights were out; she could just see Patrick's legs glowing in his recliner from the light of the TV. Marcus was on the couch and invisible.

"What's the deal with that guy?" Patrick asked from out of the darkness.

"We had one of his songs at our wedding, babe."

"Okay, shhh," Patrick said when the players on the ice started skating in anxious circles.

"Shush yourself."

By the middle of the first period, Manda felt her interest in the game evaporate. She went looking for her book and told Patrick to clean up the kitchen. She just wanted to lie down. She could hear the game going on below her and the low, masculine rumble of Patrick and Marcus's joint commentary, but the carpeting in the room cut most of the sound. It was even a little soothing. The first few pages of her book went smoothly, then she found she was repeatedly having to go back a page to pick up where her attention had wandered off. Then it was every other paragraph. Then she was asleep, the lamp still on and the book waiting in a crouch on Patrick's side of the bed.

About an hour later, Patrick got undressed, cleared the book off the bed, and climbed in beside Manda. He turned out the light and had a brief struggle with his pillow, which was, as usual, unwilling to support his head at the angle he liked. All the movement brought Manda halfway back to the world. She rolled over and put her face against Patrick's, kneading the shoulder she had in her grip.

"Is Marcus gone?" she mumbled.

"Hope so."

She kissed him, aiming for his mouth but getting the side of his nose. She was too sleepy for a slow-build, so she reached down to his crotch and squeezed lightly. That part seemed to have preceded the rest of him into sleep, and he pushed her hand away.

"What're you doing?" he asked her.

"Looking for your wallet."

"I'm so tired."

"No you're not."

He relented and rolled over to face her. His initial reluctance melted away as he became more aware of Manda's whole body lying there against him. He moved so that he was pronging her lightly in the thigh.

"That didn't take long," she said, and opened her mouth to his. "Oh Jesus, your breath," she said. "You smell like popcorn."

"So what?"

"So? Go brush your teeth or something."

Normally he would have protested the order, but in his state he had no choice but to comply. As a reward for his obedience, Manda took off her shirt and pajamas while he was in the bathroom and reached over to get a condom out of the night table. She put it on his pillow like a hotel mint. It was all she could do to stop herself from letting out a little squeak when she heard the bathroom fan click off and Patrick creep back into the room.

SUNDAY

Someone yelled "hurry!" and there was a bang. A green towel leapt off the back of the bathroom door and collapsed on the floor like a dying witch. Ken brought his hand up out of the warm water and held it in the air, signalling to whoever was in the hallway that he was just about to get out. He had dozed off in the bath again, and someone was late for work. Ken hated showers: he didn't like how the water hit the raw and pebbled side of his face. The nerves there were messed up, a doctor told him. Keep it clean, his sister told him. He kept it clean, though he hated running a washcloth over it, even lightly: it made him shiver.

He liked baths a lot, though, and that was a problem wherever he lived. That's what they'd say, the people who ran the house, who got paid to check in and talk to them all about the arguments that were always going on. They'd say, "It's a problem, Ken. If you take long baths, then no one else can use the bathroom." Ken could see that it was a problem, but not that it was *his* problem. Marcus always told him to tell the other people in the house to go fuck themselves – he'd had a hard life, and if he wanted to take a bath then what's the problem? Manda told him he had to get along with people, that living there was a good deal, and they took care of him, which was good. "I don't need that," Ken told her, but she would just tell him again that he had to get along with people.

"As a favour," she said, "for me."

Then he'd have to do it, or at least he'd have to try for a while.

There were always arguments in every house he'd lived in. There was always someone slamming a door or not talking to someone else or hiding the remote control for the TV in their room or taking somebody else's food out of the fridge and leaving it on the counter overnight because it was taking up too much room. Ken got sick of it. Whenever he could feel his brain getting full up of everybody's complaining, he would go for a walk and not come back to the house until late at night. One time, he walked right around the outer edge of Dunbridge twice in a row, though that was boring because there wasn't much to look at out near the highway. It was more interesting to go to the parks. When he was on one of his long walks he didn't like to talk to people. Sometimes he'd see people he knew, but he'd just keep going without saying hello; the whole point was to give his brain time to clear up. Even if he saw Manda while he was out he would hide behind a tree or the corner of a building to avoid being seen.

Ken had been going for long walks since he was a kid; he used to get in trouble for just walking away in the middle of school. He sometimes walked straight out Margaret's back door into the fields surrounding her place and off into the woods beyond. He'd go in as deeply as he could without getting scared, which was usually less than a hundred feet, so he was always easily found. They didn't even bother putting him in high school when they came to Dunbridge: he only had a year left, anyway.

Ken got out of the bath and dried off, putting his pajamas and bathrobe back on. Darcy was standing in the hall outside the bathroom – he'd obviously been the one knocking and yelling. When Ken came out, the other man was leaning hard against the wall and facing away from the bathroom door as if petrified. Darcy worked in a kitchen doing things like washing dishes and opening giant cans of gravy and tomato sauce. He always acted as if he'd been put in the house by mistake. In the fridge he kept only a carton of orange juice and a small container of something – rice or soup or some kind of meat stew – that he'd taken home from the restaurant. He always ate in his room. When Ken moved in, Darcy told him he was going to be a cook and use knives, but that he was scared of them right now, so Ken had to keep his knives in a drawer. Everyone in the house had to do the same. Ken only had one knife, a big steak knife with a black handle he'd bought at Giant Tiger with his employee discount. He kept it in his room in the drawer with his socks and underwear.

"I wasn't in there for very long," Ken said to Darcy's back.

"Were," Darcy said, and ducked around him into the bathroom. "Pull the plug!" he shouted when the door was shut tight behind him.

"Sorry."

Charles, Ken's other roommate, was in the kitchen when he came downstairs. He had the newspaper spread out across the kitchen table and was crouched up over an ad in the classifieds, going over it with the tip of his thumb and mouthing the words slowly and silently.

"Kenny," Charles said, not looking up. "You gotta go easy on the baths, there, buddy – Darcy was having a fit down here."

"I think I fell asleep."

"You're gonna drown. Hey, you work at Wal-Mart, right?"

"Giant Tiger."

"Shit, that's right. No, it's just Wal-Mart wants extra people for Christmas and I thought you might be able to help get me in. Cool, never mind."

Ken's room was just off the kitchen. He didn't like being on the ground floor: the thought of people breaking into the house was always on his mind at night, and Charles and Darcy always made a ton of noise whenever they were outside his door. Still, he felt better in his room than anywhere else in the house; in there he could concentrate on enjoying the lingering effects of his bath. Charles started doing exercises upstairs, jumping jacks and push-ups. Darcy banged around for almost an hour before he finally left for work. There was the sound of anchor chains being sucked back into a ship as Darcy unlocked his bike in the backyard, right under Ken's window.

Ken thought about having a nap, but he was feeling hungry, plus something was still sloshing back and forth inside his head when he moved it, so he got dressed and left the house, locking his door behind him. It was colder out but sunnier than it had been for at least a week. He checked his money: a five-dollar bill and four dollars in change. He wrapped the change up in the bill and tucked it tight into the corner of his jeans pocket. He was careful never to take more than ten dollars with him when he left the house. He used to get a small cheque from the government every month to top up what he made at the store, but that got cut off last year, so he had to stretch his paycheque to cover rent, food, and everything. His friend Steve at work told him he shouldn't have been taking the government money in the first place. "It's *retard* money," he said. "They're basically paying you to be a retard. I never even applied for it."

He knew what Steve meant, but it didn't make him feel any better about the loss of the cheque. He'd been trying to save a little bit each month in case he needed it, stuffing tens and twenties in a little fanny pack he kept between his mattresses. He had never thought about what he might use it for – getting his *own* place, maybe.

Ken's favourite doughnut shop was open. There was a table

of men wearing hunting jackets sitting at the long row of tables near the front. Each of the men had a coffee cup and a doughnut in front of him. Some of them watched Ken closely as if waiting for him to bolt into the clearing of the parking lot. For a moment, he felt like doing just that. Patrick had taken him up to his father's hunting cabin once, just before it got sold. Ken had loved the little place with the creek beside it and the pale green paint flaking off everywhere and the roughly cut bunkbeds stacked up against each wall. He'd even loved looking at the shadows of the rifles on the wall behind the gun rack. The thought of shooting one got him excited. But as they were walking along the trail back to the car, Patrick carrying an old, wooden chair that Manda had told him would have to live in the garage, there was a series of shots somewhere off in the woods. It sounded like someone banging hard on a piece of metal with a hammer. Ken looked to Patrick for reassurance, but he looked as startled as Ken did, and only said they should get back to the truck as fast as they could. "Nothing's in season," Patrick said. Ken spent the drive back watching the trees, waiting for someone to come running out of the woods looking for blood.

One of the hunters sitting with his doughnut nodded as Ken passed by on his way to the line-up. Ken pretended not to notice. *Nothing's in season*, he told himself.

Rob, one of the floor managers at Giant Tiger, was standing directly ahead of him in line, jerking his pants up by the pockets and muttering to himself in exactly the way Steve used to imitate during breaks. Rob already had his uniform on: tight yellow jacket and brown pants. On his chest he had pinned a round button with the face of a smiling, cartoon tiger.

"Hallo, Ken," Rob said with a quick cough.

"In here to fuel up?"

"I didn't eat breakfast yet."

"That's no good, you gotta get your strength. You in today?"

Ken took a breath. "Supposed to start at noon."

"Well, there you go," Rob said, turning away and talking quietly to himself. He was up next.

There were only two girls working the counter and one of them looked like it was her first shift. She kept handing over the wrong doughnut or getting the coffee orders mixed up. Rob asked for decaf, and she had to dump his cup twice after giving him regular. When she finally got it right, Rob looked around at Ken with his eyes wide. "Get lots of fuel in you," he said on his way out. "Sale on today, remember. See you in there.'"

Ken got the same girl. He told her what he wanted – an egg sandwich, a double-double coffee, and a cookie – but she stood still, staring openly at the side of his face. Ken had to struggle not bring his hand up to cover it.

"Sorry, which? A coffee? Sugar and cream?"

"Both," Ken said. "Double."

Whenever he caught people looking at the burn on his face, Ken would pick a point in the distance and stare into it until he could almost imagine a hole opening up and sucking him forward. *Just let them have their look* – that was what Manda told him to do. "They've got nothing better in their lives," she said. "So let them get their jollies."

Ken found a point at the back of the racks of doughnuts and let his eyes lock onto it. There was the head of a screw there, with a fringe of wood around it where they had twisted it in. He tried to imagine himself getting lighter and lifting up over the counter and floating into the hole made by the screw, his body narrowing at the top to a tiny point. He felt his heels lift a little off the floor, but he didn't look away.

The woman in line behind Ken touched him on the shoulder: the new girl was trying to get his attention.

"Sir? Which cookie?" she asked, looking at him skeptically

as if starting to think she'd been tricked into speaking to a mannequin.

"Chocolate."

The girl took a breath, still clearly expecting a prank.

"Chocolate or chocolate chip?"

"Chip."

Ken ate his sandwich and cookie on the way to the store. He walked down the side-alley to the delivery entrance instead of going through the front doors. The doors were locked, but he only had to wait a minute or two before two guys from shipping came out for a smoke. One propped open the door with a metal chair while the other looked in his jacket for his cigarettes. Stewart and Tim, who'd been working there almost as long as Ken.

"Hey," they both said to Ken. Stewart offered him a cigarette, which Ken took and held between his fingers without making any move to get it lit.

"What, are you saving that for later?" Stewart asked.

"He doesn't even smoke," Tim said, reaching out to take it out of Ken's hand. "You don't have to say yes, Ken."

"I know," Ken said, and went inside. He had been planning to give the smoke to Steve.

There were banners up all through the store for the Halloween "Monster Madness" sale. They did it every year to clear out old stock and make room for Christmas stuff. Ken had helped put most of the banners up and move rows and rows of shelves into the front of the store. Each of the shelves was filled with masks, costumes, decorations, and bags of candy. Steve had smuggled a giant bag of mini–chocolate bars into an empty locker upstairs. He went up there a couple of times per shift to fill his pockets, and would slip some to Ken as they passed each other on the floor, giving him a big, candied smile.

Ken found Steve in the staff room upstairs, already in uniform. He was lying flat out on the little couch, raising his legs together in the air, curling them up against his chest, and shooting them out straight again. Ken knew from experience that, in the right mood, his friend could do something like this for hours. Steve always came in an hour or two early to hang around. If his shift was over early he often hung around til closing, too. On the days when the schedule got posted he would wander around for the entire day offering to cover people's shifts. He jumped up instantly when he saw Ken.

"We've gotta have a chat," he said, taking the arm of Ken's parka and leading him out of the room and down the hall to the storage area where all the Christmas and Valentine decorations were kept. Ken waited while Steve picked through some of the midget evergreen trees and hollow reindeer. Steve found a plastic Santa, stood him up on a box, and put his hand on top of the figure's head to hold him in place. He had a look on his face of bitter triumph, as if this very Santa had been hiding from him for years.

"This little fuckhead . . ." Steve said, pointing into the figurine's jolly face. He didn't complete the thought. "When do you start?" he asked Ken.

"Noon. I checked the board yesterday just —"

"Me too," Steve said, cutting him off. "But you know what I just heard? I'm not going to tell you who told me this, but let's just say it's a pretty fucking good source, and I trust her."

"What is it?" Ken didn't like the sound of this so far; he felt a vague pressure start behind his forehead.

"So you know how they were going to hire some people before Christmas, right? You heard that?"

"Just for like two weeks."

"Just for like never! They're not hiring anybody extra, is what I heard. And now they're thinking of laying some people off after New Year's. Can you believe that? And guess who's going to be the first to get the fucking heave-ho?"

"Not us," Ken said weakly.

"Yeah, Ken, not us," Steve said sarcastically. He kicked at a box full of cupids. "Who else are they gonna fire? Listen, it's you, me, Emily, and Roger. And probably whatsisname, the guy with the big fucking shoes. They're gonna get rid of all of us after Christmas for sure. You and me are the only guys who do any fucking work around here and this is what they pull."

Ken stood there trying to absorb the idea of losing his job, the only one he'd ever had for more than a year. He offered the only argument he could think of: "No."

"I'm telling you, when they call me in to tell me I'm fired I'm going to fucking laugh in their faces. I'm going to go fucking insane."

"Why would they do that?"

"How am I supposed to know? They think we're all retards."

"Not me," Ken said.

"I don't mean *you*. I mean Emily and Roger, so fucking relax." Steve started crossing and re-crossing the small amount of floor space not taken up by boxes. "I'm so serious," he said, "if they fire me I'm going to smash some fucking windows. Burn the fucking place down."

Ken's head felt like it had turned to lead; he wanted to lie on the floor for a while. Steve was looking around the storage room, laying waste to it in his mind. Everywhere there were cupid limbs and broken antlers, the floor was awash with the gore of shredded tinsel and torn paper hearts.

"Can we go?" Ken asked.

"Where're we gonna go? It's freezing out and it's Sunday. Everything's closed. You feeling sick or something? I'm losing my job, too, you know."

"Let's just go."

"Alright, let's go down to the loading dock. Rob's already giving me shit about hanging around in the staff room. Says the coffee keeps getting stolen, like it's all me. I took some – did you?"

Ken nodded. He was completely white.

"So there you go. I bet fucking Rob took most of it, though."

They left the storage room, but not before Steve took another swipe at the midget Santa Claus. "This fucker doesn't learn," he said.

Manda turned the music up in the living room as high as it would go without destroying the speakers. She wanted to hear it upstairs where she was cleaning. The only thing she could find worth listening to was a two-disc collection of '80s music Patrick had bought for her birthday two years ago. Manda vaguely remembered hating with a passion just about every song on it when it first came out. Now, even the worst of it – the annoying bubblegum crap, the Christian metal that had seemed like such a bitter betrayal at the time – filled her with perverse affection and pleasure. They were like the idiot classmates who had somehow survived, like herself, to see adulthood. She had caught herself a few times in the last year wondering about some of the people she knew from high school, even people whose throats she had wanted to slit back when she knew them. The ones she did see, the ones still living in the area, she felt nothing for. She avoided them, and they her. Most of them could still remember what Manda was like as a kid. Even Patrick didn't know just how black everything was for her, how often she came close to dying in someone's basement or in the middle of the street, and how little she would have cared if she had. She was hazy herself on things like the origin of the faint burn scars on the undersides of her arms or the cross-shaped scar on her thigh. It was all falling away. Thank god.

She'd been trying to clean the house all day, but all she'd

got done so far was the front room. She kept finding herself staring at unfinished walls or closet doors with gouges in the wood from Patrick's childhood. In the morning she had kicked a rolling pile of dirty laundry across the cold basement floor and pushed it all into the washing machine in the back corner. She had to hit the machine with the heel of her hand to start it filling with water. The crumpling boxes that still held Patrick's parents' clothes, bed sheets, and towels were stacked around her. She felt as though she were walking through a tomb. The light in the downstairs bathroom was on, and she could see a gleam from the crack under the door. She refused to go in, just in case a rotting, grinning Ronnie was in there sitting on the can. Ronnie used to smoke in there, Patrick told her. As a kid, he could never figure out why the basement always smelled like burning. She wondered if one of the mugs he used as an ashtray was still sitting on the back of the toilet. She thought about filling the bathroom with all of the old boxes, but that might tempt fate. That was the room from which the house would make its counter-revolution, swallowing all of Manda's changes and restoring it to the awful place it was in Patrick's memory. She wanted to drag every piece of furniture out into the backyard, then unscrew every door and mirror and leave all that out there, too. She needed to see the place naked, its memory wiped clean.

It was too cold to hang anything outside and the dryer was broken, so Manda hung all the wet laundry on the broken TV cables Ronnie or Patrick or somebody had strung from the basement ceiling years ago. She started to organize some of the old furniture they kept under the stairs, trying to get it farther out of view. The dampness and mold was in her mouth. A tartan cushion fell against her shoulder and she nearly shrieked. There were some paintings in frames of a Hong Kong harbour and some fatty-looking deciduous forests. She found a brittle garden hose under a stack of lampshades and decided to drag it upstairs and out to the garage. When she shook the end of it, a long, slinky centipede crawled out, and this time she shrieked for real. She left the laundry where it was and headed upstairs. The basement hated her. She couldn't wait til Patrick got home and she had an ally against the house.

Patrick knew Marcus's street well. Two of his best friends from grade school had lived on it when they were kids, in houses that were nearly adjacent. A whole gang of them used to occupy the park at the end of the street. They'd climb up onto the roof of the bathrooms and hurl down the rocks and strips of tar they found up there. Both of those friends were long gone. One became a prison guard in Kingston; the other was a teacher working up north. Patrick missed the one who'd become a teacher more. That friend's parents were both dead, so he never came back to Dunbridge, even to visit. They'd stopped being friends in high school, anyway.

Danny had lived near here, too, and had been part of that extended gang. He was pretty much the only guy Patrick still kept in touch with – and maybe even that was done, since Patrick had just fired him from the store. Patrick hoped it wasn't: he still liked Danny, in spite of everything. The only thing about Danny was that he was sloppy. And he bore a grudge. He bore grudges for a long time, beyond the point where they were fuelled by anything resembling anger and resentment, kept alive and filed away more out of a sense of duty, a kind of solemn remembrance. He was a dedicated archivist for his own emotional woundings. It had gotten worse since his wife left him six or seven years ago. He lost his mother's house and had to move into a one-room apartment in a building behind the mall. Patrick saw it every day when he drove in. He used to walk through the back parking lot and over the hump of grass to Danny's building, sometimes bringing him a pair of fancy sunglasses or a hockey calendar – freebies from a sales rep. There was only one window in the place, and it didn't open, so the room was always dense with cigarette smoke. There was never any thanks for the things Patrick brought him, not that he was looking for any. Anything like sunglasses Danny put on right away and wore for the duration of the visit, making him look like a broken-down limo driver or a dictator in exile.

When Patrick had started getting Danny to help out in the store, Manda simply couldn't believe it.

"You don't ask Marcus, but you ask this guy. Jeezus, *Ken* would do a better job."

"Marcus wouldn't take it seriously."

"Oh, and Danny will?"

But Danny did. Even Manda had to admit that Danny somehow got his shit together just enough to do a decent job. Danny even brought in some business from the coaches he knew. And he didn't want to be on the books – it would have messed up the assistance cheques he was getting – so Patrick could pay him cash. Patrick promised him more hours and greater responsibility once the store really got off the ground, but the opposite happened, and Patrick had had to walk through the lot and over the hump again to tell Danny he couldn't afford to use him for a while. He knew not to bring any freebies that time. If the guy wasn't talking to him now or willing to help out in a pinch, then Patrick couldn't really blame him.

He would have still preferred having Danny in to help him. The two of them could work for hours without having to say much. Marcus didn't like the bare walls at the back of Patrick's store and was always trying to cover them with conversation. Danny wouldn't have minded a job like sorting out hats and shoes – it would have allowed him to do the work half-asleep, which was his preferred state. Marcus tended to get restless after less than an hour, like a little kid.

There was an actual little kid on Marcus's steps when Patrick finally got there. He looked about ten and had on a big, red jacket that covered him like a tent. He was furiously eating a bag of chips. The boy pushed to the side to let Patrick go up but didn't say anything. He kept putting chip after chip in his mouth, barely pausing to chew. Marcus's door was open a crack, so Patrick went in, knocking on the frame as he entered. It smelled like stale beer. He could hear voices.

Marcus met him in the kitchen, laughing at something. Patrick noticed he only had one sock on. He stopped laughing as soon as he saw Patrick standing there.

"Hey, what's going on? I thought you were Jacob."

"Nope. It's alright?"

"Yeah sure." Marcus looked suspicious, and kept trying to see around Patrick. "Is Manda with you? Close the door, holy jeez. Who else is here?"

"Just me. You're missing a sock there."

"Yeah, it was itchy. Hey, did you see a kid out there? Little fucker in a red jacket?"

"He's eating a bag of chips at the bottom of the stairs."

Marcus went out onto the landing. He stood there on one foot, holding the bare one in his hand. "Come on, Jacob," he yelled. "What, are you going to eat them all?" He came back into the kitchen shivering melodramatically. "Jeezus, it's cold out. Is it snowing or something?"

"Not yet. Looks like it could, though."

There was a sudden barrage of harsh laughter from the living room, all boys' voices, with one boy protesting against whatever the others found so funny. It went on for a while until an edge came into the non-laugher's voice that meant either impending tears, or a fight, or both.

"Take it easy, ladies!" Marcus shouted.

"Kiss my ass!" someone shouted back. The laughter bloomed up again, everybody in on it this time.

"You got the team here?" Patrick asked him.

"Yeah the whole team's here, all *sixteen* of them in my living room," Marcus said. "No, it's just the good ones. Not even that, actually. We're just watching some of our proudest moments."

There were five boys sitting around Marcus's living room. They all looked older than the kid on the stairs, and all of them wore baseball caps. Two of them were smoking by the window, flicking their ashes into a pop can. They kept exhaling their smoke out the window, blowing hard and not stopping until they were sure all the smoke was out of their lungs. All of the boys were intent on the TV, and the dim and shaky image of an amateur hockey game. The colour was so bad that the ice looked like skin. The whole thing sounded like it was taking place at the bottom of an empty water-tank. Both teams seemed to be wearing black uniforms, but Patrick figured out quickly that one of the teams was Marcus's.

"Hey guys," Patrick said to the room. Marcus sat back on the couch with his feet up on the trunk, watching with a bored expression the blackened skaters going back and forth on the screen. He looked like the head of a harem.

"So when's this?" Patrick asked, pointing at the TV. He moved an empty bag of pretzels and sat down on the edge of the couch.

"End of last season, second-last game," Marcus said. "A big tournament in Barrie. We went home with nothing –"

"Not true!" one of the kids shouted.

"– but this was probably the best we played all year. Fuck, eh? Look at that: no whistle, nothing! Look at him, he's laughing – *he* doesn't even believe it."

"That should have been five minutes," one of the boys said.

"Two, maybe," Marcus said, correcting him.

"I can't see anything, Marcus," another boy said.

"You weren't even in this game!"

Every once in a while a spectator's head would obscure the camera's view, and Marcus would start a round of loud complaints and whistling.

"Your dad's filming this like he's afraid of getting caught," Marcus told one of the boys on the floor, who gave him the finger in response.

"Are the tapes of your parents fucking as bad as this?" another boy asked.

"Holy fuck, Ian, nice one," Marcus said, with genuine admiration.

They were all covering it up, but it was clear the boys were a little awestruck by the sight of themselves playing. Not one of them called for the tape to be fast-forwarded during a break in the play.

Eventually, someone asked where Jacob was with the chips.

"Patrick says he saw him on the stairs eating them all."

"Who's Patrick? Oh."

The two smokers stubbed out their butts and left the room with malevolent smiles on their faces.

"Pause it for a second," one of them said.

"Don't you dare," Marcus said. "*Nobody* touches the vcr. Touch it and die."

"Who was that?" someone asked. A player from their team had just slid across the ice on his belly with his stick extended. He missed the net by a few inches.

"That was Domenic, can't you tell?"

"What a crazy fuck."

"Who's Domenic?" Patrick asked the boy closest to him, but got no answer.

There was a crash in the kitchen, and Jacob shot into the

room like a cat scared out from under the couch. He made it halfway across the floor before tripping and hitting the carpet face-first. The bag he was clutching split, raining chips down on everything. The two boys chasing him stopped dead and tried to look nonchalant at the sight of Jacob sprawled out.

Marcus raised the remote control and froze the scene on the TV.

"Clean this all up now or this goes off and you all get out."

"Yeah, *Jacob*. Clean it up."

"*Everybody*. Start cleaning now. I don't care if you weren't doing anything. I just cleaned this place and if I find a single chip anywhere in here, that's it."

"Could I get a beer off you?" Patrick asked Marcus.

"Come on, there should be some in my fridge. They bring a case, and I usually kick them out before they finish it."

Marcus started the game again and he and Patrick went into the kitchen. A beer appeared, and the two of them sat down at the kitchen table instead of returning to the living room.

"So I was actually wondering if you wanted to help out at the store for a couple of hours," Patrick said. "I forgot to ask you last night."

"What happened to Danny?" Marcus had been thinking again that he needed to find some way of making money less strenuous than Sinc's warehouse, but his first instinct was always to try and dodge incoming work.

"Danny won't do it. I had to fire him, remember?"

"That's right. I wouldn't do it if I was him, either. That place – I don't know, Patrick. Is it worth it still?"

Patrick wasn't expecting this. But at the same time, it wasn't like the question was ever far from his mind these days.

"It's better than doing nothing."

Patrick hadn't meant anything by it, but Marcus took it as a dig, anyway.

"At least I'm not killing myself, you're there every fucking day! Seriously, dude – fuck, they've got me saying 'dude' now."

"No, I know, I know. I wasn't saying . . ." Patrick looked around Marcus's kitchen for his next thought. "I just – this is something I was working on for a long time. It's not easy."

"Well, obviously. It just seems like – where's your life, you know?"

Patrick felt like asking "Where the fuck's yours?" but held it back. "Good beer, anyway," he said instead.

"Drink all you want. Take some home – I don't touch it."

Marcus agreed to come by the store one afternoon sometime early in the week. The boys cheered something in the living room.

"You guys always do this? Watch old games?"

"Benjy's father tapes them, so they get to see themselves fuck up all the brilliant line changes I make. Benjy's the one –" Marcus pushed the tip of his nose up like a pig's. "It's kind of useless, actually. It's not like they learn anything from watching these things. But whatever, they get a kick out of seeing them."

"My coach never did this kind of thing when I was playing."

"Did they even have videotape back then?" Marcus had intended the question as a dig but thought better of it and asked sincerely.

"They had something. Home movies."

They listened to the canned sound of the game for while. Patrick was relieved to be out of the living room: he had been feeling strangely uncomfortable while sitting in there. There wasn't enough room or something. Too many boys. Or maybe they were all too old, too full of attitude and showing-off. They were all too old, but at the same time not old enough, not so you could just sit and watch a game with them without them all acting like little goofs. They seemed caught in some kind of buzzing current that kept them permanently off-balance. Maybe it was puberty, maybe it was because none of them had fucked anyone yet (he assumed). He tried to remember if losing his virginity had actually brought about the massive shift into adulthood and clarity of thought he had spent years hoping it would. More and more of that was lost. He remembered the girl he lost it with, but not the act itself, or at least not all of it. Enough to know that it must have been pretty terrible for both of them, aside from the fifteen or twenty seconds that were probably the best he'd felt in his life to that point.

The beer Marcus gave him was a little old and skunky but he was glad for it. He tried not to think of all the work he had waiting for him back at the store. He had assumed he'd be bringing Marcus back with him, which wasn't ideal, but still better than picking through it all on his own. Plus he'd promised to take Manda to a movie that night. In *Toronto*, she had insisted, not Orillia or Barrie. She took every opportunity to make the drive.

"What a game last night," Marcus said.

"Which one?"

"Both."

"Yeah."

"Is Manda still pissed off?" Marcus asked with a grin.

"About what?"

"I don't know. Maybe she wasn't pissed off. It was funny though."

"What was?"

"About you – forget it."

Benjy, the pig-nosed boy, drifted into the kitchen and sat down with Marcus and Patrick at the table.

"Bored of the game?" Marcus asked him.

"I've seen it before," the boy said. "Can I have one of those?" he asked, pointing at Patrick's beer.

After Patrick left, Marcus watched the rest of the game with the boys, then they all headed out to the rink for practice. He wouldn't let anyone use his bathroom before leaving. "You can just hold it now," he said to the boys who protested. Along the way he walked with Donnie, the oldest boy on his team, one of the smokers who had run Jacob down earlier. The others were up ahead. Marcus walked slow, with his hands in his jacket pockets and a look of detachment on his face as though walking off a big meal. Donnie carried the videotape of the game they'd been watching and was talking to Marcus about all the good players that had left the team after the end of last season. It was Donnie's last year on the team, and Marcus could recognize the mixed feelings in him. He was committed and he was restless; his eyes seemed to move in two separate directions, like a chameleon's.

"Clouthier and Bart McDonald," Donnie said, holding the tape out in front of him as if it held the souls of the boys who had gone. "We don't have anybody like that now – just a bunch of little fuckheads."

"We still have Thomas and Marc Spooner and Sean Vole and you," Marcus said calmly. "We're doing okay."

He'd said words like these so many times; in a year or two he'd probably be saying something like it to one of the boys who were fooling around ahead of them. Usually the serious ones – the ones that asked to borrow the game tapes and who stayed after practice to work on their speed on the empty ice – usually they could be spotted pretty early. But once in a while a boy who looked like nothing would turn serious in his last year, like Donnie. Up until last year, Donnie had been known only for missing games.

"Who was that guy that came over?" Donnie asked.

"Patrick, my brother-in-law. Stepbrother-in-law, same thing. He's got that sports store at the back of the mall. You know the little one?"

"Really? *That's* where I've seen him before. That place is *useless*. It's so expensive and they never have anything."

"No, I know."

Donnie helped Marcus herd the rest of the boys to the benches outside the change room. The change rooms were in a dank hallway that smelled like oil; Marcus had that smell in his clothes, his hair, his skin. The walls always looked wet, with grey varicose veins snaking up through the concrete. Black rubber mats stretched the length of the hallway, and hard, white lights hung from the ceiling. Marcus could remember coming here as a kid with his school and running back and forth down this hallway, making echoes. He never skated with the rest of his class – he couldn't skate. He was a little better now, but he still coached in his shoes.

Marcus wouldn't open the door until the whole team arrived. When everyone finally got there, a wave of mild hysteria went through the boys, and Marcus had to unlock the change rooms before the noise got him in trouble. Jacob was walking around with stiff peg legs and a panicked look on his face: Marcus sent him to the washroom. One boy was sitting on the floor on his equipment bag. He had a huge gash on the side of his face.

"Where'd you get that?" Marcus asked him.

The boy didn't answer him, but his older brother jumped in to say they'd had a scrap and everything was cool. Everyone got up and dragged their bags into the dim, low-ceilinged change room. Marcus followed the last boy in and closed the door.

Darkness was already coming down like smoke on the road ahead by the time Manda and Patrick got on their way. The stretch of pavement visible in the headlights of the truck kept shrinking. Patrick had forgotten to get gas on the way home from the mall; he watched the fuel gauge lose strength.

"So Marcus had all his little friends over?" Manda asked him. She was sitting forward, trying to dislodge something pointy that was sticking in her back. The window scraper. She had on her heavy coat, the blue one with the tassels all down the sleeves and across the chest. It was her going-out coat – it made her happy just to feel the weight of it on her shoulders.

"They were watching some game from last year."

"One of their *own* games? That's sad."

Patrick reached forward and scratched at a mark on the windshield: a pebble had created a small, jagged star in the glass.

"I don't know how he can stand it. For real: all those kids in that little apartment. I'd go nuts."

"Isn't he supposed to be moving in with that girlfriend with the kid?" Patrick asked, scratching again at the blemish in the windshield.

"I really don't think that's going anywhere," Manda said. "The only people he hangs around with are those kids. That's it. And us. He suckers Margaret into letting him stay at their place sometimes, but they're not exactly the best hosts. I think it's harder for him to stay there now anyway with my dad home all the time. I know my dad was relieved when he finally moved out. He never said anything to Margaret, though – it's her house and her son, right? You know the way she is about Marcus. You've seen it."

She twittered her fingers in the air as if invisible confetti were falling from the roof of the cab. There was just the odd car on the road and no big trucks so Patrick relaxed in his seat, almost letting the truck drive itself. He yawned huge like a lion, eating the air in front of him, and Manda smacked him lightly on the arm.

"You better not fall asleep. I haven't been to a movie in a year."

"I'll get a coffee at the mall."

"Poor baby," Manda said, stroking his arm. "You should sleep in tomorrow."

Manda looked out at the last three big buildings before the turn-off: Bingo Palace, Eddie's Used Auto Sales, Beaver Bonanza Furniture. All three had been there when she'd first come to Dunbridge. The three massive buildings sitting back from the highway on broad fields of rumpled asphalt – for her they were perfect monuments for the town, its pyramids and Sphinx. She felt happy each time she passed them on her way to somewhere else.

She started telling Patrick about the new idea she had for the kitchen. All open spaces and a green-and-yellow colour scheme, right down to the bowls and plates. She went into detail about how the cupboards could be pulled down without damaging the wall, and about where they could find the wood for the shelving. She was getting the feeling she only had to talk about it to find it done when they got back.

"Sure," Patrick said, not taking much of his attention off the road. "Yellow plates? Where do we get that?"

"Nowhere in Dunbridge, obviously."

Patrick felt a familiar twisting in his chest. Every few weeks something new appeared in the house, and he could almost see the walls of their debt-pit shift.

"We have lots of plates," he said. "There's another whole box downstairs of my mom's old kitchen stuff."

"I'm not touching that old shit! Stuff you ate off when you were a kid? It's probably so coated in dust. And Ronnie's old coffee mugs, are you kidding?"

"I'm not talking about coffee mugs, I'm just saying we have so many plates already."

"So?"

"So, there's other stuff we need to buy first."

"Oh, like what?"

"Like I don't know. I just think we should be careful about spending money."

"Be careful? If it was something for your store you would just put it on the credit card without saying anything. I'm the one that has to figure out what everything is when the bill comes. I can't keep track of it half the time. You put in a whole new phone system for the store last year without telling me. I got in a fight with the guy, remember? I thought they were scamming us!"

"Not the point."

"What is, then?"

Patrick didn't want to tell her it was different because the store was his and technically the house was his, too, and for him the store was the priority. He wasn't even certain of that himself, anymore.

"We can't just leave it like it is," Manda said.

"Yeah well, if they hit us with a big water bill, we're fucked," he said. It was always a safe strategy to invoke a possible external threat.

"We just won't pay it. We might as well be on a well anyway, we're so far out of downtown."

"Yeah right."

"Margaret's place was on a well until after I moved out!"

Manda rarely had a chance to feel anything like pride in the years she spent living in that house out in the middle of nowhere.

After a few minutes of driving with only blackness on either side of them, they hit the highway that took them south to Toronto. Manda slid down in her seat and jammed her feet up against the glove compartment. Fights about money – the lack of it, how the little there was got spent, the difficulty of finding more – had been part of their lives since they met. Patrick was already working toward opening the store and saving everything he had in those days. She had to convince him to take her to a movie or to dinner, and he used to sit and watch each bite go down as if it were his own arm she was eating. They were married at City Hall and had a small party in a closed-off room at the back of a bar downtown. Margaret and Allen came, and Marcus and Ken and some of the people Manda worked with at the time. Ronnie came and got drunk and told dirty jokes, but Patrick's mother felt sick and went home straight from City Hall. Patrick had wanted to move the party to the house so she wouldn't feel completely left out, but Ronnie refused to have strangers walking around the place. He said she would just spend the whole time in bed, anyway.

In their first apartment they'd had only furniture Patrick borrowed from Ronnie and a few things Sinc had given them for free – new chairs with uneven legs and lamps that flickered and hummed. Manda never had any serious hopes that Patrick's store would free her from working, but she didn't expect that it would make everything so much harder.

The traffic was bad near the top of the city, which is as far as Patrick was willing to drive. It took him a few tries to get over into the lane he needed for the mall turnoff. They had to circle the lot to find a space. "It's Sunday," Patrick complained. "It's always busy," Manda said, with something like infatuation for the press of cars and people around them. After the relative silence of the truck, the noise of the mall came at them in a wave, making them both jumpy.

"I still need a coffee," he shouted over the sound of kids running past them.

"The theatre's in the food court. We're gonna go past a hundred coffee places, so don't have a fit."

"Everything'll be closed now, though."

A man standing in the middle of the mall offered them credit card applications. Manda was tempted until she saw it was a card they already had, one they'd already depleted.

"We need someone offering cash," she said. "No strings attached."

On the escalator down into the food court Patrick told her a story about a friend of his who'd slid down the platform between the up and down escalator in some mall and ended up hitting the floor headfirst, nearly breaking his neck.

"Drunk out of his mind, obviously," he laughed.

"And where were you?"

"Going up the other side!" he said. "We all ran like fuck."

"That's a nice thing to do to a friend."

Patrick waved his hands to show that it was both simpler and more complicated than that, that nothing that happened within groups of young men could be assessed using the words *nice* or *friend*.

The escalator dropped them in the centre of the food court. They were in a narrow lane between chairs bolted to the floor – they had to walk turned slightly sideways to fit through. Manda had to hold her purse up near her chin to keep it from hitting the backs of the heads of people sitting and eating. Half of the counters weren't open – even the McDonald's counter was locked up and dark – but the place was still nearly full somehow. A few dozen six- and seven-year-olds engulfed a whole corner of the place, all of them eating with their jackets peeled down to their waists, standing in their chairs or running in the narrow spaces between tables.

The movie theatre was on the other side of the food court. Patrick was already squinting at the sign over the doors for the show times, so he didn't hear the voice calling out over the noise of the other diners. Manda heard it and stopped dead. Patrick walked right into her. He was still smiling from the sheer pleasure of being out at night, not working.

"What's up?"

"It's fucking Shelly," Manda said with a snarl. "I don't believe it. Oh Patrick, fuck! I do not fucking believe it."

Patrick froze instantly when he heard the name, like a toy soldier whose magical few hours of life had just come to an end. His arms dropped beside him and he just kept staring straight ahead at the entrance to the movie he was sure now he would never reach.

"Can't we just keep going?" he asked.

"Patrick, she's yelling at us – *Yes I friggin see you!* – I don't want her to have a conniption right here. Aw *Christ*, Patrick, why does she have to be here? I wasn't even thinking."

"We're not anywhere near her apartment, are we?"

"We're close enough."

"Fuck."

Patrick looked over and saw Manda's mother waving at them and trying to stand up at her table near the washrooms. She looked as though she were caught by the table and couldn't get free, like the table was eating her. She was alone. She had on a blue winter coat that looked too small; there was a look of frenzied panic on her face, the same look she'd had on the few times Patrick had met her. Manda told him after the first time that her mother normally never smiled, but that she tried whenever he was around, and that this look of panic was the botched result, the closest she could come. The two of them walked over slowly, stopping every few steps to let another little kid run across their path.

"Amanda!"

Manda's mother stopped trying to resist the table and flopped back in her chair. She stared at Patrick and hissed heavily through her teeth, not daring to close her mouth again in case she couldn't muster another smile. Her face seemed ready to split. It rippled and twitched as if other personalities were battling beneath her skin. At that moment she looked more like Ken than she did Manda. She had her hair long and tied back, the way Manda used to wear it when she'd first started going out with Patrick.

Manda stood back as far as she could from her mother's table. Patrick couldn't find a place for his hands.

"Amanda!"

"So you're here," Manda said, without emotion.

"I was sitting when I thought I saw Patrick coming down the stairs – not the stairs, the *escalator* – and I said, 'I know that person, that's Amanda's husband. That's Patrick.' And then I saw you and I couldn't believe it! Coming here! I've never seen that jacket before," she said, pointing to the fringes hanging off Manda's arm.

"It's new," Manda said. She moved her arm slightly in case Shelly tried to touch it.

"A new jacket and everything. I need a new jacket, too, but it's finding the money, isn't it? That one looks so warm."

Neither Manda nor Patrick made any response, so Shelly changed the subject.

"I was just eating my dinner!"

She was eating some kind of stew out of a Styrofoam container, with a fist-sized hunk of bread she was tearing into smaller hunks, probably to make it seem like more, and some old-looking packages of crackers that Manda guessed had been hoarded from some other meal and brought from home. Her mother had never hoarded or saved anything when Manda was a kid; she'd been wasteful and sloppy. Manda believed this new-found sense of economy had nothing to do with money. Shelly had lost everything when Allen left town with Manda and Ken, everyone had gotten out of her grip, so she was determined to let nothing else escape. Those poor crackers – and all the plastic knives and forks and packets of ketchup that Manda knew filled her mother's kitchen drawers – all of them were hostages, ransomed for her sense of control, and maybe for the unearned guilt she could wring out of her daughter when she was found in the food court of a mall, among all the crazies and the old people, eating something she'd bought with rolled-up change. Manda knew that if Shelly thought she could get away with it, she would have pulled out one of the fortune cookies she kept in her bag for dessert.

"Oh Manda, you look beautiful," she said, starting to rise out of her chair again. "You cut your hair, though. I like your hair long. I wish you'd let it grow long again. I always loved it long."

"So you could yank on it," Manda replied.

Shelly dropped back in her seat and started jabbing the air in front of her with her finger.

"That's very mean and not true. It's not fair. I *never* pulled your hair. I don't know who did but it was never me."

She said it in a voice that sounded cheerful despite her angry gestures, as if she were trying to sway some neutral third party. She dropped her hands and worked to reassemble her panicked smile. Then she turned her attention to Patrick.

"Amanda can be a little mean sometimes, can't she Patrick? She's always been like that, even when she was a little girl. Is she mean with you?"

"No."

"Don't know where it comes from – *I* never teased like that. Patrick, I am so happy to see you! You are so good for Amanda. She needs someone who is steady and honest."

"Oh, ha!" Manda shouted.

"It hasn't been easy for us, you know. Amanda's a strong girl – we're both strong. If you two ever have a little baby, you'll see. It'll be strong, too."

Patrick said nothing, but his body tightened. Shelly was staring at him with a kind of lust. Manda had to cross her arms to quell the temptation to slap the old woman right there. She was also shaking slightly and didn't want her mother or Patrick to see. She didn't want to give Shelly the satisfaction and she didn't want Patrick to do anything stupid like put his arms around her.

"What are you doing here, Shelly?"

Shelly started dabbing at the table with a napkin and gathering her cracker crumbs into a pile, all with an air of false dignity.

"I came here because I like the food," she said. "They have stew on Sunday nights. The family in the apartment below me makes some kind of curry dinner every Sunday. I hate the smell of it, it stinks up the whole building. I complain but nothing ever happens."

"I'll bet you do."

"How is your store?" she asked Patrick.

"Fine."

"I want to come see it soon, but I never get the chance to come all the way up there. There's no one here who can give me a ride and I don't like sitting on a bus that long."

A kid being chased down the aisle ran over Patrick's feet and pitched forward. Patrick caught him before his head made contact with the side of the table. The kid was stunned for a second, but then wrestled his way out of Patrick's grip and ran off, the laces on his boots flipping behind him like live wires.

"You see?" Shelly said to Manda. "He would make a great father. He knows what to do. Amanda keeps telling me that she will never have kids. Never ever ever. But what a waste. What do you think of that?"

"Alright, cut that shit out, Shelly."

Shelly looked insulted. "That's terrible, the way you talk to me. I was sitting here eating! No one said you could come here and talk to me like that."

Manda gave an exasperated laugh. "Oh god, I didn't know you were so friggin delicate! Could've fooled me."

"You're being rude, I think. *You* try living my life."

"No thank you. Patrick and I are on our way to see a movie – we don't need this shit. Really."

Shelly's face instantly lost all its hostility, and she smiled at Patrick.

"I'm sorry Patrick – we've always had little arguments like this. Amanda likes to argue. Pay no attention to her."

"Oh, this is bullshit, mother. This is too much."

Shelly looked at Patrick and raised her eyebrows slightly as if her point had been proven. Patrick looked like he wanted the kid who had tripped to come back so he could throw him against the wall.

"I'm going to buy the tickets," he said to Manda. He left without saying anything to Shelly. His hands were shaking with anger as he pulled out his wallet to pay at the box office window.

Shelly watched Patrick walk away. Manda wanted to slap the lustful smile off her face. Her mother put the lid back on her stew and started to clean up her dinner. She looked like she was going to cry.

"What is it, why are you looking like that all of a sudden?" Manda asked, knowing full well she was being sucked into something. "We have no money, mom, so don't start."

"How can you afford a movie, then?"

"Patrick and I go out like once every couple of months. We hardly ever see each other."

"That's more than I see you."

"Oh fuck, is that what this is about? Because . . ." Manda couldn't find the words. "I'll come to see you soon."

"When?" her mother demanded, her attempted smile entirely gone and replaced with a more familiar predatory look. "You say that and then I don't see you for years. You won't even give me your new phone number."

"Let's just . . . What's going on with you and that job?"

"Oh, you don't care," she said. "I might have to quit it, that's what. They're all liars there. They promise things but then they turn around and do none of it. They *know* I'm too sick to work all the time."

"So why did you start working there in the first place?"

"Because they'll cut off my cheque if I don't. The province is cutting my cheque anyway, and now they're saying my rent is going to go up. You should have seen the man that came around when I called. Brand-new suit and a brand-new watch. He's making money off *someone*, that's for sure. I should have told him to go back to India, all of them."

"How can they cut your cheque?"

"They can do whatever they want! They can make me cut my wrists if they want!"

"Oh for Christ's sake, mother, that's such bullshit."

Shelly's face was twisted up with anger.

"You can't say that to me!" she shouted. "You can't talk like that – it's not fair. I'm too sick to work. You talk like you know every-thing. You just laugh at me and hide from me and ignore me."

"When the fuck have I ever laughed at you?"

"But you have no idea what it's like. I raised you – it might as well have been on my own. Your father was a liar, he lied to me."

Manda softened a little. "Yeah I know that, mom," she said. "We're not talking about that."

"He lied to me about that woman – that one he worked with – and he lied to me when he took you away."

"He had to. You wouldn't have let him."

"So you think it's okay to lie to me. Oh, okay. Now I see."

Manda felt exhausted. She fought the urge to sit down.

"Let's just get off this, okay? That was a long time ago."

Shelly looked hard into the heart of something raw and terrible that only she could see.

"It was *yesterday*," she said, hissing the words.

Manda had been waiting for years for her mother to finally fulfill all of the potential for full-on craziness that bubbled out of her every second of every day, to finally cross over from being someone who held truth and reality a little too loosely and a little too carelessly, to being someone with no grip on anything, a shithouse rat. Looking at the woman now, seething over betrayals that had happened twenty-five years ago, Manda realized the big shift into craziness may have been a gradual process that had been going on all along, that she shouldn't have been waiting for an explosion, but should have instead kept her ears open for underground cave-ins. She didn't think she wanted Shelly to crack, but she was sick to death of waiting for it. Everyone assumed it would happen when Allen had his affair, then when Manda and Ken were taken away, then when Allen took them to a town Shelly couldn't have found on a map. When she finally lost it on Ken, when she did what she did to him, that looked at first like a crack-up, but she was out front in getting him to the hospital and praying he'd be okay and all the rest of it. It wasn't good enough to let her keep the kids, but it seemed genuine. And probably *was* genuine, to the extent that anything Shelly ever did was genuine, which was not very much.

"Everyone can lie to me and that's fine because I'm such a bad person," Shelly was saying.

"For Christ's sake."

"He lied to me and he took my children and he made them hate me. You hate me because of him."

Manda had to laugh at that.

"It's true!" Shelly insisted. "He worked on you and worked on you, and now you never visit me. I know him – you don't know him. I know him."

"When's the last time you actually saw Dad?"

Shelly just kept talking like she hadn't heard. "You don't

know what it's like to have your daughter taken away from you. You don't know even the first thing about it."

"What about your son? What about Ken? You forgot about him?"

"You can't blame me for him! Everybody always blames me for him! It was impossible."

Manda had to stop herself from grabbing the woman by the hair and slamming her face-first into the table. She used to do exactly that at school to girls who called her a dyke. That was years and years ago but she knew for sure she was still capable of it. That hard, swinging rage she felt all through high school – it almost never came back to her now, except when she tried to talk to her mother.

"Listen, the movie's going to be starting any second," she said. "I have to find Patrick. I'll call –"

"And then rich little Pakis coming around and telling me to calm down. . . ."

"You're not even listening! What's the point?"

"You think you're better than me because you went away and you can laugh at me and never come to see me and hate me."

"Yup, that's right – you got it. Boy, do you ever know me, Shelly."

Shelly put the last of her crackers back into her bag and shrugged.

"I had two children that I fed and kept alive," she said. "That's more than you've done. You couldn't have done what I did. You're a coward and a little bitch."

Manda, already stunned by Shelly's words, was even more shocked by what her mother did next: she started smiling. *This is it*, Manda thought, *she's gone*. She imagined her mother having to be sedated and taken out of the food court by ambulance attendants, the stretcher banging against every chair and table. More than just smiling, Shelly was smiling while not even looking at her, staring at some point behind her instead. Manda was just about to ask if she was feeling okay when Patrick touched her on the shoulder.

"It's gonna start soon," he said. "Like two minutes." He was trying not to look at Manda's mother and trying not to look like he was trying not to look. Shelly had gone back to cleaning the crumbs off her table.

"Have fun then," Shelly said. "I can't travel up to see you so I hope you come down."

Manda let Patrick draw her away toward the entrance of the theatre.

"You still want to go or . . ." he asked quietly when they were far enough away from Shelly.

"I'm not letting her ruin this, that bitch. She's *not* going to ruin everything for me. I can't take it."

When they got into the theatre the previews had already started. They sat through the movie – something about a man who has to repeat first grade to inherit his father's company – not laughing and barely taking it in. Every time Patrick looked over at Manda she would hiss at him to watch the movie and leave her alone. When they left, she made him go out first to make sure Shelly was gone. She was. The whole food court was dark and deserted. On the long drive back Manda picked over and cursed everything Shelly had said, except for her mother calling her a coward – she kept that one to herself. She didn't want Patrick to try and calm her down about it or soothe it away.

"Unbelievable," she said. "And her looking at my jacket – I thought she was going to ask me to give it to her!"

On their street they passed an OPP car parked outside a house that had been empty and for sale forever. The light from a flashlight moved around inside, dancing around crazily then resting in one corner or another. Patrick drove the truck past slowly, waiting to see if someone would come running out.

When they got home, Patrick went upstairs to shower and sleep while Manda stood at the window of the front room with the lights off, watching the cop walk around the house and then sit in his car writing something. The dark hump of a raccoon crossed their front lawn, and something about its deliberate walk reminded her of the mailman who had demanded they salt the walk. Her breath bloomed grey on the cold glass. Something startled the raccoon before it reached their driveway. Manda hoped it wasn't kids trying to get into their garage – she couldn't take any more that night.

MONDAY

Marcus was being crushed under the wheels of a truck. It rolled up onto his arm and pressed against his rib cage until he could feel his breath being squeezed out of him like toothpaste from a tube. He got squeezed right into the darkness and cold of his own bedroom, where he was pinned against the wall. His left arm had slipped down between the wall and the bed. He tried to move it but it felt swollen, like one of Popeye's arms, nothing but meat. He worried that it was trapped and that his fingers were turning black in the unclean darkness under his bed. Everything was wrong. He was in his underwear and couldn't think where his blankets were.

His right elbow touched something, some other presence in his bed that shifted slightly and made a sound like an animal growling in the distance. Marcus's mind froze with panic, but his memory woke up to reassure him: it was Kelly's first night sleeping over. They were conducting an experiment – Mark was sleeping at a friend of Kelly's. Marcus had picked Kelly up the night before on his way home from the rink. The two of them had walked through the aisles of the grocery store, buying frozen pizzas for dinner, along with root beer and a carton of strawberries. As they walked out with the groceries, Kelly was already feeling tired. Without Mark around, her body gave up its vigilance and gave in to the exhaustion that was always gnawing at its edges. They rented a movie and watched it in Marcus's living room, the pizzas and root beer in front of them on the trunk. They didn't touch the strawberries. By the end of the movie Kelly was dozing on his arm, and Marcus had to admit defeat. In his bed they grappled with each other for a while, but it was like trying to have sex with a narcoleptic, so Marcus gave up. She smiled at him with her eyes half-closed and apologized again.

Marcus freed his arm and held it out to let the blood flow. The feeling was like the stop-motion blooming of a garden, the return of life. He wondered if babies felt anything like it after their first breath – if they didn't they were getting cheated. His arm seemed to shrink back to its normal dimensions. He pried a corner of the blanket away from Kelly's sleeping form and covered himself up as best he could.

Manda was running late. The power must have blinked out – her alarm clock was flashing pitifully, unable to stop displaying the wrong time. She wondered how Patrick had got up without waking her; she wondered how he had got up at all without an alarm. The coffee maker quit while she was trying to make herself a cup. She sat in the kitchen and stared at it for more than a minute before realizing the light wasn't on and the water wasn't dribbling through. It was like watching someone die in their sleep – the light goes out and everything stops flowing, but you don't notice until later. She felt no sentimental attachment to this coffee maker, though it was a wedding present from Margaret and had moved with them twice. It had been dependable, but it was slow and out of date, and Manda was a little glad of the chance to get a fancy new one with a timer and everything she needed.

Someone called while Manda was in the shower. She heard the last ring just as she choked off the water, and worried that it might have been her mother, that seeing her daughter had set the woman on a renewed mission to find out their new phone number. Not that it would have been all that hard: they were in the phone book. The only thing stopping her was her uncertainty about Patrick's last name. Manda waited until she was dry and dressed before checking the waiting message. She hissed at herself when she heard Ken's voice.

"Shit shit shit," she said.

She tried calling Ken's house but there was no answer. In the message he had said only that he was on his way out to work. The connection was terrible – it sounded like he was calling long-distance. It was almost nine, and Patrick had the truck; she had to call a cab.

The only people Manda saw out walking were old people and people with dogs, with a lot of overlap between the two categories. Near Patrick's old school they were brought to a stop by a crossing guard. Manda recognized her as the mother of one of her friends in high school. She thought about rolling down her window and saying hello as they passed, but wasn't sure if the old woman would recognize her. She'd been a bus driver when Manda knew her, but there'd been some problem with drinking on the job, and she'd lost her licence. Manda hoped they weren't as strict with her in her new job – stopping traffic was one of the few things you *could* do better drunk than sober.

At the office she found Lana and Cheryl standing in the small kitchen and waiting as the coffee pot filled, drip by drip. Manda could tell something was going on: Cheryl was huffing with fresh drama. Lana took an excited step forward when she saw Manda come in.

"The new girl called in sick for the rest of the week," she said. "Sean is going bananas. I think he's going to fire her."

"I would," Manda said flatly.

"I would too!" Cheryl shouted. "What did I say? Oh my god, she just started!"

"Yeah, but she can't help it if she gets mono all of a sudden," Lana said.

"Neither can we," Manda said. "Neither can Sean. We can't afford it. For Christ's sake, she can answer a friggin phone no matter how sick she is. I've had it. Marcus had it when he was a kid. It won't kill her."

Manda waited for the other two to clear out of the kitchen before going in for her own coffee. Sean came in after her and rattled the coffee pot.

"You're not sick, too, are you?" he said, not really looking at Manda.

"No, but I'm pregnant," she said.

He gave her a split-second look of panic, then melted.

"Don't!" he shouted. "Don't even joke about that! That would be like Armageddon."

"For *you*."

"Yeah for me," he said bitterly, and went back to his office.

At her desk her telephone was already flickering, but Manda held off on starting. She hadn't slept much, and she wanted the caffeine to kick in before she got into the thick of it. Her cell phone rang. It was Patrick.

"Just saying hello, seeing if you're alright."

"Cuz of last night? Because of Shelly? Patrick, it's been like that my whole life, you know that. That was her on a good day, trust me." She tried her best to sound convincing. "That was her on Prozac."

"Did she know we were going there?"

"How could she, Pat? It's not like we'd been chatting before.

It's probably just the only place she can go that's not full of Chinese people."

Manda wanted to keep him on the phone – she hadn't seen him that morning and she missed him.

"So Ken finally called this morning. While I was in the shower, of course – it's like he *knows*. Anyway, he's working today so I'm gonna go over there at lunch and drag him out. By the way, Patrick –"

"Yeah?"

"If you see him don't tell him we saw her, okay? Don't tell Marcus, either, okay? Nobody."

Manda and Ken never talked about Shelly, not since they were teenagers, and she half-hoped her brother had forgotten about the woman, though that was unlikely. She hoped that his mother had at least diminished in his mind to a vague and distant horror, something that had been endured and left behind. Manda didn't see Shelly herself for almost ten years after Allen had taken them away. Then one of her boyfriends – a sensitive one, a rare thing for Manda – convinced her to seek Shelly out. The guy was also addicted to painkillers, which meant the relationship didn't last long, just long enough for him to plant the idea in her head that she was "incomplete" if she didn't know her mother. "You have to know everything about that kind of pain," he told her, without any sense of irony.

She had found Shelly living in a high-rise in the north end of Toronto, far enough from downtown that the CN Tower was a vertical line on the horizon that got lost in the smog. She was working part-time in a fabric store. Her apartment was tiny and awful: a kitchen and living room combined, a small bedroom, and a bathroom with only a shower stall. The light in the bathroom was brown with dust and dead bugs. The bedroom smelled of sour perfume – Manda figured her mother dumped some on the bedclothes on the days she came to visit.

The living room was just a hard chair and a small television on a table. Shelly seemed to really only live in the kitchen half of the room. There was an old card-table to eat on. It was pushed up against the window and covered in decorative things she must have bought at Goodwill, little statuettes and salt and pepper shakers and lamps with frayed cords. The grimness of the apartment was a big part of the reason why Manda demanded they start meeting at coffee shops: seeing the place almost made her feel sorry for her mother and she didn't want any pity getting in.

There were a couple of photos in Shelly's apartment of Manda as a little girl, but none of her father or of the whole family. The only picture of Ken was one taken before he got burnt, a shot of him standing in the middle of a soccer field looking lost. Manda remembered how he used to wander straight across playing fields and baseball diamonds in the middle of games. He became known for it and no one really bothered him about it, especially once they realized he was a little slow. Her father had taken the picture on Ken's eleventh birthday, when he'd refused a party and a cake and the rest and simply demanded they spend the day at the park. Manda had wanted to steal the picture from her mother and actually tried a few times, but the apartment was too small to be left alone for long enough to get it off the wall. She also thought about simply throwing it in the garbage or smashing it right there on the wall. She felt her mother didn't deserve such a picture of her son's vulnerability.

Manda had a picture of herself taken on the same day, showing her pretending to dive off the rocks at the edge of the park while Ken stood in the background looking worried. She was seven. The big fights between her mother and father had already begun, but it wasn't until a couple of years later, when Ken got his burn, that Allen took them away from Shelly for good. Manda remembered the three of them sleeping in the back bedroom of someone's house for months before her father found them a new apartment. They were miserable. Allen was working all the time and Ken kept having to go to a clinic for his face. (He would pick at the scab and it would get infected, just like they warned him.) In their new apartment, Manda and Ken still had to share a room. He would keep her up half the night by moaning in his sleep and hitting the wall with his fist, trying to punch his way out of a bad dream. They weren't allowed to answer the phone or the door. "In case it's mom, stupid," Manda would tell Ken if she caught him automatically reaching for the ringing phone. She knew he still didn't like to answer the phone, but hoped he had mostly forgotten why.

What Manda could never get over with Shelly – the same thing that had finally forced her to end her visits, and the same thing she had seen the night before – was how her mother showed no sense of guilt. She was only ever interested in challenging her own record – as a mother, as a wife, and as a human being – and in making clear the context of her actions and all the mitigating factors, real and imagined. Manda had many reasons to hate her mother, but she hated her most for this, for how brazen the woman had become in revisiting all the shitty episodes in their shared past with the express purpose of lessening her guilt, of explaining them away, and in some cases, of contesting the fact that they ever occurred at all. She was like a convicted murderer who had learnt some law in jail and now spent all her time going over trial transcripts in search of loopholes and procedural flaws.

The other reason Manda hated seeing her mother now more than ever was that she was starting to see Shelly's face in her own. She had cut her hair short to try and reduce the resemblance, but it was still there when she caught a glimpse of her reflection in store windows or glass doors: that same crooked grimace and dark brow, those hard eyes. When her computer at work crashed or froze and she had to reboot, her mother's face would stare back from deep inside the monitor until the machine came back to life.

Kelly tried to shower in Marcus's bathroom but the water came out hot, then cold, then hot again. She was unable to integrate the two extremes into something warm and bearable. It pissed down on her through the one opening in the showerhead not completely clogged with rust. She got out having managed only to wet her legs. She was relieved to find a clean towel under the sink. There was a giant plant that she had never seen before sitting on the back of the toilet. It looked ill and was dropping broad, yellowed leaves into the bowl.

She had woken up with no blankets and one leg fully on the floor as if her sleeping body had been trying to walk out of the room. Marcus kept sniffing in his sleep like he was sobbing. The room seemed to slope in on her in the semi-dark. She could hear something small and animal moving in the kitchen. When Marcus finally got up he found her in the living room on the couch eating a piece of dry toast.

"I made this, sorry," she said, holding out the toast, "but I couldn't find anything to put on it."

Marcus was still a little dazed with sleep and not yet sure how he felt about finding someone already in his apartment. "There should be, um, margarine or something in the fridge."

Marcus walked around the living room picking things up: it looked dirtier in there now than it had the night before. The sunlight was revealing the mess. He wished he had done a better job cleaning up. There were still a few chips on the floor and under chairs. One of the kids from his team had left his inhaler on the TV, and there were still cigarette butts in a coffee mug on the window sill. The urge to get her out of his apartment came on in a rush, mixed with the pleasure of having her around. He already felt stuck, like he couldn't get his day started with some-one else in the way. His usual morning routine of sitting around in his pajama bottoms watching a bit of TV, putting off having a shower, and avoiding answering the phone – all of that suddenly seemed vital to his existence.

"There was a squirrel outside the window a few minutes ago yelling like all get-out," Kelly said.

"He's always there. That's probably what woke me up."

"I called Estelle – she says Mark got up in the night and cried a bit, but now he's watching cartoons and eating Cheerios so he doesn't want me to pick him up yet. He's got swimming later, though."

"Swimming?" Marcus asked. "It's nearly the end of October!"

"In a pool, obviously. He has lessons."

He was annoyed that the first thing Kelly had done was to call her son when the whole point of her staying over was to get her away from her kid and give them some time alone.

"Mark's been on his own before, hasn't he?"

"Only once or twice overnight with my mom. He's usually okay with a babysitter, though."

"So there you go," he said. "Why were you so worried about him?"

"What do you mean? I still worry about him, doesn't matter where he is. I worry about him when he's in his own bed."

"That makes no sense."

"How does that make no sense?"

"I don't know, it's just stupid."

"No it's not – he's my kid. I worry about him all the time. You better xyz yourself, by the way," she said, pointing at Marcus's crotch: the tip of his cock was peeking sleepily out the fly of his pajamas. That made him even more annoyed.

"So when do you plan to stop worrying about him?" he asked her. "When he's thirty? I mean, what's going to happen to him? It's fucked up, you have to admit it."

Kelly shouted back, louder than she intended: "I'm his mother, Marcus! What do you want me to do?" She immediately lowered her voice. "I really don't want to fight," she said.

"Yeah. Well."

Marcus stood there staring out the window until Kelly spoke up again, trying to change the subject and make peace. She was still holding a half-eaten piece of toast in her hand.

"What's that plant in your bathroom? It looks like it's dying."

"That's because it *is* dying. My sister brought it here the other day, and I don't know what I'm supposed to do with it."

"I'll take it if you don't want it. I like plants."

"I don't hate them, I just think there's barely enough room in this apartment for me," he said. "How would you get it home, anyway? No, I have to deal with it. Maybe I'll water it or something before we go."

Kelly couldn't get Marcus's remote control to work, so she drifted around the living room, looking for something to read. All she could come up with were some hockey biographies, a textbook-type collection of the "world's greatest short stories," and a thick, paperback spy-thriller that looked brand new. She had just got settled back onto the couch with the short-story book and had started one she liked the title of – "Royal Beatings"; it was like something her mother used to say – when she heard Marcus swearing, and there was a crash against the side of the bathtub.

The store where Ken worked loomed over everything else on the street like an oil tanker in a harbour full of yachts. In Manda's lifetime it had been a K-Mart, a Woolworth's, a Super Saver, and a Zellers. As a Giant Tiger it wasn't doing much better; the building was cursed.

The front doors swished open automatically. Just inside there was a bank of gumball and novelty machines. The biggest one had a dusty parrot that came to life every few minutes and said "I love to get money," except that the recording was so old and distorted that it was starting to sound like "I *have* to get money," which Manda thought was more appropriate, anyway.

There were a few sales clerks in yellow coats working in silence, never looking up to see beyond their small area. Manda went up to one young woman restocking a display of Halloween candies and pumpkin buckets. She was in her early twenties, but her hair was curled like an old lady's and she was wearing thick glasses with squarish lenses. Manda was always amazed at how old everyone working in the store looked. They hired a lot of seniors, which seemed to make the younger employees age prematurely, as if old age were contagious.

"Excuse me, do you know Ken? He works here."

"Ken . . . is somewhere," she said. "Upstairs?"

The woman stared hard at Manda to see if this information was enough, or if she was going to be asked for more. Manda recognized the look in her eyes: Ken had it when he was cornered or got confused. There were half-a-dozen people with head problems working in the store. They kept the outright cripples mostly out of sight in the stockrooms, but it still seemed like everyone was shuffling around. The only exception was Ken's friend Steve, who moved with more nervous energy than everyone else in the store combined. Manda went looking for Steve – *he* would find Ken in the same time it would take anyone else to process her question.

Before she could find Steve she spotted Ken. He was hard to miss: standing on a stepladder, holding a paper witch that had fallen from the wall. He was at the end of an aisle of boy's running shoes. The rows of shoes, with their small, yawning mouths, smelled like wet rubber and made Manda feel a little sick. She stood at the foot of his ladder and waited to see how long it would take him to notice. He was holding the witch by the throat. A roll of masking tape encircled his forearm in a pale yellow band.

"Jump!" she said as a joke, then quickly reconsidered: "No, don't."

Ken was wearing the same yellow jacket with the blue stripes as everybody else, but it looked tight on him. The sleeves stopped a few inches short of his wrists. It made him look like he was expanding right there before her.

"What's wrong with your jacket?" she asked him. "Why's it so small?"

Ken looked down at his uniform and – after almost five seconds' thought – told her it was Steve's.

"Mine got a rip in it," he said.

"Don't they have extras here you could wear? Spares?"

"We have to pay for our uniforms."

Manda shook the stepladder a little to get him to come down – it was awkward, talking to her brother while he loomed three feet above her holding a witch.

"Yeah, but they could lend you one for the day," she said. "Be better than you walking around all day looking like you're about to explode. Want me to talk to them?"

Ken looked at his jacket again, as if for guidance. Manda figured it was better to just drop the subject.

"Whatever – come down and let's go get something to eat. It's your lunchtime isn't it?"

The store had a little restaurant in it, with the usual pictures of fish-and-chips and roast beef sandwiches under a black slick of gravy. Manda had never seen anyone in there under the age of sixty except for Ken. He liked their fries, and they usually gave him free refills on orange pop, so of course it was one of his favourite places to eat. The waiter came out from behind the cash. He was old, but he looked even older than he was because of all the effort he had put into looking young – the grey hair dyed black and combed over the skull, etc. His face was thin and came to a point like a beak.

"Kenny," the waiter said, standing next to Ken but looking at Manda. He pinched Ken's shoulder. "Hey, you look fat. Look at this jacket!"

"Hi," Manda spoke up, knowing Ken would never introduce her. "I've been in a couple of times before. I'm Ken's sister."

He nodded slightly, indicating that this was information he already had. His Adam's apple kept moving up and down in his throat like it was a panicked mouse trapped just under his skin.

"Look at your arms!" he said, pointing and tugging at the ends of Ken's sleeves. "You look like The Incredible Hulk!"

"It's not his," Manda explained. "It's Steve's."

"It's Steve's," Ken echoed. He looked unhappy, but Manda knew he liked the old waiter, though he didn't like being called "Kenny."

"Steve!" the waiter said, suddenly scornful. "That little fucker was in here yesterday and had an egg sandwich and a Coke, four seventy-five – sorry, *eighty*-five – and he didn't leave me a tip. Is he working today?"

"Not yet," Ken said.

"Well I'm gonna wait around and catch him and tell him what a cheap little bugger he is. What do you think of that?"

"Sure."

"So, are you eating or just coffee?"

"Onion rings, for sure," Ken said, then went silent as he looked deep into the menu that was embedded in the tabletop. Manda had to intervene: she knew from experience that it could take her brother a full minute to complete an order.

"To drink, Ken?" she prodded him. "A Coke or something?"

Ken kept looking through his own reflection in the tabletop.

"You want a hamburger or something?" she tried again.

"Grilled cheese," he said, finally.

"And a Coke, yeah?" the waiter asked.

Ken looked confused for a second, then went back to the menu. Manda figured she should just jump in.

"Club sandwich and fries and a coffee," she said.

"On white or brown?"

"Orange," Ken said before she could reply.

Manda laughed. "What does that mean now?"

"Orange Crush."

The waiter brought them a bottle of ketchup, which Ken opened and gave a sniff – he had a strange fear of things going sour. If he tasted something slightly off, it was like poison in his throat and he'd cough it up right there. Manda took the ketchup bottle from Ken and smelled it herself so it wouldn't be an issue.

"It's *fine*," she said. "You have to get over that, Ken. It's so annoying."

Ken seemed slightly out of breath and bloated, and not only because of the tight jacket. It was getting harder and harder for Manda to recognize this swollen, middle-aged man as her brother. Marcus still looked enough like himself, though he was starting to droop and bruise like a wax statue made from his high-school yearbook photo. Ken, on the other hand, seemed to be slowly burying himself under layers of thick bone and fat. He was withdrawing, and Manda wondered how long it would be before he simply *disappeared*. Except for the side of his face, which still looked hard and ridged and angry after all these years, his skin was pale and soft like overboiled pasta.

"You look really tired," she told him.

Ken shrugged.

"So how's it going?" Manda asked, looking out at the store. "And why aren't you calling me back? I left you like twenty messages and nothing, no answer. Are you getting the messages? Are they passing them on to you?"

Ken nodded.

"So?"

Ken shrugged again. Manda had to resist the urge to get mad – if Ken was being this stubborn, there was no point in pushing it.

"Well then I'm not going to freak out, but you need to start calling me back. So are you doing all right in the new place?" she asked him. "Is that guy Darcy still complaining about everything? That other guy's okay, isn't he?"

"Darcy says I've been leaving the front door open, but I haven't," he said. "I always remember."

"Do you? Are you sure you haven't left it just once or twice even?"

"I left it open *one time*, now he thinks every time it's me."

"Okay Ken, well there you go. You can't say it was never you. What do you say when Darcy says it was you?"

"I tell him to go fuck himself."

Manda felt some relief: at least her brother was standing up for himself instead of retreating into dumb silence or the exile of his room.

"What does he say to that?"

A truck backing up outside filled the window and put their corner of the restaurant into shadow. Ken watched the side wall of the truck move slowly past them just beyond the glass until the cab slid by and the view of the street was restored. A man followed, waving his gloved hands as if herding a giant animal back into its cage.

"You have to be careful though," Manda was telling him, "because like it or not you have to live with these people, so you don't want to stir up too much shit, right? And get everybody all mad at you, especially because you just moved in there."

Manda noticed that he'd banged his thumb sometime recently. There was black blood pressed up against the underside of his thumbnail. It looked like a tiny painting of the night sky. She asked him how he did it, but he just looked at the thumb and shrugged, saying something had fallen on it. He had never grown out of the age of cuts and scratches and bruises. He had shown up at her house once last winter with blood dripping off his right eyebrow – he said he had slipped on the ice in their driveway and caught the corner of the house. Patrick told him to sue, and then went out with a bag of sand.

"So what's going on with the house now?" she asked him, trying to keep a very detached tone so she wouldn't spook him. "Marcus says he saw you out walking and you told him you hated it there. That's not what you said when you just moved in. You said it was alright."

Ken wouldn't look up at her.

"Well, what is it? Is it just cuz you're new there? You get used to them, remember. And everyone gets used to you."

"No they don't."

"They do so, and so do you," Manda insisted. "So what is it, you want to move out again?"

"Maybe."

"Well, fuck, that's great," Manda said, her attempt at a detached tone gone. "After I went around with you to see all these places and helped you move in and everything. It's hard to get into these places, Ken – you have no idea. You just tell me that someone's stealing from you or that the landlord won't fix anything or your rent is going up. Then I'm the one that has to run around and find you a new place to live. There's not a lot of these places around, Ken. Dunbridge is a tiny little town – how many of these places do you think there are? How many different houses do you think you can live in?"

She took a breath.

"So seriously, why don't you call me back?"

Ken stretched his shoulders against the constraining jacket. "I don't like talking on the phone there," he said. "Everybody listens to me."

This was new. "Since when?"

"They do it all the time."

"Who? What do they do?"

"If I'm on the phone they'll pick up the other phone and listen."

Ken started scraping at some dried ketchup with the tongs of his fork. Manda felt like she was trying to get information out of a kid. She wanted to grab the fork out of his hand and slam it down on the table to make him focus.

"Yeah, but who does it?"

"Everybody! In every place I've lived!"

Manda thought of all the times Ken had suddenly told her he had to go in the middle of a phone conversation, sometimes mid-sentence. She tried to remember if she had ever detected a click on the line, a sudden opening in the stream of sound running between them, an extra silence. His roommates interrupted them noisily all the time, asking Ken how long he was going to be, or just swearing and hanging up when they got conversation instead of the expected dial-tone. Sometimes someone would keep picking up at ten-second intervals, as if hoping the voices on the line could be scattered through persistence alone.

"If someone is listening in on your conversations," she said firmly, "it's a shitty thing to do, but it's not really a big deal. If that's how they get their jollies, then you can't let yourself get all worked up about it. Have you told the people in charge?"

Ken didn't answer. The look on his face told her he hadn't and probably wouldn't.

"So what are we supposed to do?"

"I just want to get out of there," he said.

"You said that, but you can't quit the place when you just moved in, can you?"

The waiter came over with Ken's grilled cheese sandwich and a plate of soggy-looking onion rings. He also brought a pint glass of unnaturally bright orange pop that hissed and bubbled and kept trying to eject the straw.

"You're the club sandwich, right?" the waiter asked Manda. "It'll be one more minute. We're getting kind of busy."

The restaurant was filling up with seniors who had just arrived on the bus. The mouse in the waiter's neck was practically ramming the underside of his jaw.

"Where is this coming from, Ken?" Manda asked when the waiter had gone. She spoke in a low tone: an old woman with a muddy cane had taken the table next to theirs and was staring at Ken's face. Manda wanted to grab the cane and pitch it out the open door as if to get rid of an annoying dog.

"I can't start all that again," she said, almost pleading with him. "I really can't. It's not fair. I've got the house, I've got all kinds of shit going on at work, I've got Patrick bugging me – I really can't."

"What's Patrick bugging you about?"

"Nothing. But I just can't start looking for another house for you right now, okay?"

"I don't want to live in another house."

"Okay then, what do you want?" Manda demanded. "How are you going to live? Where are you going to live? You know you need to live in these places so they can help you out," she said, trying to calm herself. "You know that, right?"

"I don't need to."

"Well if you're not going to live there, where are you supposed to live? Would you consider moving back in with dad and Margaret?" she asked. "They'd probably be happy to have you there."

Manda knew that wasn't true and she was pretty sure Ken knew it, too. Allen had gone through hell to protect her and Ken from their mother, but Manda wasn't sure he had ever reconciled himself to the way Ken was. More than that, he had been gradually withdrawing from active fatherhood since they were teenagers. After they moved to Dunbridge, he seemed to collapse. It was as if he'd decided the fight was over – he'd got his kids out of Shelly's reach, they would have to go the rest of the way on their own.

When Ken was old enough to move out, it was Margaret who first arranged for him to live in a group home. They all helped Ken move his bed and his boxes into his first room, but it was Manda and Margaret who insisted they all stay with him for the day while he unpacked. Allen had wanted to give him a slap on the back and a few encouraging words and leave him to it – he didn't even think at first to give him some money for groceries. Manda gave him twenty dollars of her own money to order a Hawaiian pizza, his favourite. He had stood in the middle of that tiny room where the head and foot of his mattress touched opposite walls, and was afraid to move, as if he didn't know what would crawl out of the floor to destroy him once they closed the door. He had the same look each time he moved into a new room and a new house. "I can't take the look on his face when it's all done and he's in there," Manda told Patrick after moving him the last time. "You just don't know if he's going to make it through the night, you know what I mean?"

Even if Margaret and Allen would have him, there was no way Ken would go back to living in that house. He had felt like an alien the whole time he was there. Margaret always tried her best to treat him well, and he liked her, but it was never like he really *lived* there. Manda felt it too, that they were boarders in

Margaret's house, exchange students from a land of unhinged and violent mothers. On her way out of the house for the last time she had half-expected Margaret to hand her the bill. Manda couldn't believe it when she first saw that house. Even now, in the fields that surrounded it she saw nothing but boredom and death. When she left the house she felt nothing but relief. Her dad was clearly relieved, just as he had been with Ken and much later with Marcus. When she moved out to live with a disaster of a boyfriend in his basement apartment underneath a family of screaming alcoholics, he made no serious objection.

"Do you want me to ask Margaret for you?" Manda asked.

He mumbled something and started scratching at his arms nervously.

"Come on, Ken, what was that? What did you say?"

"Maybe I can go somewhere else."

"Yeah maybe," she said angrily. "Like where exactly?"

"Toronto."

"Toronto? What the hell for?"

"See mom."

Manda stared at him open-mouthed, but he wouldn't look up. It took her a few moments to recover enough to speak.

"Have you been talking to dad?"

Ken shook his head, and Manda had a frightening thought.

"When's the last time you actually saw Shelly?"

"I don't know."

"Yeah but, as a kid or recently?"

The effort Ken was expending in trying to come up with the answer was clearly visible on his face. The old woman at the next table was made curious again by this new development.

"When we were at that court, with dad."

Manda was relieved: the day he meant was nearly twenty-five years in the past. She was shocked that he could remember it at all.

"So how do you know if she's even there anymore? And why would you even want to see her?"

"She'd let me stay for a while."

Manda almost laughed but stifled it. She had a cruel urge to tell Ken right there that his mother not only would not take him, but tended to block out the fact that he even existed.

"Well that's not happening," she said. "You can't just show up in Toronto and show up at Shelly's door when she hasn't seen you since you were a kid. And whatever," she said, waving away the first part of her sentence just in case it made Ken's plan sound merely impractical instead of crazy and impossible, "you already have a home. And you have a job – doesn't that mean something to you?"

"No." The tone of his voice was unequivocal. Manda wasn't used to it.

"Why? What's going on? You're not going to quit this, too, are you? Fucking hell, Ken, what's going on with you? I worked hard to set you up like this, a lot of people did. It's not like you can just go get any job you want or any room you want. You know that!"

"You're yelling at me."

Manda dropped her voice. "I don't mean to yell at you, Ken," she said. "It's just frustrating. You're acting like you think . . . well, I don't know what you think. So what's going on?"

But that was all she was going to get, she could tell: something in his eyes had receded back into his head, some flicker of attention that probably only she and a couple of other people could recognize. Once it was gone, so was he.

The waiter came to take away their plates.

"Don't wash that in hot water next time, eh?" he said to Ken, chuckling and tugging at the sleeves of the jacket again.

Manda paid the bill and made Ken walk with her to the store's entrance. He was restless, as if eager to get back to his ladder and his witch.

"Are you alright for money and everything?" she asked him, and when he made no reply except to touch one of the gumball machines, she gave him the fifty-dollar bill she had in her wallet.

"I was thinking we should go out soon," she said. The idea had just occurred to her. "Maybe tomorrow night. Marcus might come, maybe. You, me, Patrick, and Marcus. How's that?"

"I work late," he said.

"What's late?"

"I start at two o'clock and go until nine."

"Well, there you go – Patrick won't get out of the store until nine or so anyway, so why doesn't he pick you up?"

Ken didn't reply, so Manda just said, "Good – I'll call you." She left her brother standing just inside the glass doors. The sun was sharpening the shadows of the buildings downtown and the air seemed frozen in place. A few white clouds were stuck fast in the intense blue of the sky. It hadn't been sunny for days, and Manda tried to walk so that she caught each patch of sunlight that cut across the sidewalk. *It's going to snow*, she thought, and reminded herself to pull up the last of the garden. The cold made her think of the hole in the ceiling of the back room: it would now be too cold to work in there, too, and they would have to seal up the door with tape and towels. In the winter it always looked like they had barricaded something in there, a werewolf or a zombie. "This is the room you can put me in when I go nuts," Manda told Patrick once when they were both in there staring up at the ceiling and willing the hole to seal itself.

When Manda got back to work Lana mimed at her across the room to be quiet. She could hear Sean on the phone, saying "I understand that . . . yes, I understand that," over and over again between silences presumably filled on the other end with the new girl begging for her job. Maybe she was threatening him. Maybe she didn't care. Manda wondered whether Sean was going to come out of the office on the warpath or looking for sympathy for having to do such an ugly task. Either way, she figured it was better to keep her head down and get stuck back into work.

Ken spent the next few hours rehanging Halloween decorations that had fallen from the walls. Steve found him trying to get a pumpkin-and-goblin scene to stick to the side of the escalator. He giggled when he saw the effect his jacket had on his big friend. He jumped up and tried to slap a paper ghost that was just out of reach.

"Don't," Ken said. "I just put that there."

"These things are so fucking stupid. Halloween – who gives a shit?"

"Not me."

Steve pointed at a bright-green, dopey-eyed Frankenstein's monster leaning against a gravestone. "Kind of looks like you, buddy."

Steve started pacing the aisle in a tight circuit. He scratched at his chin until it was red. He was wearing his favourite T-shirt, from which half of the joke had worn away, so that it now only said "I Fall Down: No Problem." Grey shadows of sweat hung under his armpits, his forehead shone. In the fall and winter he sweated more than in the middle of a heat-wave. He always wore his coat open, even in the snow, and tore off all outdoor clothes the moment he got inside. There seemed to be an invisible foot constantly pressing down on him from behind, revving him to an unbearable pitch but never letting him run free.

"Here, give me that for a sec," he said, smiling and reaching for a coiled, paper snake. Ken gave it to him. Steve held its tail to his crotch and let the rest dangle to the floor.

"Who does this remind you of?"

Ken laughed.

Steve's face hardened. "So we're fucked, eh?" he said. He let the snake drop.

"I'm not picking that up now," Ken said, laughing. He hadn't yet caught up with Steve's sudden change of tone.

"Did you hear me? We're *fucked*."

"What do you mean?"

"I mean they might even get rid of us before Christmas and bring in other people."

"What does that mean?"

"The store only hired us because of some fucked-up thing that the government pays for. Anyway, it's getting cut, so we're fucked. Bye-bye."

Ken's arms drooped. "I don't get it," he said. One of the jack-o'-lanterns leaned off the wall as if to hear better.

"What's there to fucking get?" Steve took a grey, paper gravestone with tape on the back and pressed it against his chest until it stuck. "This is us," he said, pointing at it. *"Rest in Friggin Peace."*

Ken watched the rising escalator steps for a while, staring hard at the metal and rubber like he used to when he was a kid and was afraid of them, afraid that he'd be too slow to evade the teeth at the top.

"So who'd you have lunch with?" Steve asked him.

"What? My sister."

"Oh. That's too bad. You tell her to get you out of the psycho house?"

"Sort of."

"Yeah, and?"

"I don't know. Nothing. We talked about other stuff."

"You've got problems, buddy. I wouldn't last ten minutes in your house, I'm serious. You have to make a fucking decision, and *fuck* what your sister says. What is she, your fucking mother? Anyway, you have all kinds of other shit to worry about now. Did you tell her we're getting the boot?"

Ken's expression said no.

"I don't want to fucking start early today," Steve said. "Come with me, I have to smoke. You have a break coming, don't you?"

Ken stood there holding another jack-o'-lantern, suddenly unsure of what to do with it. Steve took it from his hands and slapped it against the closest smooth surface. As he and Ken walked through the store, Steve gave surreptitious tugs to some of the other decorations – not enough to pull them down right away, but enough so that most of them wouldn't last the day.

Kelly let Mark walk on people's lawns all the way to the pool. To touch each section of grass with his feet seemed almost an obsession. If a fence divided two lawns he would come back to the sidewalk, go round it, and run back onto the next green carpet. Kelly had to stop him twice from trying to push his way through a hedge – he would duck his head and prepare to ram it like a bull, snorting and breathing heavily.

"You better not be like this in the water or you'll get it up your nose," Kelly told him.

"You could drown like that," Marcus offered – helpfully, he thought, but Kelly turned on him suddenly and with her eyes and pursed lips told him to shut up.

"What?" Marcus asked.

"Don't say *drowned*. Remember that kid last year."

A seven-year-old from Dunbridge had fallen off the back of his dad's boat while they were crossing the lake. He had sunk like a rock and disappeared before they could turn the boat around and get back to the spot where he'd gone in. *The Dunbridge Examiner* did everything it could not to keep the story alive for weeks after. The family eventually had to move away because of it.

"It's why I got him in lessons. Plus I keep imagining how that father felt to see his son go under. Oh, it's awful. Such a shitty thing to happen, and then what they all did to him, poor guy."

At the pool, the other mothers sat up in the stands, piling their jackets around them and breathing in the humid air coming off the surface of the water. Marcus found a spot and sat down. Small groups of children stood around the pool's edge, hunched over with their hands together tight under their chins as if protecting a valuable gem. They stood in groups of three or four around instructors floating up to their necks. The children were being coaxed in, and most of them wore a smile of fear. A few just stared blankly at the water or looked defiantly away, not willing to let the other kids know they were nervous. Marcus saw Kelly emerge from the change room with Mark in his oversized trunks. He clung to her as if the pool were roiling with eels and spiny creatures. She brought him to his group but had to return to him three times before he would stay there alone without crying. It took the instructors a few minutes to pull all of their prey into the water. Once in, the children held on to the side with elbows and fingers. One girl kicked up a panicked froth around her and had to be pulled out again and fitted with a life-jacket. She was left to bob on her own in one corner of the shallow end.

"He hates going in but loves it once he's there," Kelly said when she joined Marcus in the seats. "You're not bored are you? It's only half an hour."

"No, it's fine. I'm just hot in here now."

Marcus was actually enjoying watching everybody splashing around, and the humidity, warmth, water, and exposed skin made him vaguely horny. He wondered if Mark was due for a nap after his lesson.

Flutterboards appeared – Marcus could still remember calling them "stutterboards" – and the older kids were sent kicking across to the far side of the pool. As they passed over the deepest part, their struggling bodies caught the bright light beaming up from the floor of the pool and for a moment seemed to be suspended in nothing, in shimmering air. They kicked through large, unstable squares of light reflected from the windows in the ceiling, breaking the light into clumps of silver mercury that clung to their arms and legs for a second before sliding back into the chlorinated water. When they reached the other side, the swimmers would touch and look around them as if waking from a dream and wondering how much time had passed. Then they'd start back, with less confidence this time, kicking desperately back to where their toes could graze the bottom, back into the arms of their instructors.

Mark was part of a group still learning to kick. He had only lost his fear of being away from the edge of the pool in the last couple of lessons.

"He's not holding onto the wall so tightly," Kelly said. Marcus couldn't say whether this was true or not, so he just nodded.

Mark and four other boys and one girl were stretched straight out and churning up the water behind them as if trying to widen the pool. When they did dead-man's floats, each would stiffen out against the instructor's arms and then flail as soon as those arms were withdrawn. After a few tries, Mark was able to lay there just under the surface for nearly three seconds. Kelly clapped spontaneously in her seat.

"Last week he wouldn't even put his face under!"

Again, Marcus had to take this on faith, but he didn't nod. Boredom was starting to set in and the humid air was making him sleepy. When it was another boy's turn to float like a corpse, Mark held on to the side and gave Kelly a goofy grin, his hair flattened and black against his scalp.

When his lesson was over, Mark climbed up dripping and grinning into the stands. Kelly held a towel around him while he peeled off his trunks and tried to pull his underwear and socks back over his clammy skin without any of the girls seeing. Marcus wanted to get outside, to get moving. He was yawning noisily every few seconds, finishing each yawn with a "ha!" as if it had come as a complete surprise. Mark, however, insisted they stay for fries at the snack bar.

"It's our ritual," Kelly said apologetically and looked to see what money she had in her purse.

"You looked really good out there," she told Mark when they were all sitting at a little table with other kids running around. "That was so cool when the teacher let go and you just floated."

"I know!" the boy shouted. "It's so easy! I can do anything now. I didn't even open my eyes under the water so they don't sting."

Marcus winced every time Mark yelled. The kids all around him were yelling, too.

"We're sitting right here," he finally said, cutting Mark off in the middle of a story about how he had put his face in the water and blown bubbles, something Marcus hadn't actually witnessed but didn't feel like he needed to be told about in detail, especially at such a high volume.

"Maybe you should use your inside voice, Mark," Kelly said.

Mark just looked at them both. In his fingers he held a broken fry with a drop of ketchup about to fall back onto his paper plate.

"You should tell Grandma what you learned today," Kelly said. "Want to call her when we get home?"

"Can I tell Neil instead?" Mark asked. He looked at Marcus with a quick flicker then went back to his fries.

"Do you still see that guy?" Marcus asked Kelly when they were back outside.

"Who?"

"You know, Mark's dad. I thought you hadn't seen him in a long time."

"Not really, but . . . I mean, he's still around. He doesn't have any custody or anything but I still, like, run into him every once in a while."

"What's he think about Mark?"

Kelly was looking more and more uncomfortable, as if something were creeping up behind her that she thought she'd already outrun.

"I don't know, he didn't want anything before. He was totally out of it, but now he calls me sometimes and tells me he wants to see him."

"So? Why don't you let him? That's like free babysitting. Mark would probably like it, wouldn't he?"

"Probably." It seemed to sting her to say the word.

"Well? You should call him up."

Kelly's face seemed to collapse.

"He never wanted anything to do with us, Marcus! He wanted to pay nothing and never see the baby and now he's coming around saying he wants to take him to the park. It's bullshit! He threatened me when I was pregnant, Marcus – he said I had to get rid of Mark or he would. Now his family's saying I have to let him see Mark – after four years! They'll take away my apartment."

"Okay, alright – don't call him," Marcus said. Kelly was crying; he didn't know where to look. "Tell him to fuck off," he offered.

"He threatened me!"

"What, again? You mean before or recently?"

Mark ran up to where they were standing, so Marcus never got an answer. Mark could tell that his mother had been crying and gave Marcus a black look. Marcus tried to keep his facial expression neutral, but he was dying to say to the boy "*You're* the one who started talking about your friggin dad." Kelly told Mark he had to have a quick bath when they got home to get the chlorine off, and he immediately flopped down on the ground in protest.

"I'm sorry, Marcus," Kelly said. "Do you want to come over

for dinner? I don't know what I have, but I can make something like tuna and noodles. That's Mark's favourite."

"No it isn't!" her son shouted, and tried again to flatten himself against the sidewalk.

"I'm just going to go, actually," Marcus said. "My back is acting up again."

As he walked away he could hear Mark yelling but didn't turn around to look. In his mind he pictured huge, dark birds swooping down and taking the screaming boy up into the high branches of the trees.

Three men – Patrick, Derek the security guard, and Brad, Ronnie's former student – stood around looking at a laptop that was sitting open on the counter in Patrick's store. All three were silent as they waited for something to appear. The laptop stared impassively back at them. So far, nothing had happened other than the screen going blank, though a small, flickering hourglass told them not to lose hope – unseen forces were at work. Patrick and Derek showed in their faces they weren't expecting much. Brad, who owned the laptop, kept stepping forward to stroke the mouse pad gently with the tip of his finger as if the computer were a newborn baby he was trying to wake.

"It's usually a lot faster," he said. "The connection's so slow up here. Dunbridge is . . . well whatever, it's coming." He gave the computer another fatherly stroke.

Brad had shown up, laptop under his arm, just as Patrick was thinking about getting something to eat. He told Patrick he and his family had extended their stay because his sister-in-law was a mess.

"But I wanted to show you something," he said while unfolding the laptop. "Where can I plug this in?"

Derek had wandered in just as they were starting.

"Anyway," Brad said, "we're going to get up at something like four-thirty tomorrow and drive back down so I can get the kids to school and drop my wife off at work. That's the plan, anyway, but if Susan's sister falls apart before we can get out of the house, I don't know what the fuck we're going to do. Jesus, this is taking a while. Oh, here we go I think –"

The laptop's screen turned a solid orange. Images and text began to appear as if floating up from a vat of paint. Derek gave a quietly skeptical "Yay" that Brad ignored. In fact, he hadn't said a word to Derek yet.

"The beauty of this set-up is that you can do all the smaller updates yourself," Brad told Patrick. "Things like prices and new products. Anything big, like a new category or a whole bunch of new images – that stuff you'd have to get me to do, but I can usually do that kind of thing within twenty-four hours. Unless," he added, rolling his eyes and nodding back to the entrance of the store where presumably the living ghost of his sister-in-law was standing, "I'm not looking forward to checking my email tomorrow, you know what I mean?"

The images on the screen started to spin, creating a whirlpool in the centre of all the orange into which everything got sucked, leaving a page showing various tools and appliances.

"This is one I did for Brampton Hardware two years ago. I think it's the closest to the kind of thing you'd need. This place burnt down over the summer, by the way. It's still being investigated. I don't recommend going out that way. Course, you would bring the whole mall down, wouldn't you?"

"That's a good price for a work table," Patrick said, pointing at the screen.

"Maybe that's why they got into trouble and had to burn the place down," Derek offered.

Patrick started shaking his head. "I don't know if this is the kind of thing I really need," he said. "My place is pretty small."

"But that's the beauty of it," Brad insisted. "It doesn't matter how big your actual store is, the site can be it's own thing. It's not about getting people to come in here. If they can order their, whatever, skates and tennis balls through the site, and you can give them a good deal on it, then they don't ever have to set foot in here. It becomes a whole different thing."

"But then you have to get it all to them," Derek said.

"What you do," Brad said, nodding at Derek's observation but giving it no more acknowledgment than that, "is set up an account with an online wholesaler – I can help you with that. When you get an order, you process it and send it to them, and they package it up and mail it off."

"So why doesn't someone just buy it from them?" Patrick asked.

"Because they're a *wholesaler*," Brad said, as if this were clearly a word Patrick had never encountered before. "They just keep the stuff in warehouses – that's their business. They don't chase around for people to buy one pair of skates when they've got four million of them. That's *your* job. You still have to go looking for customers."

"When's he gonna have time for that?" Derek asked. "He's the only one in the store."

"You have to keep some extra stock on hand," Brad went on, "just to make your life easier. Stuff that you're always selling – shoes, I guess, and some hockey equipment."

He looked around at the store and pointed at the door leading to the back room.

"How much room you got back there?"

Patrick thought of the boxes of shoes that were even now almost touching the ceiling: "Not a lot."

"Well, maybe you can rent a space. Or how big's your house? Big basement?"

"Pretty big."

"Anything in it?"

"Just some of my parents' stuff. It's an old house."

Brad's business face disappeared and he started grinning the way he had the other day. "Oh, that's right: you said you're in Ronnie's old house aren't you? Is that one of those huge, old places in the east end?"

Patrick tried to think what houses Brad could have meant: all the ones in his neighbourhood were definitely old, but none of them were big. They were squat bungalows nosing their front lawns like fat hogs. Or they were narrow, two-storey houses like Patrick's that tricked you by losing, as soon as you entered them, half the space they appeared to have from the outside.

"His father was my gym teacher and coach in high school," Brad said, finally turning to Derek with such unexpected friendliness that the other man took an involuntary step back.

"Is that right?" the guard asked, more to put a buffer of words between himself and this man from Patrick's past.

"He was a real hard-ass," Brad said, shaking his head. He had instantly shed twenty inner years of his life, making his exterior seem even older, as if his thickening body were trapping his teenage self inside. "I think he only taught for a couple of years. Dunbridge Senior – did you go there?" he asked Derek.

Derek shook his head no but didn't elaborate.

Brad turned back to Patrick. "I was saying to my wife the other night, Ronnie was such a hard-ass with us, imagine what it was like to be his kid, eh?"

"He wasn't that bad," Patrick replied. "So what's the deal with this Web site – is it all credit cards?"

Brad was still smiling at something standing just beyond the dimmed computer.

"Yeah. No," he said, stroking the mouse pad again to bring the machine back to full-life. "You have to set it up with the credit card companies – I can help you with that."

Brad spent the next hour opening screens, making mock purchases, digging into streams of hidden code, and giving various scenarios which showed what the site would do to Patrick's business. "It's all down to the kind of commitment you're willing to make to this side of it, and how much you are willing to let it grow," he said in a voice that was not his own. Derek left halfway through Brad's presentation to do a round of the fire exit doors. Patrick found himself growing more and more interested in the future Brad was envisioning. He started to get excited, though he tried to conceal that from Brad.

"Do I need someone else to run this, or can I do it from here?" Patrick asked.

Another future was forming in his mind, one even bolder and more committed than the one Brad was outlining. He started to picture the back room of the house converted into an office, the basement heavy with stock. His real store was too small; he saw it withering away and reverting back to a darkened space like those on either side, with only wires, plaster, and some lumber inside to show that anything had ever been there. He saw the office in the back room expanding and swallowing the small den next to it, what had been his mother's sewing room. In a few years – maybe less – this silent site, quietly processing a growing stream of orders for helmets and bats and cross-country skis, would lift them out of their debt, and then Manda would no longer have to go to work. She would become his partner – she was better than him with computers and better on the phone. The house itself would be renewed, becoming buoyant and bright where it was now heavy and dark. Manda would restore the place, remaking every room and bringing the lawn back to the fullness and greenness of Patrick's childhood. He even allowed himself to imagine the effect their renewed home might have on the neighbourhood. The *For Sale* signs would disappear, the teenagers looking for somewhere to drink or fuck would find every house on the street occupied. There'd be kids playing everywhere. Swing sets.

Best of all, they would have a beautiful house to bring a baby daughter home to, with two parents who didn't have to go anywhere to work. He could spend his mornings processing orders and talking to distributors, and his afternoons in the backyard rolling in the grass with a little girl just learning to walk.

This vision of the future carried him the entire way home that night and held him in the truck for a few minutes after he had parked beside the house, listening to the engine click as it cooled.

TUESDAY

The phone rang in Steve's apartment, and he was in the air before it rang again, the thin spears of sunlight coming through the curtain flashing on his naked white skin as he cleared the coffee table and landed on his feet next to the phone. He grabbed it and, in the same motion, let his momentum twist him around and drop him into a chair. Less than five seconds earlier he had been coiled at the foot of his bed with his arms trapped against his chest like struggling animals, dreaming of endless blue tunnels running under his apartment. Now he was sitting naked in his ratty easy chair, holding the phone to his ear and digging at the ingrown nail on one of his toes. It wasn't yet seven o'clock in the morning.

"What's up?" Steve asked, grimacing as the skin on his toe came away and was replaced by a bubble of blood.

Ken said, "Steve?" as if the early-morning call were a surprise to him, too.

"You fucker, why are you calling me so early? I'm not even working today, am I?"

"Manda wants to go out tonight. Wanna come?"

Steve actually pulled the phone away from his ear to look at it quizzically.

"Ken, what the fuck – it's like six o'clock. It's the crack of *dawn*, Ken. I can see the sun coming up, Ken. And it's cold. *Brrrrrrrr.*" He shivered but didn't move to get dressed.

"Sorry."

"So what's this – going out? You and your sister? What for?"

Ken, sitting in the kitchen of his house, heard someone come out of their room upstairs and walk along the hallway. He waited until whoever was it had locked himself in the bathroom and started the shower.

"Ken? What the fuck, are you falling asleep?" Steve shouted.

"You called *me*, buddy."

"Will you come?"

"What do you mean, will I come? I don't even know what the fuck it is, yet."

"Manda wants to go out. For a beer, I guess. Tonight, maybe."

Steve rolled his eyes and slid down in his chair until he was almost on the floor. He looked around for a cigarette and found one under the cushion of the chair. On the floor he found a matchbook containing one single flaccid match. Patrick was picking him up after work, Ken told him. As far as he knew, they were headed to Chaps.

"I'll come down just before nine and Patrick can drive me, too. I'm going back to sleep, Ken, so don't call me again."

But Steve didn't go back to bed. Instead, he sat in his easy chair, lifting his feet and stretching his legs out in mid-air as far as they would go. There was a strange, constricted feeling in his legs that he couldn't get rid of, as if he'd been bound with invisible wire in the night. He tried stomping them lightly on the floor until someone shouted something from the apartment beneath him. "Shut the fuck up," he said, quietly, and lifted his feet back into the air. The TV was still on with the sound muted – he must have forgotten to turn it off before getting into bed. Turning the volume up slightly, he watched highlights from a standoff somewhere in the southern States – Georgia or Arkansas or one of those. A man had taken a gun from a cop and shot some people in court as they were about to start his trial. He was holed up in someone's apartment. They kept showing the man's mug shot and a long-distance shot of a body on the court steps, covered in a blanket. The man finally surrendered by waving his white T-shirt out the window. All of this had happened yesterday; Steve had already seen the footage the night before. He laughed again when he saw that flapping T-shirt come into view over the flower boxes on the balcony. *He* would have kept running: Steve was sure of it. Stolen a car and been gone like a shot. No stupid white flags. A commercial came on with a woman in her underwear who rolled her eyes at her frazzled hair. Since it was warm in the room and he was sitting there in the nude with nothing to do, Steve gave his cock a minute's exploratory stroking. Getting no response, he gave up on the idea and got dressed instead.

On the other side of Dunbridge, Marcus was sitting in his own easy chair, zipped into a sleeping bag and watching the same footage of the previous day's standoff. He hadn't heard anything before about it, but his reaction to the end of it was almost the same as Steve's. "Oh, you're *joking*," he said aloud when the T-shirt appeared. He turned the channel, only to see the exact same scene from two different angles. He pulled the sleeping bag tighter around himself and, thumbing the remote control indignantly, went looking for something else, a movie or some decent cartoons.

Marcus's phone was sitting in his lap. When it trilled, he had to fight to get his hands back out of the sleeping bag, losing the remote control in there in the process.

"Yup."

There was the sound of someone breathing and the receiver at the other end being covered and uncovered. Then something that was midway between a giggle and a sneeze.

"Ken?" he asked.

"Say hello," a voice said in the background. It took Marcus a few seconds to recognize that voice as Kelly's. There was a scuffling sound, and then Kelly came on at full volume.

"Sorry, he won't talk," she said.

"Oh well. What can I do you for? It's still early for you, isn't it?"

"Did we wake you up?"

"It's alright," he said. She didn't need to know he'd been up for a while.

Kelly told him that Mark had a skating lesson later that day – *How many lessons does he have?* Marcus asked himself – and he wanted Marcus to come watch him. Marcus could tell just from the tone of her voice that her son hadn't said any such thing, and had probably resisted the idea when his mother suggested it.

"Sure, when is it?"

"Okay but don't laugh when you see him on skates – he's just learning."

"I won't."

After the call, Marcus returned his hands to the warmth of the sleeping bag and dug around for the missing remote. He found it wedged under his thigh. The sun was starting to creep into the living room. The squirrel appeared at the top of the pole and began screeching at him with more intensity than ever before. He thought about banging on the window (though that had never had any effect before) and about opening the window and throwing something, but that would have meant leaving his chair and his sleeping bag, so he only turned up the volume on the TV, where Mr. Dressup was standing in the middle of his three-walled living room trying to remember where he'd hidden his pirate treasure. Marcus was struck by the sudden, terrible thought that the look of confusion on Mr. Dressup's face was real, that he had truly forgotten behind which prop he had hidden the little cardboard chest. Marcus turned the channel before one of the puppets was forced to remind him.

Patrick and Manda were up early, too – something had hit their bedroom window hard, almost breaking it. Patrick was out of bed and at the window in seconds. Manda, thinking it was still the middle of the night, took a minute to decide whether the sound she had heard was real or merely part of a violent dream. Even the sight of Patrick staring intently out the bedroom window didn't seem definitive.

"It sounded like a bird," she said.

He changed his posture from trying to see someone on the front walk to trying to see something lying dead on the lawn.

"There's a mark here," he said. He pointed at the window pane but wasn't able to bring himself to touch the glass, even on the inside. There was greasy smudge on the glass, as if it had been hit by a wet tennis ball, surrounded by fine, grey fluff. Patrick put on his running shoes and Manda her slippers, and the two of them went downstairs to locate the victim. They could find nothing on the front lawn. The blades of grass were spiked with white frost. Manda fingered some of the plants she had put in over the summer along the front of the house. She was excited to see them slumping under the frost – in six months or so she would find out which were strong enough to survive the winter and had therefore earned a place on her lawn. She wasn't interested in the kind of plant or flower that swooned forever the minute the sun went behind a cloud.

"Maybe a cat got it," Patrick said, coming back around the corner of the house.

"That fast? It might have just flown off."

Patrick shrugged and went inside, deciding it was too cold and too early to keep worrying about it. When he shut the door behind him, Manda was immediately aware of the shockingly absolute silence engulfing the entire neighbourhood. It was as if they'd been gassed in the night. She expected to see all kinds of birds and animals stiff on the ground. The sky was clear and blue with the moon still lodged in it, bleached white like the top of a skull. Once when she was a teenager – more than once – she'd got dizzyingly high and stayed up for forty-eight hours. She was living in a basement apartment with a boyfriend who later left Dunbridge to work in northern Alberta. When morning came on the second day, and the moon was stuck up there like that, she became convinced that the moon's time was up, that it was dead and rotting right in front of them, and that it would either drift away one day or else drop out of its orbit and obliterate the world. It scared her to realize she had no preference. She remembered telling her boyfriend about this sudden revelation. He was lying beside her on the back lawn, oblivious to their upstairs neighbours who were probably watching them from inside. He just rolled on his stomach and told her she was peaking, and to just ride it out. She did, with her fingers clenched into the neck of her T-shirt and her boots pulled up to her body. They both slept for a full day after that, and when they emerged again from the apartment, the world was as silent and blue as it was now.

Manda felt a strange flutter move up her spine, and she was dizzy for a second. She worried again about all she'd heard about acid and drugs like that collecting at the base of her spine, waiting for a shock or the right memory to be released like bubbles into her bloodstream. Another good reason not to have kids, she thought. She could easily imagine one coming out with eyes as big and loose as quarters, shrieking at the taste of breast milk and screaming to stay awake because of what it saw in its mind when it slept.

The bird – or bat, or whatever it was – was gone, she decided. It was somewhere being eaten, or was curled up, stunned. The neighbourhood was lousy with cats, so either way it wouldn't last. Manda looked at the front of her house and saw nothing but rot and decrepitude. The windows were blinded with sunrise and the warps in the siding were big enough to throw shadows. Something was nesting in the eaves and the shingles on the roof looked green and ragged like the scales of an old reptile. She wanted the whole thing transformed, instantly, from the inside out.

Manda found Patrick standing in the glow of the fridge and drinking the last of a carton of orange juice. "Thanks for leaving me some," she said.

"Sorry," he replied, and pointed to the stack of buttered toast he'd made and put on a plate in the centre of the table. He was like a six-year-old, she thought. He'd spread sugar on his toast if left to his own devices. She kissed him and took away the empty carton for recycling. Both of them ate quickly and skipped their showers. Patrick wanted to get to the store early.

Patrick let Manda off at an intersection close to her office. Some baseball hats fell out of the truck when she stepped down to the sidewalk. She flung them back into the cab like frisbees, aiming for Patrick's head: "Think fast!" The first two got him full-on in the face.

"Don't forget to pick Ken up after work," she shouted, giving the passenger-side door a heave that made it cry out in rusting pain.

Ken found himself locked out of the store again. He stood staring at the steel door in the back alley, not sure whether to knock or go around the front. He did neither. Two dark birds fought over a crust of bread a few feet away from him, obviously considering him no threat. He watched their angry fluttering, and started to worry that no one would let him in the store. He needed to piss, and didn't want to have to go in a corner of the alleyway in case someone caught him, which had happened before.

The door finally opened, and Tim from shipping came out carrying a stack of collapsed cardboard boxes.

"Ken, buddy. You sleep here last night?"

"No. I'm locked out."

"Not anymore. Grab the chair, quick."

Ken dragged the chair out to prop open the door. Tim dropped the boxes by the dumpster. As if by magic, a cigarette appeared in his hand, already lit. He took a long drag, then started beating his chest. Ken laughed.

"You know what's wrong with me? My father was a motherfucker," he said, smiling. "Literally."

Tim stopped acting like an ape and started examining a large, red mark on his arm. He touched it gently, then started prodding it until he flinched. "I should try and get worker's comp for that. Huge fucking crate lands on my arm. They're cutting corners. Pisses me off. I should seriously go and show this to them, get the day off."

"Sure."

"So much for summer, eh?"

"Supposed to snow."

"Seriously?"

Ken didn't answer.

"You should take a day off, too, Ken – you're here too much. You take any holidays this summer?"

Ken shook his head no.

"You're an animal," Tim said, pinching the injured red flesh between his fingers. "You're not as bad as your buddy, there.

Speedy Gonzales. That guy's a shit-disturber. I know he's your friend, but I'm telling you, man, watch yourself. There's shit going around about people getting canned. Is Steve spreading that?"

"Is it true?" Ken asked.

"Fucked if I know. I doubt it – they wouldn't can people right before Christmas. If it *was* true, I can tell you Steve wouldn't know *shit* about it. That kind of thing goes around every year. The place keeps opening and shutting. I wouldn't worry about it – they'd keep you around no matter what, I bet. You're not a shit-disturber at least."

Ken didn't say anything. He rubbed at the back of his head, where he was starting to feel some pressure. He never knew what to say to Tim, but he liked him. He didn't like people talking about Steve, though.

"What if you get fired, what would you do?" Ken asked.

"I've seen so much shit go on in this place, I wouldn't be shocked, I can tell you that. If the place shut down and opened again as a fucking Home Depot or something, they'd have to hire me on. You should come down here and work and you'd be fine. Working on the floor is shit. I don't know how you can stand it."

"I need the money."

"Yeah, but do you wanna work so much? You want to be working all the time?"

Ken didn't have to think about it: "No."

"Tell me about it. Minimum wage, maximum fucking rage, right? If you're on the floor, you have to work twenty-four hours a day just to get anything. Anyway, think about it. Everyone's cool with you here."

Ken nodded and went inside. He still had to pee, but mostly he wanted to get away from Tim and get somewhere he could let his head relax until it was time to go out on the floor and start work.

Manda had her own keys to the office and her own code for the alarm system. She sometimes enjoyed coming in this early: the office was always warm, and she could make a pot of coffee that was strong and complicated, the way she liked it. She'd brought with her a folder full of credit-card bills and bank statements. Her plan was to sit down and wrestle with the various tentacles of their debt until she got a good sense of its true shape and size. She couldn't put this off any longer.

When she got inside, the lights were off and there were yellow girders of sun coming through the windows and pressing against the floor. One was hitting the side wall of her cubicle, melting clear light down the grey fabric stretched over the wall divider. Manda put her coat away and went into the kitchen to start the coffee maker. She picked a bag of ground coffee out of the drawer – the blackest roast, which no one else would touch. The machine took a few seconds to warm up, then gave a deep, bronchial gurgle that made Manda feel sleepy. She looked around in the cupboards and the fridge to see if anyone had left cookies behind, but all she could find were plastic knives and forks and a tupperware container of old mints that had softened with age and become fused together. All of it made her think of her mother and her fortune cookies. She wondered how many of them Shelly had stashed in her cupboards and what kind of fortunes they told – probably nothing even remotely close to what she was actually living through, not that she'd notice. And even if she did, she'd just decide the cookie was against her like everyone else. *You're a crazy bitch in need of serious medication, and you should leave your daughter the fuck alone* – Manda would have paid serious money to have something like *that* appear in one of her mother's cookies.

Manda sniffed at a container of carrot sticks she found in the fridge – Cheryl's, probably. Cheryl brought in things like this and never ate them, thinking that just having it in her lunch would draw out the harmful fats and salt from the food she was actually planning to eat. The fridge hummed in Manda's ears. She didn't hear Sean creep into the kitchen. When she closed the door, he was standing there, looking worriedly at the coffee maker. She shouted and had to quickly cramp up so that she didn't piss herself.

"Jesus fuck, Sean!"

Everything inside her was on the run; she had to keep herself from slapping Sean full in the face.

"Sorry, I thought you heard me," he said unconvincingly. "Is there enough in there for me?" he asked, pointing at the coffee pot.

"I'm making it strong, so you'll hate it. Jesus, you really scared me."

Sean just moved around her and put his lunch in the fridge, taking a second to throw out some of the old yogourt containers lined up in the door. "It's good you're in early actually," he said. "I'm usually in way before anyone else, but I didn't get out of here until nine last night because of this. I was thinking before that I might take next Monday off, but that's not looking too likely now."

"What's *this*? You said 'because of this.' The new girl?"

Sean sighed melodramatically. "I don't think I was being cruel; I thought we gave her a chance."

"More than I would have," Manda said. "She was useless."

"Well, come on. I'm just saying we didn't give her the boot the minute, you know –"

"The minute we found out she was useless."

"Well, sure. That's not really the point. The point is, we gave her a chance, and she decided to take that chance and throw it away. I was very patient, I think."

Sean paused, waiting to see if Manda would interject again. She was silent; her face looked as innocent as steel.

"Anyways," he went on. "She's gone. The problem is it looks like they want us to try going with just the three phones and not hire anyone new for a while."

"What? How is that possible? We're so stretched now."

"I know but, you know, there are probably other reasons for that, too. But the point is they don't want me to hire anyone. Anyways, you'll still get vacation and everything. Let's just see how it works out and how long it takes us to get on top of it."

"And how long's that supposed to take?"

He brought his hands up again, this time to show he had given her all the information she needed, and that she would have to take the next step herself.

At her desk, with a cup of coffee she was too angry and impatient to whiten with cream, Manda brought her computer back to life. She checked the time and, figuring it was worth the risk, dialed Marcus's number. She was surprised when he answered on the first ring – she hadn't seriously expected him to be up yet. He didn't sound tired, just distracted. She could hear voices and noises in the background. It was too early for any of the kids on his team to be over, unless some of them slept there last night, a possibility she didn't have the mental strength to think about just then.

"Who's that?" she asked.

"Some guy fixing a motorbike."

"What? Who?"

"No idea; it's some show," he said, and the TV was silenced. "There's nothing else on."

"What are you doing today?"

Marcus outlined his day as he saw it unfolding: shit, shower, Sinc's for a while, then maybe over to the mall to help Patrick. He didn't mention Mark's skating lesson: he hadn't decided for sure if he was going.

"Hey, is Patrick going to pay me for helping him?" he asked her.

"Obviously. Hey Marcus, don't fuck around when you're there. Please. He doesn't need that right now."

"I wasn't going to fuck around – what are you telling me that for?"

"Just help him out, and, you know, don't get in his way."

"Yes, ma'am."

"Well, you don't know what it's like with him and that place. It's a ton of work."

She felt the weight of it all right there, and she creaked back in her chair under it. The first warm effects from her coffee were starting to move through her chest and up her neck to bring light and heat to the airless chamber of her skull. It wasn't enough to relieve her burden, but she leaned farther back to let it do its work.

"Marcus, I'm so sick of this," she said, holding her eyes closed with the tips of her fingers, the phone between her jaw and her shoulder. "Working and everything, and the house. It's too much. Patrick's like a zombie. I almost wish the place would just flop so he could get a job somewhere and not be killing himself for this thing – oh I'm going to hell for saying that. I really need to get out, I don't know. D'you wanna go out for a beer tonight? I'm trying to get Ken to come."

"What's going on with Ken?"

"Oh, don't even . . . let's talk about it tonight. Will you come out? Come on, you probably need it, too."

Marcus agreed to meet her around eight-thirty at The Flamingo, the only bar in Dunbridge with decent food. She'd have to buy. "I've got nothing," he told her, and he meant it. Before she'd even said goodbye she heard the volume on Marcus's television come back up to its previous level. There was a distant rev of a motorcycle, and she hung up.

A few minutes later, Sean came back out of his office, coughing and clearing his throat. He knocked gently on the wall of her cubicle, all of a sudden very concerned that he not startle her. When Manda looked up he became interested in the edge of the cubicle wall, in a small polyp in the metal, almost invisible under the industrial grey paint.

"So how's it going?" he asked.

"I don't know what's wrong with me," Manda yawned. "But I'm so tired. Something hit the window this morning and scared me to death."

"I'm sorry about all this. We'll figure it out."

"Fine."

"Something else," Sean said, trying to get his thumbnail under the blemish. "It may not happen, I don't know, but one of the things they told me is they are looking into moving the whole office to Orillia."

Manda sat forward, swallowing the tail-end of another yawn.

"Oh fuck, Sean, no."

"No, but keeping everybody that works here."

"Oh that's nice, except we have to drive there and back every friggin day. Oh that's just beautiful."

"Well, I don't know if this is happening for sure, so don't go – don't tell everyone else about it in case it doesn't happen. I'll know by the end of next week for sure."

Sean quit trying to pry out the blemish in the metal with his thumb, and instead gave it a few hard strokes with the palm of his hand as if to flatten it down. Satisfied, he turned to escape.

"It doesn't make any sense, Sean. It's stupid," Manda said after him. "And then making us sit around and wait to know what they've decided? We're supposed to wait a week? I can't take another week of this."

"It's crazy, I know," Sean said, pausing in his doorway to see if there was anything else he could think of to say. There wasn't, so he shut the door halfway. Manda got up and took her coffee to the kitchen to add some cream and sugar to it – for all the good it was doing to her it tasted like ash soup and she wasn't in the mood to punish herself.

There was nothing but a few trucks and a police car in the mall parking lot when Patrick arrived. A fire truck was coming out to the road – slowly, almost coasting, in a disappointed stupor from having come so fast with hysterical lights and siren to find nothing. Whatever had happened, fire could at least be ruled out. Patrick let the fire truck pass and drove across the empty lot to a small cluster of vehicles. Before he even reached them he spotted water flowing out from the doors of the mall and staining a huge swath of the pavement black. It must have been running free for a while, spreading across the parking lot before getting caught in the downward pull of various grates. One of the trucks was for an industrial plumber, two were from the city, and another belonged to the head of maintenance for the mall. That was the man Patrick wanted to get information from, but the only human in sight was a bored-looking policeman, standing away from the trucks and holding his pencil to his notebook, his eyes on the spread of the water as if he were trying to sketch it. Patrick gave two quick beeps of his horn as he came up to the officer, who jumped slightly and started waving at him to stop.

"Easy, buddy," Patrick muttered to himself. "Wasn't going to run you over."

The policeman came over to Patrick's window. "It's all closed," he announced.

"What happened?"

"It's all closed up," he repeated a little more forcefully, as if worried Patrick were an opportunistic looter. "At least for today. Maybe tomorrow."

"Yeah, but I have a store in there. At the back. What happened?"

"You need to talk to the maintenance guy." He squinted in the direction of the glass doors. "He's in there with a couple of guys from the city. It's a total mess. All the drains backed up."

Patrick thought of all the boxes of shoes and hats in his back room.

"Oh fuck, all the drains everywhere?" he asked.

"I think just at this end, but it flooded out half the building."

He was pointing away from the corner that had Active Sports hidden in it, so Patrick felt some relief.

"So it's all closed up for sure, the whole day?" he asked, surprising himself with a wide and involuntary smile.

"Maybe tomorrow, too. I haven't heard how long I'm supposed to stay here. I'm waiting to see if it's going to be me all day or if they're sending someone else. I just got here."

Patrick parked the truck and got out. The water had no depth, but it moved fast and ridged up against the front of his shoes. Another plumber's truck pulled into the lot while Patrick was standing there and pulled up next to the police car. Two men got out and looked out at the spreading water, following it upstream with their eyes back to the glass doors and into the darkness beyond. The two of them nodded at Patrick and the policeman, who had been standing nearby, waiting to dispense what little information he had. The driver of the truck yelled to Patrick: "How about this, eh?" Then he and his partner went inside to see the worst of it. There were still no lights on inside the mall, so Patrick guessed all of the power had been cut. Sure enough, a hydro van drove up a minute later and parked next to the mall's doors with its front tires just outside of the spread of water, as if the whole vehicle were charged up like an eel.

Patrick looked out over the grey lot and felt happy to see the whole place deserted. He liked the look of the water spreading out like a black cape. He liked the small wake created by his shoes and by the tires of his truck. He liked the expression on the policeman's face, who kept looking out to the road and then back into the mall, waiting for someone to come from either direction to tell him what to do. He especially liked that he now had no choice but to get back in his truck and drive home. He had no alternate use for the day, so, after driving in a slow arc around the parking lot, hoping to spread the water out even farther, he gave the cop another friendly beep and drove home, back through Dunbridge's sparse morning rush-hour. He felt weightless now; the water coming out of the drains in the mall could wash away all of the shelves he spent days putting together, the cash register he had spent two weeks training himself on. It could curl up the grey carpet he and Danny had laid down, crumple the walls he had put up. All of it could go – he had the day.

Feeling superstitious, Patrick pulled into the driveway slowly and parked the truck behind the house. He felt as though he were violating something by being here during the day. A weekday. He entered the house with the same caution – through the back door, clicking it shut and standing on the landing, listening for noise, waiting for the house's disapproval. It was cold but not dark inside, and the heat came on as he stood there. There were clothes on the back stairs that Manda must have kicked down on the way to the washing machine. Patrick scooped them all up and walked down to the basement, pulling the string on the light bulb in the ceiling. It smelled damp down there, like wet coal and stale bread. Patrick dripped dirty clothing and towels across the cement floor as he carried his load to the machines in the farthest corner. Clothes were already there hanging dry from the low ceiling: Manda must have forgotten about those, too. He found the shirt he'd been looking for for a couple of days. The dryer was only two years old, standing white and proud and lifeless against a wall furry with dust. It had conked out for no apparent reason over the summer, fulfilling the cliché by doing so just a month or two after the warranty expired. The washing machine was the same one he and Ronnie had carried down here years ago, when Patrick's mother was confined to her room and his father had attempted to take over the household chores. Ronnie ended up kicking the previous washing machine to death after accidentally choking it with pillows. The soggy weight of them kept stalling the spin cycle. After that, Patrick came over more often to check how things were going. One afternoon he came in to find his mother standing in the living room, leaning hard against the back of the recliner, her face white. Patrick had helped her back to bed and went looking for Ronnie. He found him in the basement, watching his tiny black-and-white television in the workshop where he never did any work.

"Why the fuck did you let her out of bed?" he demanded. "I found her up there almost passing out. You know she can't do that."

Patrick felt rage harden his arms into clubs, and he took a step into the low light of the workshop.

"I can't stop her from getting up," Ronnie said quickly, though he didn't look at Patrick or change his position. "She's used to doing all this shit for herself – I can't keep telling her no. That'll kill her before the rest of it does, and you know it. She wants to get up and fold some underwear like a friggin human being, what am I going to say?"

Patrick dropped his arms and stood staring at the miniature TV screen. An unstable, black warp kept moving up through the screen. Ronnie had the back of the TV tethered to long stretches of wire and coat hanger to correct the reception, but nothing could eliminate this recurring warp. Patrick was sure his father didn't even see it anymore and never noticed the absence of colour or sound.

The house was warmer now, but Patrick still felt odd being inside it on his own. He made himself a sandwich in the kitchen and was amazed again at how deeply and violently Manda had dug into the walls and the floors. It looked like the kitchen in the old hunting shack now. He retreated to his chair in the living room and sat for a while in the bright square of sunshine coming through the window. He thought about clearing out the garage so he could park the truck in there over the winter. He thought about calling some of the people he knew from the mall to see if they knew any more about whether the place would be open tomorrow. He thought about looking again for his sister's phone number. Within minutes, he was asleep.

Sinc stood behind the counter on the sales floor of his store, talking on the phone. As he spoke he drew diagonal lines across the dead days of August and September on his desk calendar. It was a clear day out, and sunny. A flash of sunlight came through the store's front windows every time a car went by. He hung up and pressed the button for the bell in the warehouse. When, after a few minutes, Marcus didn't appear, Sinc walked through the store to the warehouse, where he found his nephew sitting on an office chair and bouncing back as hard as he could, thrilled as a kid that the hidden springs and machinery were absorbing each blow rather than toppling him backwards.

"These are alright," Marcus said, touching one of the levers sticking out from under the seat to give the chair a small adjustment. "Better than the one you've got in your office."

"It's good, eh?"

"I could sit in one of these eight hours a day, no problem. What am I doing working here?"

"Fucked if I know. Why didn't you come up?" Sinc asked him without any anger. "I rang the bell ten minutes ago. You fall asleep from boredom?"

Marcus leaned far back in the chair and twisted himself around. "Me? Bored? Back here?" he asked, sweeping his arms out to take it all in. "I was trying to call Patrick. I'm supposed to give him a hand at his store later."

"My god, you're a friggin workhorse," Sinc said. He sat down in another of the desk chairs. "How's Patrick doing? Is that store picking up?"

"I doubt it."

"I told him he should have got his own place. A detached place, like this. Setting up in a mall looks so good: you got everybody right there, but if they stick you out in some corner, you're fucked. To get one of the good spots they just keep jacking the rent on you and finding all these extra little fees. At least with this place out here I know what's coming." He knocked on the desk with his knuckles.

"So listen," Sinc went on. "I was talking to your mother last night, and she asked me how you were doing."

"And what did you say?"

"I don't know," Sinc said, shrugging. "I said you were a lazy little cocksucker who's fucking some teenager with a kid."

"Thanks." Marcus got up from the chair, recovered it in plastic, and wheeled it back to the corner with its companions. "Am I supposed to call her or something?"

"So how old is this girl you're doing?"

"She's older than the kid, is that enough?"

"You're nuts. Someone else's kid? I wouldn't go near that with a ten-foot pole. Where's the father?"

"He's around, apparently," Marcus admitted. "I thought he was long gone but apparently he wants to see the kid now."

"So what? It's his kid."

"That's what I said! But apparently he's a prick and took a swing at her sometime."

"When she was pregnant?"

Marcus nodded. "Apparently."

His uncle tsk-tsked. "That's no good," he said, smiling. "You're supposed to wait until they have the baby, then you can slap them all you want."

"You're a piece of work. What if I told Aunt Catherine that?"

"You would *die*, simple as that. Slowly and painfully."

"Did my mother say anything? Do I want to know?" Marcus asked.

"She asked if you could get Amanda out to call them. Allen wants to see her, I guess."

The two of them said nothing for a while. Marcus creaked back as far as he could go in the chair, ready to topple backwards if necessary, just to break the boredom.

"Alright," Sinc said finally, "you can fuck off. Go help out Patrick."

It was a forty-minute walk out to the mall. The cold got under Marcus's baseball cap and pierced his bomber jacket. There was a hole in the left armpit of the jacket that he had been babying for two years, trying to keep it from growing into a full-scale gash, but it looked like he was losing the fight. He could feel the air coming in on his left side and freezing his ribs.

When he got to the mall, he found the parking lot empty and shimmering with water, all of it fringed with ice. The same cop Patrick had talked to that morning filled Marcus in on what was happening. Marcus imagined tall fountains of water rising up out of the toilets and washing through the stores and down the wide hallways, dragging mannequins and folded shirts and stereos out the front doors and into the gutters. At least he'll be able to get some new shoes off Patrick, ones that weren't too badly damaged. Patrick owed him at least that much for not calling and telling him to stay home.

"So no one's inside?" Marcus asked. "Nothing's open?"

"Just the plumbers and the City's in there," the cop replied. He looked trapped between the tight pleasure of being authoritative and the relief of having someone to talk to, someone that wasn't going to berate him for the mall being closed. "I've been stopping people all day," he said. "I'm thinking I should block the entrances, but I don't have enough signs to do it."

"I wish I'd known," Marcus said. "I walked all the way here."

The two of them stood staring into the entranceway. They couldn't see anybody moving inside, but every few seconds one of the hoses streaming out of the doorway and across the pavement gave an animal twitch and belched out more water.

Four or five boys were dominating the free afternoon skate. They flew backwards through the grown-ups and through the kids moving clockwise around the rink. They didn't look as though they were skating at all so much as being whipped around by a hidden cord. Kelly, sitting up in the stands and waiting for the ice to be cleared for the afternoon lessons, wondered if any of the boys were from Marcus's team. They looked about the right age. They seemed to be threading the slow band of skaters, herding them. The young and the weak and sick, the toddlers in moon suits who kept splaying out on the ice or who had to chip along slowly with their mittened hands up against the pocked boards – the hockey kids would come as close to these as they could, trying to scare them off with cold speed. To each other they would race up and stop suddenly with a spray of snow from the edge of their blades. Then they'd start off again, flying like hawks, getting dirty looks from the pigeons.

Kelly had been drunk with these kinds of boys as a teenager, absolutely drunk with them. She'd had boyfriends who played, and she would come to watch their games. If she skated with them, they would lead her around by the tips of her fingers, going faster and faster until her knees locked and she started screaming with playful fear. She was genuinely scared of falling, but more scared that the boys would dump her if they thought she was no fun or a whiner. She took all that they had to offer her – the silences, the mood swings, the teasing, the hand on the back of her head guiding it crotchward – as merely expressions of their legitimate impatience with her. Or else they were all just false manifestations of their true relationship, just ghosts out to confuse her. If they sneered or got mad or answered too quickly *yes* and grabbed her hair and her tits when she asked them if they loved her, then this was false, too.

She saw all-too clearly now that none of them had ever been in love with her, none of them had ever felt the same throwing-up dizziness and excitement she did when they hadn't seen each other for a long time. Even the nicer ones, the ones that liked to be naked when they fucked, the ones who hung out with her and even came over to meet her mom – even those would eventually feel the pull of the pack, and she would get dumped. Even those would suddenly scream at her to stop acting like they were married.

Now she just wanted them all dead. Fucking *dead*. She dreaded the thought of her son turning into one of them when he got older. Mark idolized the boys. He stood down at the glass as he waited for his lesson, watching them hunt and circle the ice. His hands twitched inside his mittens and he would step back if one of them went by too fast. He complained to Kelly that his skating instructor wasn't teaching them how to skate fast.

"But he's teaching you to skate, right?" she asked.

"Yeah, but not *fast*. And he says we can't start going backwards yet."

Kelly couldn't imagine Marcus as one of those boys. He didn't seem the type. She'd first seen him at a hockey-awards dinner she was helping cater. She didn't even realize he was a coach at the time. All the other coaches were big, thick-necked guys who sat and ate and told their players to shut the fuck up while the speeches were going on. Marcus sat at the back of the hall, leaning back on his chair almost to the tipping point and talking to a small group of boys standing around him. All the boys kept ducking in to tell him things, jokes or gossip, most of which made him laugh or roll his eyes. A couple of times someone came back to ask them to be quiet, which seemed to delight Marcus just as much as the boys around him, and they'd almost kill themselves trying not to laugh while pretending to be serious and attentive and thoroughly shushed. She introduced herself after, and they were seeing each other within weeks. The first time they had sex Kelly had to keep reassuring Marcus that she was comfortable doing it; he looked like he couldn't believe his luck. It didn't even bother her that he was a little flabby and that his underwear looked like it was about ten years old – he was so sweet about everything. She wished he was like that all the time.

The free skate finally ended. Mark did his stumble-walk along the pathway of black rubber and stepped onto the ice. He drifted forward a few feet, then flapped his arms wildly and went down on his knees. The other boys and girls in his class followed Mark out onto the ice, and Kelly was embarrassed again to see so few of them flailing and falling like her son had just done. One or two others dropped like they'd been shot, but they were back up in a second. Only one other boy, the one who wore a snowsuit and mittens on a string, was more of a disaster than Mark. That kid hadn't yet managed to stay balanced and perfectly still on top of his skates for more than a few seconds.

Mark pushed backwards off the boards, almost cracking the back of his head open when he fell. Kelly stood up, ready to run for him, but he just rolled over onto his belly and looked around to make sure none of the hockey players had seen it.

While the instructor tried to get all the kids lined up against the far end of the rink and ready for a chaotic dash to the blue line, Kelly tried to find a comfortable position on the bench. She pulled her jacket off and bunched it up under her, but it didn't help. She was starting to feel hungry, too. Mark started calling to her from the ice and pointing into the stands, to where Marcus was walking toward her with his hands in his pockets. He nodded at Kelly as he came closer and looked a little embarrassed at hearing his name being called out over and over by Mark.

"I told you he wanted you to come," Kelly said.

"Sure," Marcus replied, still not really believing it. He looked out at the rink, squinting a little as if it were only just now coming into view. Mark had been lured back to the group by his instructor.

"He's doing all right, looks like," Marcus said. "Staying up for while."

"He wants to go whipping around the ice like the older kids."

"Aaah, that's just showing off."

"There were some boys out there earlier that looked like some of yours."

Marcus settled onto the bench beside her. "They *were* mine; that's why I waited until the lesson started to come over."

"Trying to avoid them?"

"It can get a little much, you know? Hanging around you all the time. I wouldn't mind it so much except that you tell them not to do something, and two seconds later they do it anyway. Or you tell them to keep it down, and right away they're all yelling again."

"Oh god, I know. When we were leaving to come here I was like 'Mark, make sure you have your mitts, make sure you have your mitts –'"

"Yeah but at least it's just him," he said. "And you can tell him whatever you want. I've got a dozen of them around my neck all the time, and their parents are fucking idiots, most of them. Some of their kids can barely go to the bathroom by themselves, and then they wonder why we're not winning all the time."

Most of the kids were now at centre ice. They stopped there to look back at their fallen comrades rolling and twitching on the ice behind them. Mark was down on one knee, looking intently at the laces of his left skate. He started to stand but was still wobbling, so before he could fall again he sat down hard on the ice and started to pull on the lace-loops on both skates to make them tighter.

"I used to do that," Marcus said, smiling. "Fuck with my skates for half the lesson."

"Yay!" Kelly shouted: all the kids had made it safely to the other side, Mark included. He was kneeling with his forehead against the boards looking as though he were deep in grateful prayer. Or maybe praying that this was the end of it and all he'd be called on to do.

Marcus laughed. "Now they have to get back."

Everyone sitting in the stands, Marcus included, watched with the same mix of delight and fear as the class returned slowly and painfully across the ice. It was like watching newly hatched turtles scramble down the beach to the protection of the sea. Marcus thought about inviting Mark and Kelly back to his apartment after the lesson: he had cleaned the place up before going out that morning. Even Manda's plant had received some attention. It would be the first time Mark had ever been inside his apartment, and though Marcus felt a little wary of having a four-year-old running around, he was curious to see what the kid would think. He could pull out his old Nintendo if Mark got bored. He decided to wait until after to see how things went and then bring up the idea as they were leaving. He didn't want to promise anything and then have Mark act like a little shit. She might even invite him back to her place first, which would be better.

"Is the snack bar open yet?" Kelly asked. "It was closed when I came in."

"The guy in there goes for half-hour smoke breaks. Should be open now, though. Want me to get us some fries?"

"Oh wicked. Want me to give you some money?"

"Actually, yeah."

Marcus walked down the stands two at a time and waved to Mark as he was going out the doors. A few kids were kneeling on the benches in their skates and watching the lessons through the windows. A bored mother stood nearby; she looked as though she were in the middle of trying to sneak away unnoticed. Marcus nodded at her to show his support for her escape attempt, but she ignored him. A man stood on his own further down the line of windows. He looked over at Marcus and didn't look away. The guy was young and he looked familiar, but he was too old to be one of his former players.

Behind the counter, a man was preparing a pot of filtered coffee. He had on a 'Dunbridge Days 1995' T-shirt that was stretched and hanging off him. Bobby had been running the snack bar since Marcus started coaching here, but had never learned the names of any of the people at the rink, and never grew more friendly than he was the first time you bought something from him. He came to the counter with a coffee in a Styrofoam cup and, looking past Marcus and giving him no acknowledgement, called out, "Coffee." The mother standing with her group of kids said, "That's me, thanks," and came to retrieve her drink. Bobby didn't look up at Marcus until the woman had moved away.

"Yes sir, you want a coffee?"

"Maybe later, thanks. Do you have the fry thing going?"

He walked over to the deep fryer and dropped a wire basket into the bubbling, tea-coloured oil.

"What size, sir?"

"Oh huge. Extra Large."

The fries went in, the basket given a shake, and Bobby disappeared behind his drinks fridge, presumably in case someone else came to the window – he liked to do things one at a time. As if justifying Bobby's fears, the man who had been standing by the windows suddenly stepped directly in front of Marcus, who had to take a step back.

"The line-up's back here I think, eh?" Marcus said.

The man turned around to face Marcus. "Take it easy, buddy," he said.

Out of the corner of his eye Marcus saw the woman with the coffee and the kids look over, then look away. The man kept staring at him, waiting for a response.

Marcus put his hands up with the palms out and said, in a backing-down tone, "I'm just waiting for my fries."

The man didn't soften a bit. "Maybe you should just watch it," he said with the same edge in his voice. As he said it, something in his face shifted, and it was transformed: Marcus suddenly realized he was looking at Mark's face trapped within that of an older man, a man who had made something hard and unforgiving of it. Most of Mark's features were spread thinly across the face and lost completely behind a jagged, black goatee, but his eyes were right there, unobstructed and alive, staring at Marcus with cold anger and resentment.

Marcus laughed nervously. "So what is this, I'm just . . ."

"I think it's time to go, eh?"

"What?"

Mark's father took a step toward him. He'd clearly been working himself up for a while. Marcus tried to think if he'd seen him standing when he'd arrived at the rink. Probably the guy had been watching him talk to Kelly all that time and started seething.

"Are you Neil? Look, I don't know what your problem is –"

"You're the one with the fucking problem."

"What does that mean?"

"It means you better watch your fucking step or you and I are going to have problems."

The absurdity of the situation finally overwhelmed Marcus's initial fear, as did his calculation that, though he hadn't been in anything like a fight since junior high school, he was still bigger and heavier than Neil. Anyway, people didn't just *fight*, not just like *that*. Neil wasn't going to do anything here – he was just showing off because he was angry. Probably drunk, too.

"Come on, what the fuck is that? I'm not going to fight you."

"Why, cuz you're a fag?"

Marcus laughed again. The kids by the windows were watching with faces full of expectant joy while their mother tried to pull them away.

"This is just stupid. Is this because of Kelly? Does she even know you're here?"

Neil's eyes shifted slightly. He wasn't comfortable being led off the path of immediate and decisive violence. "I don't give a fuck about that bitch," he said.

"Hey, easy," Marcus said, in the same ironic tone he used on his team. "That's a little much. What's going on? Is this about Mark?"

"He's *my* fucking kid."

"Yeah I know. So what the fuck are you mad at me for? What

| 185 |

did I do? I'm not trying to take him. This is between you and Kelly I think. Seriously – talk to Kelly."

"She has a big fucking surprise coming, I guarantee you that. I fucking guarantee."

"What does that mean?"

"None of your business."

"That's what I said before! It's none of my business, but you're still getting all hyped up."

"Why don't you get the fuck out of here?"

"What for? I'm not trying to *replace* anyone here."

"I'll fucking replace your head."

At any other time, Marcus would have laughed at that.

"Look, there's no trouble here. No one's trying to do anything, okay? I was just here to meet Kelly. All of this has nothing to do with me."

"You better fucking believe it."

"Oh fuck this," Marcus said. He took a step towards the rink doors. Neil stepped in front of him again.

"If you go back in there I'll fucking pound the living shit out of you."

Marcus knew right away that he had miscalculated the odds of Neil beating him up: the guy could and he would.

"I'm just going in there for a second."

"I'm fucking serious: if you're not out of here in ten seconds you're fucking dead."

The mother and her kids were gone. Bobby was watching with absolute neutrality from his snack-bar window. He'd probably pulled the fries out of the oil as soon as the shouting started so they didn't go to waste. Marcus could suddenly see the situation he was in: he was on the verge of getting his head beaten in. In public. And for what? On principle? Whatever there was between Kelly and Neil, it was not his problem. He felt as though he were being forced down a corridor that grew narrower with every step, forced by people who reserved the right to take their lives in absolutely any direction they chose. People who had made choices they now regretted were unburdening themselves of the consequences of those choices and putting them all on him. Neil had made a choice to abandon his own kid, now he was trying to make up for it by threatening Marcus. Kelly had made a choice to have Mark. She kept him. She *chose* to fuck Neil four years ago, and chose not to deal with him when things went to shit – as she should have seen right from the start they would. No one wanted to live with the consequences of their actions; no one wanted to be responsible for their own mess; everyone had shit the bed and wanted Marcus to deal with it. He would not. It was too much.

Marcus told himself all this as he stood with Neil growing tighter and sharper in front of him.

"You know what?" Marcus said, throwing his hands up and walking toward the doors to the parking lot. "I don't have time for this bullshit. He's your kid – I don't want him. I'm definitely not going to *fight* for him."

As he pushed through the doors Neil yelled after him: "Your team fucking sucks, you faggot!"

Marcus could have laughed at that, too.

Ken could feel the store blinking off in stages behind him as he leaned with his back against one of the big front windows. In a few hours the cleaners would arrive and the store would blink back on. It was almost nine-thirty and Steve hadn't shown up yet. A truck came along that looked like Patrick's. Ken panicked at the thought of leaving without Steve. He was relieved when the truck, which was the wrong colour anyway, kept on moving and went around the corner at the same time Steve appeared. He was walking fast and cramped up in his leather jacket because of the cold. Ken raised one mittened hand and shouted, "Steve!"

Steve didn't slow his pace until he got within three feet of Ken, where he stopped dead.

"What are you shouting at?" he said, and started hopping from one foot to the other. "It's fucking cold – where's the man with the truck?"

Pretending to see someone in the store, Steve waved, smiled, gave his own reflection the finger, and took a few running steps toward the window to give it a hard, high kick that stopped just short of the glass.

Ken checked his watch and found the face blank, the batteries dead. When he pressed some of the buttons all he got were digital fragments of numbers. Steve had his face against the glass and was cupping his hand around his eyes to see in.

"They left a full cart in the middle of the floor!"

"My watch is dead."

"*I'll* get you a new watch," Steve said. He mimed picking up a garbage can and throwing it through the window. Patrick pulled up in the truck and gave a honk that almost made Steve jump through the glass for real.

"Home, James!" Steve shouted.

Patrick didn't say much on the way to Chaps. He wasn't happy about having to drive Steve, or about him coming out with them at all. From experience, he knew that Steve couldn't handle more than four or five drinks but tried to cover for that fact by drinking six or seven as quickly as he could. Steve filled the silence in the truck with bullshit about the car he used to own and the last job he had before Giant Tiger and his odds of getting laid that night – which were excellent, according to him. Patrick had barely put the truck's nose into the Chaps parking lot before Steve had the passenger-side door open and was jumping out, forcing him to hit the brakes. Steve had gone inside and was coming back out before Patrick and Ken even made it across the lot.

"It's dead," Steve announced with disgust.

"It's Tuesday," Patrick replied, and walked past him through the door.

It wasn't quite dead inside: there were only two people at the bar and one table occupied, but Chaps was cramped enough that even one person alone with the bartender made the place feel populated. The ceiling was low, and there were metal support pillars every ten feet or so on which the owners or the staff had hung posters and decorations. Ken was unable to pass any of these without brushing them with his shoulder and knocking something to the ground. Steve sat down at a table and immediately started picking at a poster stuck to a nearby pillar.

"Can you stop that?" Patrick said.

Steve gave it one more pick and stopped. He scooted over to make room for Ken, who was still wearing his yellow work jacket under his parka.

"You still got your thing on!" Steve laughed.

"I forgot."

"Yeah, no shit. You look like a geek, and I have to sit beside you."

"Leave him alone," Patrick said, embarrassed on Ken's behalf.

"Ooooo . . ." Steve said, giving Ken a smile. "Well, get your jacket off anyway."

"Ken," Patrick said, ignoring Steve as best he could. "You're sure Manda said we were meeting here? You're sure of that?"

"What the fuck's the difference?" Steve asked, almost bouncing in his chair. "Let's get some beers going."

"Ken?"

"Yes," Ken said to both Patrick's original question and to Steve's plan.

Satisfied for the moment, Patrick offered to get the first round of beers.

"What do you guys want?"

"A Blue," Steve replied, almost before Patrick had finished asking the question.

"A," Ken started, and seemed to take a difficult breath before finishing – he was trying to pull off his parka without standing. "Blue."

Waiting at the bar, Patrick watched the game highlights on the TV. Nothing interesting: two American teams he didn't give a shit about. When the bartender put the bottles on the bar, Patrick noticed that not only was the little finger on the man's left hand missing up to the knuckle, but his skin was tinted all over a uniform orange. A winter tan, he guessed. There was a tanning salon at the mall with massive, glowing beds that looked like old laundry presses. Manda sometimes urged Patrick to go there to counteract the bleached albino look he had all year round. He was glad he had always resisted – the bartender looked like he'd been dipped in iodine. He did another quick visual sweep of the bar on his way back to the table, just in case he had missed seeing Manda sitting in the corner somewhere.

"We need some tunes," Steve said, tucking into his beer. "I can't take this country shit. Got any quarters, Ken?"

Ken dug into the inside pocket of his parka and pulled out a small package covered in Saran Wrap. Slowly and carefully he unwrapped his stack of quarters and gave Steve four.

"Shit," Steve said, laughing and snapping his fingers, "I thought you were going to roll us one."

"Work's going alright?" Patrick asked Ken when Steve had left to feed the jukebox. "Are they giving you enough hours there?"

"Yeah, tons."

"So it's alright?"

Ken didn't answer.

"That place used to be a Woolworth's," Patrick said to fill the silence. "I used to go there to buy Hot Wheels cars. Or steal them – used to be easy."

"People still steal shit," Ken said.

"Oh yeah?"

"Yeah, and we're supposed to catch them if we see them doing it or whatever, sticking something in their jacket."

"There's no security guard or anything?"

"Yeah, but they want us to do it more."

"Do you?"

"Some people do. I don't. I don't give a fuck."

"Does Steve?"

Ken was silent again. He started peeling the label off his beer bottle, scraping at it with his thick fingernails.

"So, the new house – it's okay and everything?" Patrick asked. Manda had told him something recently about Ken and his new place, but he couldn't remember anything about it now, not even whether it was good or bad. "That one guy seems alright, the guy that I met. Works in a body shop?"

"Charles."

"That's it. Is that it? I thought his name was Peter."

"Charles."

"Did you used to live with a Peter?"

"No."

"Well, whatever, how's the place going?"

"I want to get out of it."

Patrick now regretted bringing up the subject in the first place, especially without Manda there.

"That's shitty," he said. "That's . . ."

Ken looked at him to see what he was going to say, but Patrick was saved from having to finish his sentence by the sudden, incomprehensible gonging of a giant bell. One person at the bar looked around; nobody else, including the bartender, even blinked. The bell struck again, and the sound hung in the air like fog. Before the third strike, a small bloom of recognition opened in the back of Patrick's mind: it was a song from when he was in high school. He still heard it every once in while, booming out of cars and maybe on the radio. He was almost at the point of remembering the name of it when, just before the fourth strike, Steve appeared next to the table, a cigarette in his mouth and a phantom guitar in his hands. When the band came in and the bell dropped out, Steve's phantom guitar became a phantom microphone.

"*A rollin' thunder, a fiery rain,*" he growled, but could go no further, because the bartender had pulled the plug on the juke-box. There were a few muted *yays* around the bar.

"Oh that's *bullshit*," Steve said, looking over at the bartender. He sat down reluctantly.

"So is it that bad?" Patrick asked Ken, figuring he would take another shot at the subject of Ken's new home.

Ken nodded. "Pretty much."

"Fucking right it's that bad," Steve said to Ken. "That was your dollar wasted."

Marcus had to nurse a single ginger ale for an hour before Manda showed up at The Flamingo. He was down to sucking the diminishing ice cubes through his straw while sitting in the corner beneath the faded mural of a tree with two testicular coconuts hanging beneath its palms. His mother had told him once The Flamingo had been a tropical-themed dance hall when she was younger; he had very vague memories of sitting, bored, in one of the booths as a child while a loud wedding reception went on around him. When Manda finally arrived, she didn't come to the booth right away, but made her hand into a telephone receiver and disappeared again down the hallway to the payphones.

"My cell phone's dead," Manda told him when she got back. She put her tasselled jacket between them. Marcus was still wearing his bomber jacket. "Are you cold?" she asked him.

"They don't put the heat up enough in this place."

"Did you eat here?"

"Yeah right, and get Flamingo's Revenge."

"That was *one* time – you're such a baby."

The waitress, whom Marcus had been shooing away all night with his glass of ice cubes, was finally permitted to approach the booth. Manda ordered a rum and coke, Marcus a rye and ginger.

"Ooh, you're living it up tonight," Manda said. "Did Kelly give you a blow job or something?"

"Not even close. You won't believe this – it's unbelievable."

Manda was practically licking her lips with pleasure by the time Marcus finished telling her about the skating lesson, and Neil, and his taking off (though this last part was de-emphasized in the version he told her). She especially liked Marcus's impression of a monkey-faced Neil standing there with his fists up, and the fact that Marcus had left with Kelly's money in his pocket (a detail he hadn't really thought about, but one she pounced on immediately).

"So what did you say to her? Have you talked to her?"

"She called and left a bunch of messages, but I'm just –" Marcus waved his hands in front of him as if declining an offer.

"My god. Well I told you this would happen."

She hadn't actually, but she had thrown up enough similarly disastrous scenarios that she felt she deserved some credit for it.

"Well, you're lucky you didn't get attached to the kid. You'd be fucked now if you had. It's what usually happens. I *told* you."

"Not too fucking likely."

"Well I warned you. You don't fuck around with someone who's got a kid. Especially when she's, what, twenty-five?"

"Something like that." Marcus realized he didn't actually know for sure.

"It's not like you've got a lot of options, but Jesus, you can do better than that, I think. Maybe not just her on her own – she's pretty, so I don't know."

"Thanks a lot."

"Beggars can't be choosers, but that doesn't mean –"

"Yeah, I get it. Thanks."

Marcus finished his drink and, not feeling any nausea or dizziness, allowed Manda to order him another. Two more and he'd have the most alcohol in his system he'd had since he was a teenager. Manda was already on her third, and since none of them had had any effect on her mood so far, she decided to help them along with a beer. She'd been hoping that just being out would lift the gloom that'd been sitting on her for the last few days – since the moment she saw her fucked-up mother in that fucked-up food court on the way to see that fucked-up movie, to be exact.

"Aw Christ, Marcus."

"I know what you mean," Marcus said, assuming she was being rhetorical.

"No, it's just work and everything. They might be moving the office to Orillia, which is just stupid and completely fucks me up if they do. And then Patrick's all out of it as usual. And now Ken's talking about wanting to move again. It's too much, it really is."

"Hey what happened with Patrick today? I walked to the mall this afternoon and the whole place was closed. There was water everywhere." Marcus splayed his fingers out over the table to demonstrate.

"What do you mean, what water?"

"I mean *water*, like toilet water or something. They had to close the mall. I walked out there for nothing, and Patrick never even called me once."

"He never called me at all. I never heard anything." As a reflex, Manda checked her cell phone: still dead.

"I don't know what's going on with him," she said. "He goes off in the morning like he going to get kicked in the ass all day. It's *his* friggin store! It's not the easiest thing to do, I know, but he should try being where I am, on the friggin phone all day with assholes from Vancouver who want to stay at the Holiday Inn in the middle of Toronto for nothing, then get all kinds of free passes to go up the CN Tower and shit like that."

"I've never been up it," Marcus said.

"You're *joking*. Fuck's sake, Marcus, where *have* you been?"

"Nowhere," he said. "Where is Patrick now, anyway? Wasn't he picking up Ken?"

This time Manda shook her cell phone to see if she could rattle it to life.

"I bet Ken's fucked this up, somehow," she said. "I bet he forgot and went home. Patrick's probably trying to find Ken's house – he's only seen it twice. He can barely see at night but he won't get glasses. And now he'll be all pissed off at me. Oh it's too much."

Manda suddenly leaned in toward Marcus and spoke in a quieter voice – a purely symbolic gesture, given the size of The Flamingo and the distance between them and the next occupied table.

"I have to tell you something, but you can't say a word to your mother or to my dad."

"Oh I'm supposed to tell you to call them, by the way," Marcus said.

"Are you listening?"

"Yeah yeah."

"Not one word. You can't tell Ken, either. Don't tell anyone. I'm serious."

Manda told Marcus about seeing Shelly. It took him a second to remember who she was.

"How did she know where you two were going?" he asked.

"She didn't! She was just there like she's a fucking witch or a psychic or something!"

"Well, when's the last time you saw her?"

"Not for a long time. Listen, you can't say *anything* about this to Ken or anybody."

"What am I going to say? Isn't she the one who burned his face? How is that supposed to come up in conversation? It's hard enough getting Ken to talk about the weather."

The waitress came to the table to take away the empty glasses. Manda ordered another rum and coke and another beer, and Marcus asked for a glass of water. He was still working on his second rye and ginger.

"She was begging me to visit her," Manda continued.

"Who? Oh. Yeah? And? What'd you tell her?"

Manda gave Marcus a pained expression.

"Oh you're kidding," he said. "Are you serious?"

"I didn't tell her anything, but . . . I've been thinking like I should. She's an evil bitch, but . . ."

Marcus just shook his head. "So you won't go out to see your dad but you'll go hang out with the woman who fucked up your life and almost killed your brother. That's nice."

"I know but . . ." She shrugged. "It's like I have to know what's going on with her. I have to see her or I start thinking she's not real. Like I made her up when we were moving around all the time. I didn't see her for so long. I visited her a couple of times, years ago."

"What for?"

"I told you: I just have to see her, to see how bad she's gotten.

I know it's crazy. I stopped it for a while cuz I couldn't take it."

"Has she ever said anything about Ken? Has she ever even apologized?"

Manda snorted bitterly. "Are you joking? As far as she's concerned she was a wonderful mother who had to fight just to get by, and everyone was out to get her, and oh so much bullshit it makes me sick. Honestly, I'm glad she never brought it up, because I probably would have strangled her." She downed the rum and coke the waitress had just given her in one gulp, almost choking on the ice. "Fuck I'd love to strangle her," she said into the neck of her new beer. "Give me a quarter – I'm going to call home again."

Steve was happy, Ken was okay, and even Patrick was starting to have a decent time, though he kept looking at the door every time someone came in to see if it was Manda at last. He figured she had got stuck doing something with the house or with Marcus and would show up later. He hadn't been out at a bar without her in years. He had to admit it felt strange, but good – he didn't want to spend the entire night alone with the other two, but for the moment he was prepared to relax and enjoy himself. Steve had come to an agreement with the bartender that the jukebox could be played as long as A) the volume was kept at half-strength, and B) the selections were made with a little more consideration for the other people in the bar. Steve selected accordingly, and didn't go near the little volume knob he now knew to be just around the back of the thing. When one of his songs came on, Steve would sing along in a high-pitched voice and point to Ken and Patrick in turn, as if to show them which lines of the song were about them in particular. Patrick kept laughing at this; Ken had seen it before. Patrick bought the table a pitcher, and Ken bought the next two.

"Money bags!" Steve said. "Where's this all coming from?"

"You alright for it?" Patrick asked Ken.

"It's fine. I have some money saved up."

"I'll bet," Steve laughed. "You know this guy, he's probably got a thousand dollars in a sock under his pillow. All in quarters!"

Patrick laughed, and then went on with the story he'd been telling: "You should have seen it," he said. "The whole mall was empty, nobody there, and there was all this water just fucking gushing out. It was like . . ."

He couldn't think of anything to compare it to, so he just shook his head and had a drink.

"What did the store look like?" Ken asked him.

"I didn't see it. They wouldn't let me in." Patrick thought for a second. "Asshole cop."

"You could pocket the insurance money," Steve suggested.

Patrick nodded at the wisdom of this and finished his glass. He drained the pitcher filling his next. A Led Zeppelin song came on, one from an album he used to own but had lost a long time ago. He mumbled what he remembered of the words, getting about one in three correct, though sometimes he lucked out with a whole line. "Fuck the store," he said, clinking Ken's glass with his own. "Piece of shit."

Steve was up again and talking to the bartender. He came back with a smile upon his face, carrying a tray with three shots on it.

"Vodka!" he shouted. "We're going to Moscow tonight. Pravda! Gorbachev!"

"You've got plans," Patrick said.

"My great-grandfather was Russian," Steve said.

"Bullshit."

"Total bullshit," Steve agreed. "Let's do it."

Steve and Patrick threw back their heads and dropped the

shot down their throats while Ken sucked it out of the glass like medicine. The other two had to slap him on the back as he choked.

"Vodka's bullshit," Ken said huskily when he'd recovered a little.

The smeared platter that had held Manda's nachos sat at the edge of the table, ignored by the waitress. Manda was feeling the same way – ignored, dirty, scraped clean of all that was good. Marcus had, as usual, cut himself off midway through his fourth drink and was now looking into a pint glass of fountain Coke to avoid looking at his stepsister, who was getting messier by the minute. Manda had been running her worried fingers through her hair, and now it was standing up like a fright wig. She did her best to pat it back down.

"Better," Marcus said. He was feeling bored and embarrassed. Everywhere he went, it felt like, someone was falling apart at the seams.

"You shouldn't have let me eat all those," Manda said, looking resentfully at the empty platter. "It's not like I needed another couple of pounds."

"I had some; you saw me."

There were more people in The Flamingo now, but it needed the equivalent of two wedding parties to feel anywhere near full. Manda went to the bathroom to pee and clean up a little. As she passed the payphones she thought again about calling Patrick at home, but she had no more change in her purse, and Marcus got weird every time she asked him for a quarter, despite the fact that she was paying for the drinks. Patrick must have forgotten, gone home, and fallen asleep. She wondered what he'd been doing all day with the store closed. She thought about him at home without her – probably the place was happier that way, with just him there. All the work she'd done would be reversed when she got home; there would be something wrapped in tin-foil cooking in the oven and Ronnie would be sitting in his chair.

In the bathroom mirror she found a streak of sour cream on her face that Marcus hadn't told her about. She wasn't mad. She stumbled a bit getting back through the bathroom's aggressively swinging door and another woman coming in gave her a look.

"Fuck off," Manda said when she got back to the table.

"Who, me?" Marcus asked.

"No, some bitch in the bathroom. Looking at me."

Marcus folded his coaster into a flat-bottomed canoe that he set afloat in a puddle of liquid the waitress had neglected to wipe up.

"Did you order me another drink?" Manda asked him.

"Did you want one?"

"Yes. Don't you?"

"You have another one, and I'll watch."

"Don't be a prick, Marcus. Please don't be a prick. I don't need it."

Manda stood up and waved at the waitress, who was just on her way to tell the bartender about the table of high-school kids in the corner by the bathrooms who were trying to order a pitcher with fake ID.

Steve hadn't been able to sit still for more than five minutes, and now he was threatening to go for tequila shots. Patrick just stared at the half-full pitcher between them that refused to empty itself. Waking up at five o'clock plus the beer he'd had earlier – it was all catching up with him. His eyes were heading toward half-mast.

"I have to work tomorrow," Patrick protested.

"Oh come on, so do I, so does Ken – so what?"

"I don't," Ken said. "I have a day off."

"Well good for you. We're going to have lots of those soon, eh? So let's do a little *te-qui-la*!"

Ken shook his head. "I don't want any. It makes me sick."

"I don't care about *sick*," Patrick said, "I just don't want it. I'm going to boot it soon, anyway."

"Oh, you . . ." Steve sulked until a Rolling Stones song he'd picked came on the jukebox, and then he was up to see if he could sneak the volume up a little without the bartender noticing.

"Are you at the store tomorrow?" Ken asked Patrick.

"Every day. Except today."

"No I mean because of the water maybe it was closed."

"Hope not. Why, you coming in?"

"Coming in where?" Steve asked, having completed his mission.

"I might need a ride tomorrow," Ken said.

"A ride where? Maybe Manda can take you. I need the truck but she can maybe come pick it up and get you."

"Hey, you need any help at the store?" Steve asked.

"Hang on – where do you need a ride to, Ken?"

"Pretty far."

"I'm only doing four shifts at the store, and that might be ending, those fuckers, so if you need a hand . . ."

"Yeah right. What's pretty far?"

Steve was now stretched so far over the table he was practically lying across it on his belly. "What the fuck does that mean?" he asked.

"At least to the lake," Ken said. "Or the other way. Not sure yet."

"What the fuck does *what* mean?" Patrick asked Steve. "Watch my beer!"

"You said 'yeah right' – you think I'm a shitty worker?"

"I have no clue and I don't really care. But probably, yeah."

Steve started loudly insisting he and Ken were the only ones who did any work at Giant Tiger and that he could do three jobs at once and could run Patrick's store better than he could himself and Patrick could suck his cock right then and there. The bartender came over to tell Steve he had used up his warnings and had to finish his drink, pay up, and get out. Patrick made a half-hearted attempt to intervene on Steve's behalf, which just got him and Ken kicked out, too. As embarrassing as it was, Patrick was fine with that – he was ready to go.

The three of them got out to the parking lot without further incident, but then Steve lit a fresh cigarette.

"You're not bringing that in the truck," Patrick said.

"So wait til I'm finished it, fuck."

"Don't be an asshole, Steve," Ken told him. "Let's just go."

"Just put it out, and let's go."

"Fuck that, I'll walk it."

"Fine with me – get in, Ken."

Patrick started walking toward the truck but before he could put his hand on the door, Steve came running up from behind and took a swing at him. Patrick ducked, and Steve's fist got him hard on the shoulder. The cigarette popped out of Steve's mouth and rolled under the truck in a spray of red sparks. He ducked down low and ran twenty or thirty steps away, bent at the waist, before Patrick could grab him or try to hit him back. Patrick took one step in his direction but didn't bother to go any further: he wasn't going to chase the guy around the parking lot like an idiot. His shoulder felt like it had been impaled, his arm was dead. Steve must have caught him in just the right place – it was hurting too much for the amount of strength the guy had put into the punch. Patrick pointed at Steve, who looked like a nervous baseball player about to steal a base, and told him to stay the fuck away, then he called for Ken, who had disappeared. He waited a minute or two before giving up and driving off, spinning the tires on the gravel. Steve ran after the truck and tried to smack its side, but it was gone before he got near it.

"Ken, you fucking retard, where the fuck are you? That shithead left us here! Ken!"

He walked around back to see if Ken was there taking a leak, but all he found was a raccoon fighting its way into a bag of chicken bones left outside the back door of the bar. He called for Ken a few more times, then started walking along the road back into town, muttering curses the whole way against Patrick, the bartender, and everyone else who had failed him so spectacularly.

After much pleading, Marcus finally gave in and had two more rye and gingers, but now he was back on straight ginger ale and feeling rotten. The smoke in the place was making him feel ill, for one thing, and Manda was starting to get that look about her, the one that said she might not get through the evening in one piece. He had lost track of how many drinks she'd had already – more than seven, anyway. He kept trying to keep the conversation on safe topics, but she insisted on lurching into the kinds of things that were bound to leave her bloodied.

"I know this is his dream, but it's just not working," she was saying. "It's like he's gotta know when to quit or something, I don't know."

"It's only been a couple of years."

"It's been four, Marcus!" she shouted and then quickly changed her tone to one of self-recrimination. "I don't support him enough. He always supported me. He used to drive me to see Shelly when we first started dating. He'd drop me off and the poor guy would drive around for a couple of hours or go to

McDonald's or something. Then he'd have to put up with me after, the way I was after those visits. He never said anything. Oh Christ, Marcus, I used to just lose it. Even the other night, he was so good, and I just . . ."

Marcus shifted in his chair – his ass was asleep. "I wish I'd had some more of those nachos now," he said. "I'm friggin starving."

"He just doesn't *say* anything. That's why I knew it was never going to work with you and that Kelly: I knew you would never make that kind of commitment to her. You don't do that. It has to be there, or . . ." Manda lost her point in the mottled surface of the table.

"Yeah well, that wasn't my fault," Marcus said.

"I know that!" Manda said, and she reached to hold him lightly by the wrists. She started stroking his arms with her thumbs. "You could never be like that. You don't have it in you. You're a Taurus, so you need someone who won't ask anything of you. All that shit."

"Oh my god, Manda – you're not going to start that shit, are you? Are you for real?"

"No, I'm not going to start that shit. No, I'm not for real. But I'm just saying that, sometimes, if you look into it, if you read about it, it can scare the *shit* out of you."

"Having a girlfriend?"

"No, your horoscope and all that. It's *scary* sometimes. I think it's total bullshit, but it can be scary."

"So can you."

Manda took a long drink. "You and all those boys," she said.

"Don't say that – people'll think I'm a *perv*."

"No, the hockey players. How long are you going to keep that up, anyway, coaching and all that?"

"Gimme a break."

Marcus escaped her grip and crossed his arms. Manda

didn't seem to notice. There was a rum and coke-scented fog drifting up through her. People were talking behind her eyes, reading out transcripts of conversations she'd had twenty years ago, ten years ago, last week. The air in the bar was damning her; every song they played was full of accusation.

"Oh Marcus, I used to always want a little brother, and then I got one and look what I did. I was such a bitch to you. I was so fucked up. Do you forgive me for all that?"

"Yes," he said, without even trying to make it sound like he meant it.

"Do you forgive me for being such a bitch to you? I was so evil. I think I actually went crazy for a while."

Marcus couldn't help it: he laughed.

"I mean it! For real!" she insisted. She brought her hands up to her face and pressed her fingers against her eyelids. "For Christ's sake, I don't want to be crazy. I am though – I'm going to be crazy and I'm going to be just like my mother. I can already feel it happening. I look at her, and I'm like, *how long have I got left?*"

"You're not crazy," Marcus attempted.

"I've been thinking something bad is going to happen, ever since I saw her."

"She can't do anything."

Manda turned on Marcus: "I know she can't actually fucking do anything! What is she going to do, come after me with a plastic fucking fork? She can't even use the fucking phone book."

"Then what?"

"I don't know, but she's such an evil bitch. She messes me up every time I see her. I keep thinking about what she did to Ken – not just the face, but before that. She used to make him go nuts to make herself feel better for having him. She'd lay into him, smacking him or leaving him behind whenever we were going somewhere, the park or whatever. He wasn't even ten years old!"

"Fuck."

"I almost want her to come to Dunbridge to see Ken and me," Manda said, stabbing the table with her finger. "At least it would end this whole thing about us being kept from her. He told me yesterday he wants to go see her."

"Maybe he wants to strangle her finally," Marcus offered.

"You want to know the worst thing? I saw her the other night and I just knew that's where I was going. But all I could think was I should have a baby just to spite her, just to show her that – fuck her – even if she's right, she can't stop me. I was like, what would piss her off more?"

"That's really stupid."

"I know it is, but I'm starting to feel like I owe it to Patrick to have a baby before I'm completely fucked. I'm thirty-eight already."

"Jesus, you don't need a kid. What would you do that for?"

"I know I don't."

"You wouldn't last *one week* alone with a kid. One week."

"I'm not afraid of actually having a kid, that doesn't bother me at all, just . . ."

"The rest of it. Manda, you'd go fucking crazy. That would be the end of it and you know it."

"I feel kind of bad for Kelly. She's all alone."

Marcus shrugged. "No she's not. That's the problem."

Manda took a sip from Marcus's ginger ale. The lack of alcohol seemed to sting her.

"I could have had one by now," she said.

"One what?"

"Baby."

Marcus was silent. Manda spun her fingers into the tassels hanging off her jacket.

"I almost did."

"I know."

Manda's face became twisted up with sadness.

"Please don't ever tell Patrick that. Please."

The music in the bar suddenly leapt out from whatever hole it had been hiding, obliterating Marcus's reply. The sound reverberated against all the cartoon palm trees and flamingos and demented monkeys on the wall until every beat was like a slap. Manda watched the waitress cross the empty dance floor with a stack of clean ashtrays.

The raccoon behind Chaps now had the bag of chicken bones open and was picking them up one by one in its little black hands, unable to believe its luck. It was so entranced by its find that it didn't notice another raccoon, swollen with unborn babies, toddling across the shattered concrete in the empty lot next door, coming to join in and help reduce the pile of slick bones to shards and scraps of torn plastic. Neither of them paid much attention to Ken, who stepped out of the shadow of the dumpster just as the two raccoons were settling a silent peace accord that would allow them both to eat without fear of attack from the other. Ken watched them fondle the bones for a while, amused by their dainty manners, but also thinking how they were close enough that he could kick one of them like a soft soccer ball. Steve would have tried for the kick; animals disgusted him. Ken crossed the empty lot back to the road, almost tripping over some of the rusted, metal rods curling up from the ground like the seedlings of a new building trying to grow out of the cracked foundations of the old one.

Something had clicked in Ken's mind while he was standing behind the dumpster waiting for Steve to get out of sight, something that would not be unclicked. He needed to get home to get things ready. It was a half-hour walk, but Ken didn't notice any of it. Each house and building crumbled as he passed; the road sank into the dirt behind him as he lifted his feet.

It was after one, and Manda was looking like she could slip under the table at any minute, so Marcus got her up and out of the booth. She insisted on giving him a tight hug as soon as they got outside onto the sidewalk, a hug that lasted so long he started wondering if she had dozed off standing up in the middle of it. There was wind coming down the street, stripping away everything warm and alive and leaving behind nothing but cold. Marcus could feel it against the backs of his legs, but with Manda standing against him he was sheltered against the worst of it. Her blue leather tassels were streaming over the arms of his jacket. A cab sitting at the curb gave them a quick honk, which brought Manda back to life, and the two of them climbed in the back. She lay with her head against his shoulder the whole way, drifting in and out of consciousness. "I'm so happy you talk," she told him fuzzily. "Patrick never talks, but you talk." Then she was gone again for a while. The ride home was a pulsing streak of light from the streetlights being drawn past the back window of the cab, which seemed to be sitting still.

Marcus gave the driver his own address first. When they pulled up to his building and he opened the door of the cab to get out, Manda woke up a little and said, "If you see Ken first, call me," as if they weren't both heading to bed, but only splitting up to cover more ground in an all-out search. His stairs seemed steeper than usual – he almost went down on his belly when his foot missed one halfway up. He could smell the rotten beer that Manda had been complaining about and had to fight the temptation, as he looked for his key, to sweep all of the bottles off his landing and down the stairs. His apartment was cold, colder than outside, it felt like. He left the lights off to spite himself – there was enough light coming in the windows from outside, anyway. He had a sudden fear that Neil was waiting for him in the dark, but he fought it down. There was a quarter of a sandwich he'd left from dinner sitting on the kitchen table. After a brief but furious internal debate, he ate it, and nothing in his life had ever tasted better.

Manda got her front door open but wasn't prepared for the way the floor in the front hallway rolled and pitched like a floating dock in a storm. She had to walk with her shoulder sliding along the wall to get to the kitchen, where she spent two minutes trying to get a can of Coke open, long enough to have completely lost interest in drinking it by the time the thing was fizzing in her hand. She wondered if Patrick was home. She climbed-crawled the stairs and spent a few dark moments in the bathroom with the light out, certain she was going to have to throw up in the bathtub because of the impossibility of her finding the toilet in the dark and getting the seat up in time. She fought the shower curtain but it wouldn't yield – it seemed to have grown a dozen more layers of thin plastic. She kept struggling with it but felt she was getting no closer to the dark, clean mouth of the tub, so she gave up on the idea of puking altogether and felt her way back out of the room and went in search of her bed and her husband.

It took her eyes a while to adjust to the darkness of the bedroom. The carpet was warm and soft under her feet, but she couldn't get her shoes off without assistance. Patrick was on the far side of the bed, lying with his legs curled up under the covers like a giant seahorse. The sight of him breathing gave Manda a raw feeling, and she crawled across the bed to wake him up. She dug at him with her fingers and pulled his blankets until he started to move.

"What . . . ?"

She kept pulling on the blankets but they wouldn't come.

"What are you doing? Where were you?"

She tried to reach around into his crotch, but ended up only pinching his thigh, making him jump.

"Stop, what the hell. . . ."

"I want to fuck," she said, and a kind of storm blew up from her spine and out through her skull, almost sending her face-first into the mattress.

"What are you doing? What time is it?"

"Fuck me and give me a baby," she said.

Patrick stopped fighting off her hands.

"How drunk are you?" he asked her.

"I'm fine, how drunk are you?" she replied. "Can you fuck me now? Please?"

"Now? You serious? What the fuck? Where were you, even?"

She got the blankets off him. "Come on, let's go," she urged, pulling at his underwear.

"Hang on, let me . . . hang on."

Patrick rolled out of bed and tip-toed to the bathroom, where his sudden and blooming horniness conflicted with his desperate need to pee. When he had resolved that conflict, he ran the cold water in the sink and rinsed his face to wake himself up and wash away any remaining trace of the interior of Chaps. Unable to resist, he turned on the light for a second to check his stinging shoulder: there was a blob of blue ink floating there under his skin. In the hallway, he shivered and almost skipped to the bedroom door to get his feet back onto the thick carpet.

"Did you leave the door open? It's freezing out there," he said, and could tell immediately that Manda was asleep on top of the blankets in all her clothes, even her shoes. Her breath was coming out in frustrated groans. He wrestled with her sleeping body, trying to get her lying straight at least, so that he would have a place to sleep, but that was all he could accomplish – he didn't have the strength to get her undressed and under the covers.

Plus his shoulder was really hurting now. After undoing her shoes and making sure her hair was off her face, he put on his shoes and went downstairs to check the front door.

WEDNESDAY

By seven o'clock Ken had already been watching the morning brighten the walls of his bedroom for an hour. It was cold out, but he had the thermostat in his room turned up so high he could lie on top of his blankets. He still had on the shirt and pants he'd been wearing the night before, though he'd managed to take off his Giant Tiger jacket before falling asleep. There was a faint smell of smoke and beer in the room. He was dehydrated and his stomach and head were hurting a little – he kept dozing off and having quick, vivid dreams about drinking pint glasses full of ice water.

He'd had less than four hours' sleep, but he wasn't really feeling it yet. His body seemed to lift off the bed as if about to start hovering. His head was an empty jug – it was almost whistling. It was the lightest he could ever remember feeling. He was like a captive animal who'd woken up to find the cage door open. He'd been ready to go for a while now but he was enjoying the feeling so much, prowling around inside that open cage, that he wanted to be fully awake and fully aware of every moment when he finally stepped through.

He reached under his pillow for the fanny pack he kept

his money in, money he'd counted a dozen times already this week. Every time he did he came up with a slightly different number, but always somewhere near $2,000. He counted it again and got $1,980, which was the year his father had moved them to Dunbridge. That coincidence floated around in the background of his mind for a while, waiting to see if it was needed.

With the money zipped tight in his fanny pack, and his fanny pack in his hand, Ken fell back asleep. He had time.

Patrick sat in the back of Active Sports on a chair he'd bought years ago from Sinc. To keep his shoes off the floor, which was painted over with a thin layer of dirty water, he had his feet up on an unopened box of baseball caps. From what he could get out of the plumbers who were still out front, his end of the mall hadn't been affected by the initial clogging up, but in fixing it they had had to flush out all the pipes, causing all the drains in the mall to start puking up water.

"It was a fuck-up," one of the plumbers said, "but I guess it's almost more fair now, eh? Everybody getting it?"

Patrick could tell that they had found this a lot less funny a few hours ago when they'd first discovered their mistake.

Everything in the storage room smelled like wet cardboard now, mostly because that was just about the only thing he had back there. The cord for his desk lamp trailed along the wet floor to the wall plug, and his head was hurting too much to put up with the fluorescent lighting, so he sat back there in semi-darkness, with the door propped open and the bathroom light on. The carpet out front was blackened and wet, and the bottom edges of his false walls had acquired the same creeping brown colour as the ceiling in his kitchen and back bedroom at home. Other than that, there wasn't too much damage; he tried to tell himself he had got off easy. All the boxes were lined with plastic, so no stock had been harmed.

Patrick opened the box he'd been resting his feet on. Inside were four rows of fifty hats spooned together. The first cap he grabbed had the logo of a snarling, muscle-bound hawk – an expansion team from the U.S. He hated those logos that hissed and snarled and shook their fists. The next row were all blue-and-silver Maple Leafs. He grabbed two of those, adjusted one for his own head, and took the other one with him out the back door.

It was windy out, and the sky looked as murky as rink ice. Patrick figured the snow would hit within the hour, beginning the short slide into winter. He thought about going back to grab his jacket, but kept on walking without really deciding one way or the other. Though his head was hurting a little, he felt alright. He hadn't had too much to drink the night before. Not enough to do him in, anyway. His shoulder ached, but he refused to do anything about it – even to rub it would be to give the little prick Steve and his sucker punch too much credit. He stretched his arms out to either side of him and took in a deep breath of air that was already cold enough to sting the back of his throat.

Patrick's truck was the only vehicle out back, though he'd seen a few in the main lot, mostly store-owners and employees coming in to see how bad things were. He wondered vaguely whether the mall would compensate everyone for the damage. Even before seeing the cardboard boxes starting to sag into the cement floor, or the carpet and the walls out front, he'd been feeling like he had woken back up to the reality of the store. The old fear of letting the place die with nothing to show for it had come back.

At the far end of the lot he stepped into the wind-blown trash and the grass and through a naked stand of trees to the apartment buildings beyond. If Danny wasn't home he would just hang the cap on his door knob and leave. He stood in the hallway, looking down to the farthest end of the hallway. The door opened after his second quiet knock, and Danny stood there in athletic shorts and a beer T-shirt that Patrick recognized as the man's pajamas. The TV was on behind him, and Patrick could smell scorched milk.

"The mall's all fucked up," Patrick said.

"I know, they flooded it," Danny said, and he smiled darkly and shook his head, as if the whole thing could have been avoided if only they'd consulted him.

"What's the store looking like?"

"A total mess. I can't open today."

"Yeah well, they better fucking pay you for that. You could sue them if they don't."

Danny dropped into his chair next to the TV. There was some talk show on: two people were standing over a hissing wok, and the host was *mmm*ing and *ooh*ing at the sight of the bubbling food. "Look at her," Danny said. They watched the host interview an actress neither of them recognized and then a man with his hair in gold ringlets who had to be convinced by the cheering audience to leave his seat and take his place behind a microphone on a small stage. Danny muted the scene before the man began to sing. He pointed at Patrick with the remote control. "Lock the door, eh? Some guy's been coming in the building and trying the doors. He got someone's stereo last week."

"I think I heard something about that. Didn't they catch the guy?"

"Someone saw him leaving the building. He takes off across the parking lot and drops the stereo. Million pieces everywhere. You should have seen it – I was just laughing."

Danny hated his neighbours, and welcomed anything that hurt or disturbed them in any way.

"We've got people breaking into the empty houses on our street," Patrick said.

"What the fuck for? Place to sleep?"

"No, kids getting stoned or whatever. They almost started a fire once."

Danny smiled. "I used to do that. So how's everything going at your place?" he asked.

Patrick recognized this as Danny's indirect way of asking about Manda, whom he had always feared a little.

"It's alright. Manda's still tearing the place apart. We're still fucked for money until the store picks up. I thought I had an idea to get some more money coming in, but it won't work. She's still working at the phone reservation place and everything. It's a job. I know she wants to quit."

"Why? Is she bugging you for kids yet?"

"Not really," Patrick said, and gave a forced laugh. "I was bugging her for a while, actually."

Danny took this in silence. He made no outward sign to show what he was thinking, though Patrick could easily guess. Normally, he would have left it at that, but he was tired and irritable and sick of it.

"So what do you think of that, me with kids?" he asked.

Danny just shifted in his chair and looked at the muted TV, where the man with the golden hair was still singing. Patrick could see Danny's mouth twitch with the desire to change the subject.

"You think it's stupid?"

"I don't know," Danny muttered.

"Oh, bullshit," Patrick said. "What do you know?"

Danny's expression didn't even change, and Patrick let the subject drop. He remembered the hat and pulled it out from where he'd been sitting on it.

"Hey, I brought you this," he said.

"Oh yeah?" Danny took the hat and started to brighten. The white in the logo was made with a material that shimmered

– Danny moved it around to catch the light as he inspected it. "This is alright."

"You gonna try it on?"

Danny looked at him quickly, and Patrick saw his eyes dart up to the identical hat on his own head. Patrick took his off, and Danny's greedy smile returned and he put the hat on, swivelling his head back and forth so that Patrick could now get the benefit of the shimmering effect.

"Is that all you brought?" Danny asked happily. "No season's tickets?"

"Not yet. Still trying."

Patrick made himself a cup of instant coffee in Danny's little kitchenette, and the two of them watched TV until there was nothing but late-afternoon soaps. During the commercials Patrick told him a little about going out the night before, but the only part Danny reacted to was Steve's sucker punch.

"You should have run the little faggot over," he said.

"I probably should have. I might have even tried to, actually. He's a quick little shit."

Danny had an evening shift at the Irving station coming up, so Patrick let himself out and headed back across the lot to the mall, still holding the extra hat in his hand. It was blowing snow already. Broad flakes like the palms of tiny hands crowded around him and pushed him from behind. He slipped on a small puddle that had sealed itself over with ice and watched for a few minutes as the snow slowly devoured his truck. All life seemed to have gone out of the mall; he was there to rebuild, to reseed. At his back door he paused and braced himself for the coming hours of dark, wet work.

Marcus woke up at noon, almost exactly so: he opened his eyes just as the clock beside his bed changed to 12:01. He was bound by his sheets, and his foot was throbbing where he had kicked the edge of the bed, which in his dream had been the ice of a frozen river into which he had fallen. His bedroom window was open a crack, and a cold wind panicked the curtains. It felt as though a frost had settled on him in the night. He'd stayed up until four in the morning the night before, watching TV under a blanket and alternating between an infomercial for a mini-blender and a movie that promised nudity but delivered only talk.

It was just as cold in the rest of the apartment. Marcus cranked the thermostat and silently urged on the valiant old baseboard heaters. He couldn't face the shower just yet, so he once again lay on the couch under the blanket.

The phone rang – the father of one of his players wanting to know if his son had spent the night at Marcus's place. They'd had a fight about the length of the kid's hair.

"I called the school and he's there now," the father said, trying to sound fully in control and without any worry. "I'm just curious where he was."

"Well he wasn't here. Nobody's stayed here in a while."

It was true: it had been a couple of years since anyone from his teams had used his apartment as a crash pad or as the first stop in an attempt to run away from home. Either the boys on his teams were coming from better homes, or the age gap was getting too big for them to seriously consider him as someone they could trust in that situation. Marcus knew it was probably the latter. Marcus's rule was they got one free visit – after that they had to find somewhere else to stay or show up with money for rent and groceries. One kid stayed for nearly a week after his parents found him in the back seat of a car, drunk, with a fifteen-year-old behind the wheel. The last kid who had shown up at Marcus's door – after unsuccessfully trying to conceal from his mother that he'd flunked the eighth grade – only asked for something to eat and the phone to call his dad. Out of habit,

Marcus offered the kid his couch for the night, but was glad when he left for the bus station instead.

That night, Marcus's team was playing the Penetanguishene Warriors. It was their third game of the season and the one with the least chance of victory so far. This year, and for the last three years running, the Warriors had a third line made up almost entirely of native kids – dark, serious-looking boys who looked even more serious and dangerous by smiling all the time and who were, on reputation alone, left to skate across the ice untouched and unchallenged. Marcus wished he could just concede the game in advance and use the ice time for drills. If he ever did the league would fire him, but he was starting to think that wouldn't be so bad.

The game was at seven. In a few hours some of the boys would show up after school to smoke and hang around until it was time to walk over to the rink. He needed to get out before any of them showed up. It was already two in the afternoon before he made the decision and turned off the TV, and he still had yet to shower and dress.

By the time he got out the door it was almost three o'clock. He went down to the corner store for a bag of chips, not sure how he was going to kill the next few hours. While standing at the cash in the store he saw three boys from his team coming across the street, aiming for his stairs. The three of them had somehow managed to line themselves up in ascending order of height, like a Russian doll brought to life. They could have been cartoon assassins. He watched them disappear past the edge of the window and heard six feet going up the stairs; he half-expected them to be in step. While they were ringing his bell, Marcus slipped out of the store and around the corner unseen. He turned up a side street that ended in trash and a little path that would allow him to cut through to a park. For a second, he had a giddy vision of the three boys chasing him – still in single file, smallest to tallest. Once he got off the street, he even stopped to look back, but there was nothing to see but lead-coloured trees and a floor of rusted leaves cut through by a brown trail. Marcus sat in the park for as long as he could stand it, which was less than ten minutes, before deciding the only warm place for him was the rink. It was only a ten-minute walk away, and he could probably score free coffee off someone in the administration office. No point in asking Bobby the snack-bar man, that was for sure.

The night before he'd felt nothing but anger and resentment at the way Kelly had let loose her needy little kid and her fucked-up ex-boyfriend in his life, but now there was something sharp jabbing at him at the thought of taking off on her. It was over, he was sure of that – there was no way he was going to get his head kicked in over a four-year-old who didn't even like him. If he was honest with himself, he probably wouldn't have risked a beating even just for Kelly. She hadn't made him a priority in her life – she wouldn't even give him a key to her place – so why should he get killed? The messages she had left on his machine the night before started off confused, moved through anger, and ended up just sad and confused again. He thought about calling her, even just to let her know what Neil had said, but what stopped him was the thought of trying to explain why it had taken him so long to do so. Anyway, he figured if Neil was serious about what he said, he'd probably done something already so there would be no point in warning her – she'd already know. And if he wasn't serious, then warning her would just get her upset for no reason. The jabbing was still there, but Marcus decided there was nothing he could do about it.

Outside the rink there were piles of lifeless snow that had been scraped from the ice's surface and dumped there by the Zamboni. Soon these piles would be real and would ring every parking lot in Dunbridge – already the sky looked infected with snow. Sure enough, a few flakes blew through Marcus's line of vision before he'd crossed to the front entrance. He realized he was now trapped in his apartment for another six months of winter, and this time he didn't have Kelly's place to escape to. He stopped just outside the front doors of the rink to look at his reflection. Snow was landing on his bare neck, and he could feel the cold eating through his jeans. The rip in his jacket practically whistled from the wind blowing through it. He reached out and slapped the stick-man in the wheelchair to open the automatic door. The fans were blowing hard between the inner and outer doors as if to delouse each new visitor. Just before the automatic door gave up waiting, Marcus stepped forward and let the building take him once again.

Manda could see the shadow of a tiny sliver set deep within the palm of her hand like a fish trapped in ice. Illuminated in the butter-glow of her bedside lamp, the sliver looked dead and inert, but when she turned the light off and lay back down on the bed it seemed to awaken and resume its slow, needle-nosed burrowing. Babying the hand did nothing, so she tried making it as uncomfortable as possible, laying on it or putting it under her head as she tried to sleep. Nothing would stop it. She had already decided it was in too deep to be dug out cleanly with tweezers, not without a lot of collateral damage to her palm. Squeezing it did nothing. She wasn't going to let Patrick at it, that was for sure: the last time she'd asked him to help with something like this (a speck of sawdust in the eye), he'd moved in on her like an old wrestler, not even stopping to wash his hands before almost pressing her eyeballs back into her skull.

Where this sliver came from was a painful mystery. She could have sworn it wasn't there when she woke up, still giving off alcoholic vapours, at the sound of Patrick's alarm.

After trying everything she could to get him to stay home that day – begging, insults, bribes (nothing sexual, obviously: she would have barfed at the mere sight of a cock that morning, and she was pretty sure she wasn't at her "freshest," as she and her friends used to sneer in high school) – she took her own advice and called in sick, leaving a dry-throated message on Sean's voice mail: *feel like shit, might try later, sorry about this.*

The sliver was definitely there when she woke up again an hour or so later at the sound of Patrick starting the truck. At that point she assumed she had hit her hand on something in her sleep, there was no other way to account for the feeling of being stung repeatedly, and with cold precision, by a wasp the size of a mouse. It wasn't until she got up (almost) for good around eleven that she could bring herself to look for the pain's source under the sharp light of the bathroom. Since then she'd been back in bed at least three more times, but the sliver, combined with the guilt about the night before and the feeling that she was wasting yet another day she could have used on the house, kept her from falling back into anything deeper than a momentary doze. She tried to resist the urge to keep looking at the sliver, but the lamp kept drawing her back under its light, and she would press at its shadowy shape with her finger, unable to even guess at its true size.

The only thing she could think was that she must have got it when she was fumbling around in the kitchen the night before trying to get something to drink. Some of the exposed wood in there was raw enough to do some damage if she fell against it the wrong way. She checked herself over for other signs of a fall, but there was nothing. Her memory wasn't going to yield anything up, at least for a while. Her night out with Marcus had already been partially corrupted in her mind by the hours she had spent stewing in her own boozy juices while lying, fully dressed, on the bed. She was still angry at Patrick about being left in that state, though she could recall just enough of what she had done when she got home to make her decide not to make a big deal about it. Everything after standing outside The Flamingo with Marcus was already like an old shipwreck in her mind, broken and scattered and grown over with rust and weed. It was going to be tough bringing all those pieces back to the surface to sort out what happened, and she didn't have the strength at the moment. So she left it all to sit down there in the shifting darkness for later.

After getting up and having a shower, Manda called Patrick at the store. She was curious to know if he was even open and she still didn't know where he had ended up going the night before. There was no answer, so she called Ken. A man – not Charles, who liked Manda and would have been friendlier – told her Ken was "gone." When she asked if her brother had said where he was going, whoever it was only restated his original answer: "Not here." She wanted to ask if he'd come in the night before, but realized it was pointless and would only have caused trouble for Ken. She thanked the voice, and it hung up without saying she was welcome or goodbye.

In the kitchen she found only bread crusts and Patrick's marmalade to eat. The coffee was little more than a teaspoon of granules in the bottom of the can, and there was no milk or juice. She ate dry toast with a can of Pepsi from the back room. They were at least a week overdue for groceries, but Patrick had promised her that if the mall wasn't open he would come home early so they could hit the giant Food Depot in Orillia, where the shopping carts were as big as bear cages.

Manda made an effort to find something useful to do, but it was no good: she was a wreck. She went downstairs to check on the laundry and found clothes stiff with mold hanging from every part of the ceiling. She made a nest for herself on the couch in the front room and drank tea out of a souvenir beer stein, the only clean mug-like cup in the house. Her library book, the same one she'd been struggling with for almost a week, was there, and she settled in to try again. It was the longest she could ever remember giving a book. On her shelves the spines of books she'd already read were starting to look tempting, and there was a new one in at the library that sounded at least a little more promising – something about the end of the world. The book's biggest crime, as far as Manda was concerned, was not that it was boring – she'd yawned through enough trash to see that as inevitable, one time out of three – but that it made her feel stupid. It wasn't like the out-and-out, over-her-head stuff she knew instinctively to avoid. Those books seemed to have been created for a whole other species, and she resented their existence about as much as a dog resents birdseed: she didn't get them, she didn't see the point, but it wasn't for her anyway, so why worry about it? This book wasn't simply too smart for her, it was *condescending*, and for that there was no forgiveness. She would never allow anyone or anything to condescend to her. Ever. And so, after taking a moment to break its spine, Manda threw off her blankets and took the book to the little table by the front door, where it would wait for her to take it back to the library when she was good and ready.

With nothing to read now, but feeling temporarily light and free, Manda decided to give her father a call. The cordless was upstairs somewhere. She wrapped herself in a blanket and went on a hunt. It wasn't in the bedroom but in the bathroom on the edge of the sink. She was tempted to lie down in the bathtub with the blanket around her – it was warm enough in there.

Margaret answered on the second ring; she picked up the phone while still yelling her reply to a question Allen must have asked her from another room.

"Amanda! Marcus must have told you to call."

It never bothered Manda to hear her stepmother use her full

name the way it did when her real mother did the same thing. Coming from Margaret, it seemed like friendly recognition of the permanent emotional distance between them. From Shelly it sounded like the opposite: an attempt at a special, more intimate relationship based on the fact that she was the woman who had given her the name in the first place.

"Hey, Margaret. How's everything going? You sound pooped."

"My god, I've been trying to get everything in before the snow covers it all. Anyway, I've given up now – anything still out there will have to wait until spring."

Manda hadn't even noticed the snow. The bedroom's heavy curtains were still closed, but now that she looked she could see a regular disturbance in the light coming through between and beneath them.

"How long's it been snowing?"

"Long enough to completely cover my garden already. You can't see anything there now, just snow."

Manda and Margaret talked about their gardens for a few minutes, and about Marcus (though neither mentioned Kelly), and about some of the noteworthy changes that had been happening to Dunbridge in the last few months, and then Margaret called for Allen to get on the other line.

"I'll say goodbye now, dear. I still have a few things I want to drag into the garage before they're completely buried."

Allen was already on the line, breathing, it sounded like, though a paper tube.

"Don't put the barbecue away," he told his wife. "We can still use it."

Margaret sighed with affectionate anger. "He says that, and then every year nobody touches the thing until May. Bye, Amanda!"

Manda had wanted to talk to Margaret a little longer to

find out how her dad was doing, if he was still falling down, etc. She was unlikely to find out the truth from the source – everything he told her would be either overly stoic or damply self-pitying.

"How are you feeling, Dad?"

"Hot. She jacked the heat as soon as she saw the first snowflake."

Allen shared his daughter's hatred for stuffy, warm houses.

"Don't be a baby. Go sit outside or something and let her be comfortable."

"She never is until it's roasting in here, though. Anyway, what are you calling about? Are you and Patrick coming over sometime?"

"Marcus said for me to call you."

"Are you coming over?"

"Patrick works all the time, you know that. But I was thinking maybe next week. Maybe Ken and I'll come over. Have you talked to him lately, by the way?"

"Not for a while, why? I think Margaret tried to call him about some job she saw in the paper, but I don't think he ever got back to her. What's going on with him?"

"Oh Christ, you know – sick of his house, wants to move."

Allen didn't say anything. Manda felt like he was trying to make clear to her that this part of his kid's life was no longer his concern.

"Anyway, I think he's alright. Probably just bored because of the cold and can't walk around as much."

"Jesus, him and his walks."

Allen asked her a few neutral questions about the house, and Manda told him some of her future plans for the place, all without mentioning she'd barely started on the plans she'd told him about last year.

"Patrick fights me every step of the way, of course. He won't come out and say it, but I know he'd be happy to have the place exactly as it was when he was growing up."

"Well, be careful – it's his house, remember. You can't take over someone else's house."

"It's *our* house, Dad. We're married, remember? Just like you and Margaret share the house?"

Allen laughed. "You really believe that?"

Silences started to open up in the conversation. At first, Manda was able to fill most of them with gossip from her work, which she knew he didn't give a shit about, and with accounts of running into people from her past at the mall or in a coffee shop somewhere. Allen, she knew, had left behind most of his friends when he came to Dunbridge, and he had never really made any knew ones here – his friends were really Margaret's friends, and there were none of those he really cared much about. The silences finally grew too large to fill.

"So what exactly was I supposed to call you about?" she asked him.

"Oh right. Marcus told you to, did he?"

"Yes, *Dad* – Marcus told me you wanted me to call you so I did. I can say it again if you want. What's going on?"

"Nothing. We're just . . . Margaret and I have been talking to a lawyer."

"Oh fuck Dad, you're not getting divorced, are you?"

"We're not actually married, so it's kinda hard to get divorced. Anyway, it's nothing like that. She just thought if there was anything you wanted you should say now rather than later. Ken, too, I guess. There's not that much, obviously, and there's some things Margaret wants to give Marcus. I don't know about the house, though I'm guessing that'll go to him, too. Probably sell it. You two already have one, and it's not like Ken can –"

"Dad, what the hell? Don't tell me you're making your friggin will."

"I just think it should be settled, that's all."

Manda had been starting to feel better, the smog of her hangover wasn't hanging in the air quite as thickly, but now she felt the full weight of it come back down upon her. She rolled onto her side with the phone still at her ear and pulled the comforter over her.

"Christ, this is just what I needed. Where's this coming from? Have you heard anything? Has Dr. Punjabi or whatever his name is said anything? I swear to god, if you tell me you've got six months to live I will seriously lose it. I will."

"Well it's not that, but you never know. It's just something we've been talking about. It could happen. I'm no spring . . . ah, I mean, it could be Margaret, too, though I guess that wouldn't really affect you."

"What is that supposed to mean?"

"No, I mean, you know, for what you get. Most of yours and Ken's would be coming from my side."

"Jesus Christ, Dad, you sound like you're planning a wedding. Here you are talking about what we're getting – I don't want anything! This is creepy and gross. Just stop it."

Acid crept up the back of Manda's throat. It was too hot in the bedroom; she wanted to kill the furnace and open every window in the house. She needed real air. With the phone pinned between her ear and her shoulder she pulled at the bedroom window. The bird-smudge was still there. The dead bird was somewhere. The window wouldn't open. Manda felt like lying flat out on the deep carpet, her head was spinning.

"Well, tell Ken anyway if there's anything he wants –"

"Tell him yourself!"

"Alright alright, Manda. We're trying to be smart here."

"What's smart about this, Dad? Asking me what I want – what the fuck am I supposed to ask for? It's all Margaret's. We dropped everything and ran, didn't we?"

"Don't talk to me like that."

Manda recognized his tone from the fights they used to have when she was a kid. It had been years since she'd heard him get angry about anything.

"No, I'm serious. What are you supposed to be leaving me? You're leaving me with Ken and Shelly and everything else to deal with. Just like always."

"What has *she* got to do with this?"

"Oh nothing, Dad. I guess she doesn't exist. I guess she just fucking melted or something the minute we left Toronto. I don't know who's worse – at least Shelly is fucking crazy, what's your excuse?"

"Manda!"

"And don't tell me it could be Margaret that dies. She's going to live to be a hundred and fifty, and you know it. She won't die until Marcus does or her house falls down. No Dad, you're the one who's sick; you're the one that can't walk around anymore. You're going to die, and I'll be the one to take care of Ken and deal with mom. I'll be left alone with absolutely fucking everything and I'll be fucked if I notice the difference."

There was a disbelieving silence on both ends. For a second, she half-expected Allen to hang up on her and let Margaret field the apologetic calls for the rest of the day. Instead, she was the one who hung up, shocking herself probably more than her father. It was a panicked reflex, and she hated herself for it even as she was pressing the OFF button with her thumb. Now she did lie down on the floor: her knees had lost their stability. The floor hummed into her ear until she was calm, and she slept for the better part of an hour. When she woke up, the carpet imprinted on her face like a tattoo, it was darker in the room, and what she had said to her father was right there waiting for her.

Everything Ken owned, except for what he was taking with him in his knapsack, was in garbage bags on the floor around his bed. He hadn't decided what to do with them, whether to take them to the curb or ask somebody to come pick them up. It felt better to just leave them there, like a crowd of orphans.

There were still a few scraps here and there. On the wall were some cards – one from Manda and Patrick, one from Margaret and Allen, and a couple from Marcus. The ones from Marcus were his favourite. Marcus would buy the wrong kind of card on purpose – a Valentine card for his birthday, a Get Well Soon card at Christmas – and then mark it all up and draw cartoons all over it. Marcus always put cash in the cards, a couple times as much as $200. Every once in a while, if Marcus knew he was in trouble, he'd send him a card out of the blue, for no occasion, with $50 in it. A chunk of the money Ken had saved up was from Marcus. He tried not to spend that money, if possible. It was special. He never told Manda, and the one time he'd tried to thank Marcus for it, he'd just shook his head and told him not to worry about it, it was cool. There were times he'd wanted to tell Steve about the money, but he was glad now that he hadn't. Steve was on the other side of whatever barrier he'd crossed the night before while standing behind the dumpster. Ken had always been too scared to go on a boat – just like Manda, though she would never admit it – but he figured this was what it was like to cross the ocean and watch everybody and everything getting smaller behind you.

Ken had snuck the garbage bags out of the kitchen when no one was in there, but now he could hear someone opening and closing the fridge door. He put on his parka, tucked his mitts into his pockets, and left his room, not even bothering to lock the door behind him.

Charles was in the kitchen, sipping coffee and picking at a sandwich. He stood up to refill his cup but stopped when he saw Ken's knapsack.

"What's up? You going camping?"

"Sort of. No."

"You know it's snowing, eh? They're saying twenty centimetres by the end of the day. I don't believe it."

"It's snowing?"

"Look out the window, buddy."

Without even turning his head, Ken could see movement beyond the glass.

"Where're you headed?" Charles asked him. "You working tonight?"

Ken could feel a slight weight coming into his head. This had all felt so clean and certain in his room – now things were getting muddy. He leaned up against the sink and looked down into it to avoid looking at Charles. "It's my day off," he said. "They've had me on the same schedule for a month."

Charles nodded. "That's how they do it," he said. "Oh hey, you left the front door unlocked when you came in last night. I found it when I came down. If Darcy'd seen that he would have freaked."

"Sorry."

"Well whatever, just don't do it."

Ken took a look in the fridge to see if there was anything in there he could bring, but his shelf held only an opened can of Pepsi and a jar of peanut butter that anyone could have if they wanted.

"You can have this peanut butter," he told Charles, who just stared at him.

Ken went looking for his boots. Charles, out of a growing curiosity, followed him into the front hallway, bringing his freshly refilled cup of coffee with him. Ken tried to pull his boots on without untying them, nearly falling over as he forced his feet into them. When he finally got them on he stood up straight and looked at Charles, who was sitting on the stairs.

"Well, *sayonara*," Charles said, and Ken said "sayonara" right back without thinking and with a look on his face so serious that Charles started laughing. He tried "Hasta la vista," but Ken just picked up his knapsack and went out the door.

"Aloha," Charles said. He sat there for a few minutes, sipping at his cup and thinking about a car he used to own that got totalled in an accident that wasn't his fault. He was about to go turn on the TV when he heard someone coming heavily up the front walk. The screen door called out, and Charles heard a key fighting its way into the lock. It clicked and counter-clicked and was finally locked for good. The screen door called out again, quieter this time, and away went Ken.

Patrick came home at the end of the day smelling like mold and wet paper. On his head he wore a new Maple Leafs cap. A few hundred wet snowflakes leapt though the door into the house with him. He found Manda upstairs in the bath, covered over in hot water and foam that shimmered nearly as much as his new hat. It was the first time he'd ever seen her in there. Despite her insistence on a bathtub large enough to sink into without touching the sides, she never took baths – she'd told him they only ever had baths in some of the apartments she'd lived in with her father and Ken, and they just made her think of having to immerse herself in her brother's dirty bathwater. She looked as though she were asleep. There was a book open on the floor, a thick paperback with two giant cat's eyes on the cover glowing a sinister green.

She jumped a little when he said hello, and her breasts bobbed up out of the foam. He felt like climbing in with her, even just to lie there in the warmth. No, it would have been for more than that, he admitted to himself: her nipples were gleaming in the water like they'd been oiled.

"I didn't even hear you come in," she said, pushing her wet hair back against her skull. "Do you have the truck?"

"Course I do. Where would it be?"

"Well, I don't know – I didn't hear it. It's snowing pretty bad out."

Patrick sat on the toilet and tried not to stare.

"How are you feeling?" he asked. "Still pretty rough?"

She sunk back down in the water and closed her eyes.

"Can you drop the radio in here with me please? I feel like I've got nothing left after this week and it's not even over yet."

"Summer's over, anyway."

"Summer's been over for while now, honey. It's just finally all hitting us. I hope it snows, like, ten feet tonight, and everyone gets stuck inside for six months. We can eat out of cans for a while and fucking unplug the phones. I don't want to see anyone for a while. I'm sick of it."

"What's going on?"

"Nothing, I'm just being a bitch. As usual. I *am* a bitch. I'm sorry, honey, I can barely talk, I'm so whipped."

Patrick shooed himself from the bathroom and went looking for something to eat. He knew they were out of groceries, but was still shocked at the scarcity of food in the house. Marmalade on soup crackers was the best he could come up with without defrosting something. Manda came in as he was preparing to cover a third round of crackers with orange jam. She had a towel on her head.

"That's disgusting," she said, looking at his plate.

"What else am I supposed to do?"

"So what happened to you last night?" she asked, sitting down with the cold dregs of a coffee she had left on the counter before her bath. "I was stuck there the whole night with Marcus telling me all his problems."

"What problems has that guy got?" Patrick could easily think of a half-dozen problems that Marcus had, but most of those were his own fault.

"He's got the kid's father after him now, apparently."

"Which kid? Oh. Really?"

"So he says. So where were you? I figured you were here all night, not answering the phone."

Patrick told her about going to Chaps, and about Steve getting them kicked out and punching him in the shoulder, and Ken's disappearance.

"I would have stuck around for him," he said. "But I was so pissed off, and I figured Ken had already started walking anyway. He's was being a bit weird all night. Not that . . . whatever."

"Jesus, who told you to go to Chaps? Didn't I say the Flamingo? I'm sure I did."

Patrick shrugged. "Don't think so. Ken said Chaps, so I just went."

"What a little shit that Steve is, eh? What a piece of work. Is your shoulder hurting?"

"Not really," he lied. He'd been rubbing it just before she came in the kitchen.

"Aw Christ," Manda said, leaning back in her chair and closing her eyes. "What a complete fuck-up. We can't even do that right; we can't even go out for a beer without everybody fucking it up. Why do we even try? I'm so sick of Ken's bullshit, I'm telling you. Next time he asks me for something, I'm going to be like, 'help yourself for once.'"

She sat forward suddenly. "Hey, what happened with the store? Marcus told me the mall got flooded. What's going on?"

"Nothing. It's fine."

"What do you mean, 'fine'? Marcus said the place was full of water."

"It looked bad at first, but I think I got most of it cleaned up.

They fucked it up and flooded the place twice. It's just the carpet that's fucked."

"Well, what does that mean? Were you even open today?"

"No. Nobody was. Except Wal-Mart, obviously. They probably had the fucking army in there cleaning the place out."

Manda thought about this for a minute. "Are you opening it up tomorrow?" she asked.

"I don't know – should I?" In his mind, Patrick had been letting the store teeter the entire day, willing to let the slightest shift either way decide its fate. He looked at Manda now, waiting for the word.

"Do whatever," she said. "But make sure they pay for whatever damages."

Patrick nodded and spread marmalade on another cracker.

"I know you," Manda went on. "You're too nice. You'll put up with whatever shit they pull, but you've worked too hard with that place to let them fuck you around on this. You should be more like Ronnie, just this once: he'd be in there screaming his friggin head off right now. They'd give him whatever just to shut him up."

Patrick nodded again and smiled.

"Manda," he said.

"Hmm?"

He turned a dry cracker over in his fingers a few times, paused, then gave it a few more turns. His lips slid around on his mouth in slow confusion.

"Well anyway," she said, yawning. "I feel like absolute shit. I'm gonna get ready, so let's get moving. We need groceries like nobody's business."

They pulled out of the driveway less than half an hour later. It was completely black out, and the snow came out of the darkness and hammered the windshield so relentlessly it made Manda think of a locust swarm she'd seen on some nature show.

The windshield wipers struggled to scrape the glass clear of the battering slush. The Bingo Palace, Eddie's Used Auto Sales, and Beaver Bonanza Furniture were no more than dark humps that passed slowly in the storm. There was hardly any traffic on the road; they could see cars sitting on either side of the highway looking spooked by the snow. A little ways out of town they passed someone walking hard in the ditch, head down, looking cold, but neither of them wanted to stop. They'd heard shit about hitchhikers. They passed a flashing tow truck every few kilometres – in the darkness they looked like scavengers pouncing on the weak and the fallen.

Patrick drove slow; he didn't trust his tires to stick to the road if he hit a drift or some ice. Every once in a while he could feel the back of the truck slide away slightly as he took a sharp corner or passed another car. The heat was on full, and his thighs were burning a little from the hot air coming from under the dashboard. Manda was sitting with her head back. She looked as though she had dozed off again. The warm thump of the wipers started to creep behind his thoughts and ease his attention away from the road. Something warm wrapped itself around his spine, soothing it. He started thinking that his father was in the cab with them, silently fuming about not being allowed to drive and having to sit in the middle. Patrick tried to tell him to stop pouting, but his mouth wouldn't open all the way. He had just got his teeth apart with his tongue when the truck gave a lurch and bounced off the guardrail shielding roadwork in the far-left lane. Manda screamed his name as the truck tried to swing across the other two lanes. Patrick pumped the brakes and steered against the spin. Out of habit he hit the horn, too, making the truck cry out in fear. When he had them straightened out again, he started going forward again, a little slower than before.

"What are you doing?" Manda shouted. "Fucking pull over to the side!"

He did, just as a transport truck went flying past them, giving off a long, low roar and turning everything outside the cab to snow. Patrick kept the engine running but let his hands drop from the wheel.

"Are you far enough off the road?"

"Yes."

The big truck's wake sent snow sideways and up in huge, white whorls. A tow truck pulled up beside them, throbbing with orange greed, but Patrick gave the driver the thumbs up, and it moved on.

"What happened? I'm ready to throw up!"

"I started to fall asleep," he said.

"What are you talking about! How the fuck do you fall asleep on the highway? Holy shit, Patrick!"

Manda pulled her seat belt away from her as if it were clinging to her chest in fear. Patrick pressed his foot down on the emergency brake and clicked on the hazard lights so nothing would plow into them from behind. The windows started to fog up so he turned down the heat. He felt as though he'd just swallowed a whole pot of coffee; the taste of marmalade was in his mouth.

"Sorry all right?"

"No I'm sorry," Manda said. "I'm just . . . my heart's going and everything. Look at my hands."

She put her hands out in front of her: Patrick could see a slight tremble even in the low light of the cab.

Manda rubbed her face. "It just keeps getting better," she said. The passenger-side window was completely fogged up but she made no move to clear it.

"I'm sorry."

"No, it's not that. It's okay. I thought I was going to puke there for a second. That was *crazy*. No, it's just everything. It's like someone pulled the string or whatever and everything just fell on me all at once. Fell on *us*."

"Did you hit your head?" Patrick reached over to move her hair away from her forehead; she flinched involuntarily.

"I don't mean *actually* fell on me, I mean Ken and my dad and everything. And Shelly, oh fuck. They're all sitting on my chest all the time; I can't even breathe, you know? Jesus, what am I talking about? I sound like an airhead."

"You don't. I know what you mean."

Manda felt bad for flinching, now. There was always room for more guilt, she supposed. She reached over and rubbed Patrick's arm.

"I just wish we knew we were onto something, you know?" she said. "Like, that something is going to work out – I don't even care anymore what it is. *Anything*. And don't say 'something will' as if that's supposed to make me feel better," she told him.

"Wasn't going to."

"Well."

The wind rocked the truck slightly. Neither of them had any idea what time it was. It could have been midnight. There was nothing to see around them but snow looking frantically for the ground and spinning everywhere in confusion.

"I'm sorry," Manda said.

"For what?" Patrick asked after a pause, though he'd been about to say the same thing.

"For all this. For everything ending up like this."

"Like what?"

Manda pulled her coat over her head as if she were about to hyperventilate. "Do you still love me?" she asked him, her face hidden.

"Obviously," he replied. "Why'd you ask me that?"

She didn't answer, but pulled her jacket back away from her face. He could see the gleam of tears there. She palmed them away as best she could.

"I look like a cow," she said. "I shouldn't drink so much – I nearly peed my pants."

When there was once again more black than white outside, Patrick asked Manda if she wanted to keep going or head back home. They could always get groceries another night.

"It's your call," he said.

"We're nearly there, what's the point?"

Patrick twisted around in his seat to see if anything was coming, but there were no lights visible in either direction. The snow had finally cleared everyone off the highway. They were almost alone.

(ACKNOWLEDGEMENTS)

Many thanks to Michael Holmes, Jack David, Simon Ware, Sarah Dunn, and everyone at ECW; Derek Weiler, Alison Jones, Gary Campbell, and everyone at *Quill & Quire*; Vanessa Matthews, Martha Magor, and Anne McDermid; Phil Rudz for the great cover, Marie Rampino and everyone at Tamm Communications, James Grainger, Jane Warren, Meaghan Strimas, Alex Lukashevsky, Todd Babiak, Heather O'Neill, Rob Wiersema, Lorne Whitlock, Emily Donaldson, Shaun Smith, Dan Smith, Janie Yoon, Micah Toub, Tracy Jenkins, Dan Donaldson, Gary Butler, Estelle Anderson, Marc Côté, Michael Redhill, Nancy Lee, Lindsey Love, *Maisonneuve*, *Geist*, *The Antigonish Review*, *The New Quarterly*, the Ontario Arts Council, The Writers' Trust of Canada, The Writers' Union of Canada, Ken and Verlie Whitlock, Sean and Ann McEvenue.

Very special thanks to Iago and Olive.

BackLit
INSIGHTS FOR
READERS

A DEFENCE OF PLOTLESSNESS

OR, THE BEST SCENE IN BULLITT IS NOT
THE ONE YOU'RE THINKING OF

by Nathan Whitlock

There is a short scene very early on in Steve McQueen's 1968 cops-
and-mobsters film *Bullitt* that I've always loved. *Bullitt*, of course,
contains more than a few iconic scenes, including, most famously,
a ten-minute car chase in and around San Francisco that ends
with one car flying off the highway and bursting into flames.

That's not the scene I'm thinking of. In fact, the one I
always remember from the movie is barely a scene at all. It happens about seven or eight minutes in, when Steve McQueen's
character, Detective Frank Bullitt, is awoken in his apartment
by his partner pressing the buzzer outside. McQueen/Bullitt
gets out of bed and pulls a lever at the top of the stairs to unlock
the street-level door. Having done that, he returns to his bed
and sits there rubbing his face, trying to wake up. His partner,
Delgetti (played by Don Gordon, in real life a friend of
McQueen's), goes straight to the fridge, pours himself a glass of
orange juice, then wanders past where Bullitt is sitting. Saying
nothing about why he has come, Delgetti pulls the blinds on the
window and proceeds to read aloud from the newspaper. All

| 243 |

this time, Bullitt does nothing but sit there looking slightly annoyed and making himself a cup of instant coffee with a little plug-in device on his bedside table. After about half a minute of his partner's droning, Bullitt finally snaps and says, "Why don't you just relax, have your orange juice, and shut up, Delgetti?" To which his partner replies, "Let's go, Frank."

And that's it.

I say Bullitt "does nothing," but that's a lie. In fact, he – or rather, McQueen – does a lot in this very short scene (the whole sequence lasts around two minutes). When he gets out of bed to pull the lever, he does an odd hobble-step down the stairs as if babying an injured foot. With the lever pulled and the door opened, he comes back to the bed, his body stiff and his hands in fists. In contrast to the other actor's slow, almost bored rhythms, McQueen is shaky and vulnerable, his hands between his thighs for warmth. He looks like a guilty child awaiting punishment. As Gordon passes him with the orange juice, McQueen makes a quick reach for it, then drops his hand and looks at the other man with a mildly hurt expression on his face. When Gordon opens the blinds, letting in the sunlight, McQueen actually recoils slightly, his eyes squinting, his expression one of momentary fear – again: like a child. Slowly, McQueen's character regains composure, though he is still clearly half-asleep. His movements become smoother, and the normal power dynamic between the two men reasserts itself.

Every time I watch that scene, I feel strange little bursts of pleasure at the hobble-walk, the aborted reach for the orange juice, the recoil from the sunlight, the warming up – the whole thing. The very first time I saw the movie, I remember thinking I was in for something very strange and special: a naturalistic crime thriller that made room for both epic car chases *and* the way it takes even hardened detectives a few minutes to get their bearings in the morning.

And here's the truly odd thing, the thing that maybe makes me love the scene all the more: it is completely superfluous. There is nothing that comes before or after that requires us to see the movie's hero having trouble waking up. In fact, it only serves to undercut his hero status, to humanize him. After all, this is our first introduction to Det. Frank Bullitt, and it doesn't exactly scream "hardboiled cop" to watch him squinting and shivering first thing in the morning. By rights, we should never see him so vulnerable, unless that vulnerability is integral to the story, which it isn't here. Any film editor or director aiming to create a more plastic and invulnerable myth of a movie, one in which every scene and every line of dialogue keeps you firmly within an imaginary world sealed off from our own – the Coen Brothers do this all the time, often to excess and often brilliantly – would've cut that bit of waking-up business without thinking. But for some reason, that scene is there. And for me, it has a way of overshadowing everything that comes after.

I have a particular, peculiar obsession with this kind of thing, very nearly a fetish. I don't shun things because they are epic in quality, or mythic, or utterly unrealistic – whatever you take that to mean. I like when movies, music, books, architecture, personalities are larger than life, but there is always a part of me that is most satisfied, most engaged, when such things are *as large as* life – when the boring, seedy, inescapable details of actual life are seen not as a straightjacket on the imagination, but as a means to engage with the world on a deeper, more focused and resonant level. Even with outsize heroes, I am always looking for the small details that make them human, that hint at other, less dramatic stories lying half-hidden somewhere.

When I was working on *A Week of This*, I had a vague idea that I wanted to create an entire book out of nothing moments like the one at the beginning of *Bullitt*. I was very aware that this was probably a stupid thing to do – I still remember the look that appeared, however briefly, on my future agent's face when, having been asked how the writing was going, I admitted I was probably removing every last element that would make it easier for her to shop the book around. I knew fairly early on that this book would be a tough sell, one that could kill even the remotest glimmer of interest with its willfully uninspiring summary: *A week in the life of a bunch of unhappy people in a small town in Ontario*. Not even *I* would go near *that* book.

(That's not true: I might. A movie came out of Romania a few years ago called *The Death of Mr. Lazarescu*, in which a cranky and unlikeable old man is shuttled around all night from emergency room to emergency room in the back of an ambulance until the promise of the title is finally fulfilled. It was billed as a black comedy and had a running time of over two hours. I, of course, had to see it, and ended up loving it.)

I enjoy being manipulated by a well-oiled plot, one with all kinds of unforseen curves and reversals, but what really draws me in are stories that have no apparent story, stories that are more interested in exploring than unfolding. Or if they unfold, they do so in many directions at once. The authors I feel closest to are those who make art of out of meals and marriages and missed opportunities, authors like Chekhov, Woolf, Joyce, Alice Munro, John Cheever, Muriel Spark, Henry Green, V.S. Pritchett, and J.F. Powers. These are the authors who almost never bore me, though they all, as Auden puts it (in his poem "The Novelist"), "become the whole of boredom" in their work. These are authors who often write about the people standing somewhere behind the movers and shakers – or cleaning up after them, babysitting their kids, serving their dinner, doing their taxes.

I'll admit: listing authors like Joyce and Munro is partly an act of wishful thinking. It's hard not to fantasize just a little about being cited alongside them one day, the way a young athlete or would-be guitar hero in his parents' basement might fantasize about being included at the end of a different list of names. Not as an equal, obviously, but perhaps as a worthy fellow worker. A much-junior partner. (Even fantasies have their limits.)

Listing them is also to summon them as literary bodyguards. To write closely observed, essentially plotless fiction these days can make an author feel like the skinny weakling at school – the one with various semi-exotic allergies, perfect attendance but middling grades, and a habit of sending teachers thank-you notes at the end of every semester. It is also to appear to ally oneself with the great swaths of bloodless, endlessly interior, and action-phobic novels about "loss and love." With the likes of Woolf or Munro at my back, however, or filmmaker Mike Leigh or picture book author William Steig, two more artists whose work enters my bloodstream unfiltered, I am not merely a writer who lacks imaginative and prosical firepower, but rather a secret member of the Quotidian Justice League.

But that doesn't really explain why I wrote a novel that appears to have no plot. People wake up, they go to work, they bitch at each other, they eat dinner, they fart around watching TV or doing the laundry, and they sleep. Why would anyone write a book where the climax appears to pass by while everyone is trying to figure out at which bar they were supposed to meet? Why would anyone read a book like that?

The answer is that you can write – and read – about anything, as long as it engages on some level, as long as there is something going on beyond simply noting where a character happens to be at any given time. Samuel Beckett wrote a whole novel about a man who could barely get out of bed. So did Kafka. And both of those books have become strange, powerful literary classics. (Not making any such claims for myself or this book here – just saying.) I simply don't enjoy thinking about books in terms of *what happens next*. I am more interested in *what is this and where did it come from and how does it behave when nobody's looking?* I like to dig in a little, and writing a book where there is no overarching narrative hook – *She's dying of cancer! He's off to war! They're all ghosts!* – allows me to dig around in the characters' lives, in their backstories, and really pick through what I unearth to find patterns. These patterns, whatever they are, all add up to a plot.

That all sounds fairly dry, as if I'd written the book this way out of some highly literary considerations, when in reality, I wrote about these people and these events because I found them funny, familiar, and endlessly fascinating. And here's the thing: I don't actually consider *A Week of This* to be "plotless." I'm not the kind of author who would write an "anti-novel" containing an "anti-plot." I get tired of artists whose whole schtick seems to be about frustrating common expectations (as opposed to creating new, more interesting expectations); it's the equivalent of putting a child to sleep on Christmas Eve with promises of Santa and presents and turkey, only to have him wake up to an undecorated, present-less house, and shouting, "That'll teach you to expect things!" Some artists treat their audiences like that poor kid, and some audiences crave the treatment. I'm happy to leave them both to it.

I think all kinds of things happen in this novel, just not the kinds of things that are usually found in novels. Or maybe they are the same things that are found in a lot of novels, just that they are lingered over here a little more than you'd expect. Obviously, this is my first novel, so I have my own take on how successful I was at making it all work, but there seems to me to be an enormous amount of activity in the book, just not a lot that would qualify as heroic – or anti-heroic, for that matter. A writer-friend of mine said it reminded him a little of a soap opera. He immediately apologized for the comparison, but I think that's pretty close, in a strange way: push all the characters up a few notches on the economic scale, slather them with make-up and hairspray (and take out all the swearing), and you have something resembling a daytime serial. *A Week of Our Lives*. (My parents' love of *Coronation Street* probably played an important role here . . .)

For readers who are okay with that, who are up for a novel about the kinds of people who rarely get a story all to themselves, I think questions of plotlessness vs. plotfulness become irrelevant. These might just be the same kinds of readers who would prefer to watch Steve McQueen try to wake up rather than drive a Mustang really fast for ten minutes.

THE NEWSLETTER

by Nathan Whitlock

[Ed. Note: While "The Newsletter" works as a standalone story, it takes off from the scene on page 52.]

It was always difficult, a real tick of a job, to put together the library's monthly newsletter. There were months when the problem was that nothing much was happening at the branch, but that wasn't the case for October. October was stuffed. That was what Anne had said when she and Terry put together the final list of events and announcements: "It's just *stuffed*!" That made Terry laugh and say something slightly ridiculous about Thanksgiving turkey.

> *It's October! Which is always a very, very BUSY month at the Dunbridge Public Library Main Branch. Children are back in school. The weather is getting colder. Brrr! Almost time for mittens and scarves! Perfect time to spend some time inside at the library!!*

The problem this time was figuring out what to put first. Well not *first*, because first came Anne's short introduction. She'd done so many of the newsletters, writing those introductions was bone-easy – the only difficulty she sometimes had was making sure she didn't repeat herself. Sonia had caught her accidentally doing that once: the introduction to last May's newsletter had been almost the same as the introduction to the previous May's. Anne had even said the exact same thing about May flowers and April showers. Sonia had *loved* that – Anne could tell. She made sure everybody heard about it, especially Mr. Price, the library's director. As if anyone would really notice they were the same – anyone, that is, who wasn't the kind of person who just waited for others to make a mistake. Still, Anne felt like a billygoat for it. She always checked now, just in case.

October 4 is the deadline for our "Rhymes with Orange" Poetry Contest. Don't forget to give your entries to one of the librarians at the front desk. Double-spaced and typed, please. (REMEMBER: your poems do NOT have to include the word "orange.")

Anne felt it was important to offer that last bit of clarification, though everyone else thought it was unnecessary. One of the student volunteers had come up with the name of the contest; Anne worried it would cause confusion, but Mr. Price was enthusiastic, so it stuck. She had further concerns about the contest that were also dismissed, such as: a) that some of the high school students would submit homemade rap lyrics containing swearing and violence; and b) that Bobby Paul, the morning man from CDUN Radio Dunbridge ("The Moose"), would pick one of those as the winner. She still hadn't forgiven Bobby Paul for a so-called "joke" he'd once made about Lady

Diana, even though he'd apologized for it on-air and made a donation to cancer research. (A few people in the paper said it should have been to AIDS research, since that was what Lady Di had mostly done work for, but Anne didn't think he had to go *that* far.)

Many of you have mentioned the leak in the ceiling on the third floor. Mr. Samson, our excellent maintenance manager, says it will be fixed before the end of the month. Until then, watch your heads!

Anne wasn't sure she should make a joke about the leak, in case Mr. Samson, who was always a crab, thought she was suggesting he was taking too long with it. Terry thought it was fine, and had even come up with the idea of putting in the little clip art image of a sign saying, "Under Construction." Anne always appreciated Terry's help with the lists; some of the other ladies never lifted a finger. She'd been doing the newsletters for six years now, ever since Mr. Price came to the library and made such a fuss about being more visible in the community and having more events. There were those who said it was because Mr. Price's wife was not only Pakistani but from Montreal that he was so eager to have events: they wouldn't be able to meet people any other way. Anyone who thought that, Anne said at the time, must think people in Dunbridge were just a pack of rednecks, driving around in trucks and firing off guns, just like they said in Toronto. More than once, Mr. Price had called Anne "Our Town Crier" and "Our Social Director," which she knew was overstating the case. She enjoyed the effect it had on people like Sonia, though. Sonia was the kind of person who woke every morning shocked to discover there were other people in the world. Her sister had just had a baby – you'd think such a thing had never happened before, to hear her talk about it.

Our weekly teen reading group will now be meeting in the third-floor conference room, instead of in the reference area, because of noise concerns.

Anne regretted ever having come up with the idea for "Plot Gobblers." It had been fine when the group had just been her nieces Sara and Tammy and some of their school friends, but those girls were older now, and the kids who'd been coming to it lately were real troublemakers. They thought she couldn't hear them back there because of her ear, but she could hear them just fine. She could've turned off her hearing aid and still heard them. She doubted any of them did any actual reading; from what she had seen and heard, they spent more time talking about movies and music and their new cell phones than books. She knew it'd be awful to say, but she couldn't help think sometimes there were simply too many kids in the library. It might be a lot nicer for everyone if maybe children stopped coming altogether once they turned ten, and returned when they hit twenty.

Reminder: there is NO street parking directly in front of the library, and the parking at the rear of the building is reserved for our handicapped patrons. Please respect the needs of the disabled – someday it might be you!

Mr. Price sometimes suggested that the monthly newsletter was perhaps too much work for just one person, and that maybe Anne ought to share the load with some of the other librarians. He had brought the idea up before, and had spoken privately to her about it after July's newsletter, in which she had, as part of her Canada Day message, asked library patrons to remember all those brave men and women in uniform currently serving in Afghanistan. He was fine with the sentiment, especially given the fact she had a nephew there, but had concerns with the reference to "exploding turbans." He also thought she had perhaps made too much of the possible reasons for the continuing disappearance of men's fitness magazines.

> *This month's Free Friday Flick will be* The Godfather: Part III. *As always, the movie will be followed by a discussion, led by the head of our A/V department, Josh Richardson. Bring your own popcorn!*

Mr. Price also thought that maybe Anne should relent and let the heads of the different departments get their own sections in the newsletter, instead of insisting it all go through her. To be honest, she wouldn't have minded if the head of the children's department, Miss Newsom, contributed a little more than a simple list of missing or damaged picture books, which, if printed, Anne had to explain over and over again, would take up more than half the newsletter. Miss Newsom was also always after Anne to put in something about the kids' section not being a daycare, and how parents should not leave the building while their children were in there, as was always happening. Anne thought that was reasonable, but how many times could she print that? Letting Miss Newsom write something would've meant letting Josh Richardson write something, however. He'd been threatening to produce a separate A/V department newsletter, and had been effectively doing so online, a situation Anne had brought to Mr. Price's attention on a number of occasions, but which he felt was not a problem. If forcing him to start his own newsletter was the price of keeping him out of the real one, Anne was okay with that. Josh was one of the ones who thought the library needed to open its doors even wider, to let bands play there and have art exhibitions. Sonia, who liked Josh even less than Anne did, had suggested perhaps *he* was the one stealing the muscle magazines. Anne had laughed at that, though she knew Josh had a wife and a small child.

Don't forget: October is the SCARIEST month of the year!
October 31 is our annual "Halloween Spooktacular."
There'll be ghost stories, a haunted house, "scary" special
guests, and prizes for the best costumes.

Anne had come very close to leaving the library after last year's Spooktacular. She, as always, had smeared white all over her face and put fake spiderwebs in her hair to become the Ghost Librarian. Each time she did it, she noticed, she had to do a little less to make herself look the part. Sonia always wore something slightly inappropriate: last year, she was a sexy cat. Anne was tired of being outraged by it, so she had long ago decided to feel sorry for the poor woman for thinking so little of herself she felt she had to put on a display.

Last year, Josh had come wearing a fake beard, a toque with a pom-pom, a red-and-white striped shirt, camouflage pants, and army boots. He had a plastic machine gun slung over his shoulder. Everyone laughed when they saw him, but Anne didn't understand until she overheard someone say, "Osama bin Waldo." Miss Newsom was the only person who didn't laugh: she worried that some of the younger children might be disturbed by the sight of a favourite picture book character carrying a gun. Anne had to admit she hadn't thought of that, and offered to talk to Mr. Price about her concerns.

Mr. Price was dressed as Frankenstein's monster. The expression on his face when she asked if she could speak to him privately, and when he heard what she had to say, told her all she needed to know: he was waiting for her to retire. When he first took over, he had promised them all he would not fire anyone, but she had already seen him hound a few older ladies into retirement. She wondered if Sonia weren't putting a word in his ear, as well. Anne had seniority among the librarians, and had first pick at scheduling and vacations. She knew Sonia wanted to work fewer evenings so she could attend her son's hockey games. Anne used to happily switch with her whenever she was asked, but the few times she had, there hadn't even been a thank-you. Not to mention Sonia always left things in such a state at the end of the day, and that Anne usually found herself feeling a little faint if she worked past eight o'clock.

Mr. Price ended up asking Josh to put the machine gun away, which he did, but not before the two of them had a little laugh at Anne's concerns – which had really been Miss Newsom's concerns. (Anne realized she should have made that clearer to Mr. Price.) That little laugh, even more than the look Mr. Price had given her, had made her want to do something she'd never even thought of before: quit. She wasn't like the other women there, who had their husbands' pensions to live on, but she was sure she could find something else to bring in some money. Her hearing issues were not as much of a problem lately as they'd been before. And she was a hard worker. Even Mr. Price couldn't deny that – he'd said so himself, calling her the Main Branch's "busy beaver."

But even as the thought of quitting came into her head, she felt cold panic go through her. So much had changed in the library in the past few years, but so much of it was exactly as it had always been. It fit around her like an antique hoop skirt, flattering her even as it sometimes tripped her up. They had repainted many of the walls, but she could still see where the holes had been, where words had been scratched in. She could remember how the shelves had been arranged, all straight and in darkened rows, before Mr. Price had cut them all in a half and made the place airier and brighter and more like a bookstore. Even some of the noisy teenagers she could remember as faces peering out of strollers while their mothers loaded up on magazines and board books.

About most of the changes that had happened to the library, Anne was happy. She was not one of those people who thought everything should stay the same, just because. But at the same time, she felt some people – Josh, for one, and Sonia, definitely – showed too little respect for the way things had been. The way they talked, you'd have thought there was nothing but musty bibles and farmer's almanacs on the shelves before, and that everything had been dank and dark and dripping with water. There were a lot of people – older people – who still used the library and remembered how it was, and what's more, who preferred it that way. Did their opinions not count? There had to be someone there who understood them, who could address their concerns. There had to be someone who was a clear link to the past most of them were still living in in their heads. In the face of all that change, something had to stay the same.

Anne had left the Halloween party early that night, telling everyone she had a headache, and as she cleaned off the make-up and pulled the webs out of her hair in the bathroom of her apartment, listening to the howling of the sugared-up children outside, she decided she would not retire until she was good and ready to do so. It would've simply been irresponsible. Instead, she would be a model worker, always ready to help out where needed, and be more flexible about things like scheduling. She would help bring about any new changes Mr. Price wanted, and would volunteer to explain them as best she could to the patrons who might be resistant. She would get along with everyone, but still hold the line against the likes of Josh and Sonia.

But there was one thing she would not be flexible about, one thing she would not abandon. She had taken on the task of writing the newsletter when no one else had been willing to do the extra work. There'd been times when she had put the thing together while sick as a dog. Did anyone else offer to help? Hardly. Even Terry wouldn't do it. It was easier to do now, with the new computers, but did that mean it could write itself, as Sonia and even some of the other ladies sometimes suggested? It wasn't something that just happened with the click of a button. There was a beating heart within the newsletter, and Anne was the one who'd put it there. As she searched the web for the perfect image of a grinning jack-o-lantern for the latest one, Anne smiled at the memory of what she'd said to Mr. Price the day after last year's Halloween party:

"Doctor Frankenstein only made one monster, Mr. Price. I make twelve a year."

ABOUT THE AUTHOR

Photo: Gary Campbell

Nathan Whitlock's writing has appeared in *The Toronto Star*, *The Globe and Mail*, *Maisonneuve*, *Toronto Life*, *Canadian Notes & Queries*, *Geist*, *Best Canadian Essays*, and elsewhere. He grew up in the Ottawa Valley and currently lives in Toronto.